MW01063340

ИНСТИТУТ ПЕРЕВОДА

AD VERBUM

Translation of this publication and the creation of its layout were carried out with the financial support of the Federal Agency for Press and Mass Communication under the federal target program "Culture of Russia (2012-2018)."

The publication was effected under the auspices of the Mikhail Prokhorov Foundation TRANSCRIPT Programme to Support Translations of Russian Literature.

THE YEAR

OF THE

COMET

SERGEI LEBEDEV

Translated by

ANTONINA W. BOUIS

RICE PUBLIC LIBRARY
8 WENTWORTH ST.
KITTERY, MAINE 03904
207-439-1553

NEW VESSEL PRESS
NEW YORK

New Vessel Press

www.newvesselpress.com

First published in Russian in 2014 as *God Komety*
Copyright © 2014 Sergei Lebedev
Translation Copyright © 2017 Antonina W. Bouis

All rights reserved. Except for brief passages quoted in a newspaper, magazine, radio, television, or website review, no part of this book may be reproduced in any form or by any means, electronic or mechanical, including photocopying and recording, or by any information storage and retrieval system, without permission in writing from the Publisher.

Cover design: Liana Finck
Book design: Beth Steidle

Library of Congress Cataloging-in-Publication Data
Lebedev, Sergei
[God Komety. English]
The Year of the Comet/ Sergei Lebedev; translation by Antonina W. Bouis.
p. cm.
ISBN 978-1-939931-41-2
Library of Congress Control Number 2016915499
I. Russia—Fiction

and now faint with fear, the miserable Lares
scramble to the back of the shrine,
shoving each other and stumbling,
one little god falling over another,
because they know what kind of sound that is,
know by now the footsteps of the Furies.

C. P. Cavafy, "Footsteps"
Translated by Edmund Keeley / Philip Sherrard

PART ONE

CHILD OF AN EARTHQUAKE

I was born in the afternoon of March 14, when a fault opened deep below Bucharest.

The inky tips of seismographic recording needles trembled as the tectonic blow rolled through the Carpathians toward Kiev and Moscow, gradually receding. The face of the world was distorted, as if in a fun-house mirror: avalanches fell from mountains, asphalt roads buckled, railroad tracks turned into snakes. Flags shook on flagpoles, automatic guns rang out in arsenals, barbed wire across state borders broke under the strain; chandeliers in apartments and frozen carcasses in meat processing plants swung like metronomes; furniture on upper floors swayed and scraped. The thousand-kilometer convulsion of the earth's uterus gave a gentle push to the concrete capsules of missile silos, shook coal onto the heads of miners, and lifted trawlers and destroyers on a wave's swell.

My mother was in the maternity ward, but her contractions had not started. The tectonic wave reached Moscow, shook the limestone bedrock of the capital, ran along the floating aquifers of rivers, gently grasped the foundations and pilings; an enormous invisible hand shook the skyscrapers, the Ostankino and Shukhov towers, water splashed against the gates of river locks; dishes rattled in hutches, window glass trembled. People called the police—"our house is shaking"—some ran outside, others headed straight for the bomb shelters. Of course, there was no general panic, but this was the first time since the German bombing that Moscow *reeled*; it was only at quarter strength, but it was enough to awaken the deepest historical fears. They surged for a second, these fears: of nuclear war, the collapse of the country, the destruction of the capital; few people admitted that they had experienced these fears, everybody talked instead about a slight confused fright, but they were lying.

Mother worked at the Ministry of Geology and was part of a special commission that studied the causes and consequences of natural disasters. She had seen the ruins of Tashkent, the ruins on the Kuril Islands and in Dagestan, thousands of people without shelter, destroyed homes, buckled rail tracks, cracks seemingly leading straight to hell. When the maternity ward was shaken by a gentle wave from the center of the earth, my mother was the only person to understand what was happening, and the unexpectedness of it, the fear that the earth's tremor had pursued her and found her in the safety of Moscow and induced her into labor.

The earthquake was my first impression of being: the world was revealed to me as instability, shakiness, the wobbliness of foundations. My father was a scholar, a specialist in catastrophe theory, and his child was born at the moment of the manifestation of forces that he studied, as he lived, without knowing it, in unison with the cycles of earth, water, wind, comets, eclipses, and solar flares, and I, his flesh and blood, appeared as the child of these cycles.

My parents were wary of this coincidence from the start, they thought it a bad sign. Therefore they entrusted me to my grandmothers, hiding me in a sewing box with thread and yarn, among the accouterments of geriatric life. My grandmothers, who had suffered so much, lost brothers, sisters, and husbands, but had survived all the events of the age, were to give me refuge in the peaceful flow of their lives, bring me up on the margins, far from real time, as if deep in the woods or on a lost farmstead. But— and I will tell you about this later—the nearness of my grandmothers merely intensified the sensation it was supposed to heal.

Why did my parents, who were not superstitious or given to reading meanings into things, still worry about the portent of the earthquake? My mother could not get pregnant for a long time. The doctors were stumped because all her signs were normal; at last, an old doctor, a professor, changed tack. Instead of asking about family illnesses and rechecking all her blood and other samples, he had a long and detailed conversation with my mother about the family's history. She did not understand the purpose but she told him everything she knew—she clutched at every straw.

The professor said that she was not the only patient he had like her; in many women he saw an unconscious fear of motherhood connected to the great number of violent deaths the previous generation had suffered. He suggested they go somewhere extremely peaceful, where nothing would remind her of time, history, or the past. Mother was ready to take the suggestion, but my father resisted at first; he thought that the problem was between them as man and woman, not in history or psychology. But they went.

In those years, the Soviet Union was building hydroelectric stations, and reservoirs were supposed to flood enormous areas along the Siberian riverbeds. My parents took probably the only unscheduled vacation of their lives and headed out to the zone of future flooding. They spent a month there; my father had a friend in the construction administration, and they were housed comfortably in an abandoned house of a buoy keeper at the foot of the cliff, a tall granite remnant that had to be demolished so that it did not interfere with shipping on the future sea.

It was a place of great emptiness and silence. Hunters' huts dotted trails and roads. Letters no longer reached this region, since the mail codes and addresses had been deleted in advance of the flooding, just like the telephone numbers of the former kolkhoz offices; the villages didn't appear on the new maps ready for printing. The animals left the river valley, the people were gone, and even the fish, as if sensing that soon water would flood the banks, either lay low in the bottom holes or swam upriver.

In a Robinson Crusoe world consisting of house, rowboat, fishing nets, firewood, stove, food supplies, and rifle, my parents lived in a time that they had never experienced before or since; I don't think they even took photographs, although they brought a camera.

There, in the ideal nowhere, a place that is now forever underwater, I was conceived. And I was born in the tremor of an earthquake, as if my parents' plan had been discovered and the big world sent a menacing message to the one they had hoped to hide from fate.

My feelings, my ability to feel, were fashioned by that underground blow. I had trouble understanding anything to do with stability, immutability, and firmness, even though I wanted those states I could not achieve; disharmony was closer and more understandable than harmony.

When I took walks in the city, I was attracted by old houses, sinking and decrepit. Cracks in walls and windows, cracks on the sidewalk which children sometimes try to avoid, cracks in the marble siding of the metro joined into a complex network for me, as if the entire world was tormented by secret tensions.

Kaleidoscopes and puzzles where you had to make a figure out of parts did not elicit curiosity, but a morbid, stubborn interest—not so much to put the pieces together as to observe how the whole can be reassembled and disassembled.

Objects that had lost their companions—a single mitten, a shoe left alone while the other was being repaired, a domino dropped in the playground—called me to understand how they lived in their insufficiency.

Even though I knew I would be punished, I would sometimes drop a cup to experience the moment of the vessel's irremediable loss and the irreversibility of time. Grown-ups tried to teach me to be careful—for them spoilage, breakage, even accidental, was tantamount to a crime. They lived as if there were a finite number of things, and a broken shot glass could not be replaced by another; a lack of care for things would lead to having none at all, a regression into the Stone Age, animal skins, digging sticks, and flint axes.

The grown-ups seemed to be constantly mending the world, aged, worn, carelessly used; they thought that loss was the result of age. But when Father cemented the dacha's foundation that had cracked from the earth's spring turbulence, I thought it was not the foundation's age that was at fault—rather, the future was hidden inside the cracks and it was growing out, like leaves or bushes on old facades, crumbling the exterior.

They sometimes made me listen to classical music, but I was tormented by its harmonies, sensing that the world wasn't made that way, it didn't have form and discipline, and I sought other sounds that would correspond to my picture of sensations. I found them at the German cemetery, where we went a few times a year to tend the family plot.

Stars, insignias, rifles, propellers; captains, majors, colonels—every third or fourth tombstone had a photo, their faces still youthful. The cemetery was dispassionate proof of what the country had done for a century and where its men had gone; the saturation of war was so strong that I sometimes expected medals and orders to grow on trees instead of leaves.

Among the old graves there were Germans of previous centuries: someone called Hans Jacob Straub, physician and apothecary. The Russian names alternated with German names, as if it were a total list of losses after a fierce battle. I thought the corpses had to be uncomfortable there, underground, lying in graves as if in the trenches, and that some deceased general had taken command in order to free our soil from the German-Fascist invaders.

The quieter and more reconciled the cemetery seemed on a clear fall day, the more horrible, deep and persistent seemed the underground struggle that supplanted eternity for those who did not believe in it. The cemetery land, dug up and crumbly, often sank, buckled, tossed up stones, swallowed fences, tilted tombstones, and squeezed out tree roots—I imagined these were traces of underground attacks: recognizing only the enemy, the corpses dug underground passages with their fingernails, stormed burial vaults, and broke into other people's rotting coffins.

Suddenly, with terrifying noise, the wind tunnels of the nearby aviation plant roared over the cemetery. During the war, jet fighters were tested there with compressed air. A prehistoric animal, the mastodon of all mastodons, roared, its voice bigger than the cemetery, bigger than the city, it even put a stop to the silent underground war and suspended my heart, which lost its beat, in the emptiness; the power of the sound was so great it turned into the sound of power.

Yet my parents went on cleaning the area as if nothing happened, scraping off the persistent moss and sweeping leaves. But I was certain: yes, the world was built on discord, yes, my sensations were truthful, in the way that the sensation of the nearness of bad weather, of high pressure, of electrically charged air before a storm was truthful. The roar of the wind tunnels over the family graves became the sound of the past, the sound of history, the sound of its ruthless elemental power, and I listened to it almost gratefully. It explained in a manifest physical manner what forces were tearing apart and oppressing our family and what echoes of events lived in it; it tore off the covers to reveal the very core, the very essence.

LEGACY OF THE DEAD

With the birth of a child, a family's fate awakens, its postponed powers going into action; the diagram of relationships changes, for now there is a new center of gravity.

Everything that connects people, amity, arguments, insoluble contradictions that have become a form of existence lose their static nature and move into the active phase. The clashes over the crib involve not just will and character, but the joint legacy that will exist in the child, unchanged, or that will not take, or become part of the new creature's life.

Every family in the USSR was "overloaded" by history; the family space did not protect you from anything, it had lost its autonomy. Too many people had died before their time, and the family remained exposed to the crossfire of history, constantly reconfiguring itself to the intensity of the losses, finding a replacement for once significant figures.

Probably every family at any time lives like that. But there seems to be a threshold for loss, after which there is a quantitative change. The family stops being a communal entity unfolded in time, built on values and meanings, and it becomes simplified, moving into a reactive existence within opaque zones where you can hide from time and the state.

You are born inside certain relations that become "family" to you simply by the inertia of language: father, mother, grandmothers, son, grandson. These people have warmth, closeness, sincere feelings. But essentially they are a multilayered, complexly organized conflict, and an insoluble one because the conflict does not arise from personalities. A child's life in such a family is not at all necessarily horrible, the child can be loved and spoiled, but he still feels that below the cover of daily existence and the concord of communal life, there are tectonically active layers saturated with blood that is hardly symbolic.

A child grows in a field of conflict greater than his horizon of comprehension, inheriting historical anxiety as a background and milieu of life.

Name and surname is the first and tightest tie to the family; but often I did not want to have either. I was afraid when I saw my name written somewhere, for example on a medical document, inaccessible to me but "signaling" my existence.

I seemed to know how dossiers are gathered and stored, how questionnaires and personnel files lie for years in cardboard boxes, how the bureaucratic machine strives to "tie" things up, combining a person and his name, so that neither can escape the other and the person is always identified precisely.

The fear of lists of names, the fear that your name would become a thread tying you to arrested relatives, that they could take you away just for your name if it revealed a persecuted nationality—all these fears that I had not experienced personally seemed to prompt my fear of having a name. Sometimes my greatest pleasure was in writing it in pencil and then erasing individual letters, watching how my name became unrecognizable.

I decided to give myself a name that no one would realize was a name. I would call myself Plexiglas or KPRB-ZT, Quiet Evening or Tomorrow's Weather Forecast. People would think those were random words, but I would call myself that and gradually I would separate myself from my outside name and one day slip out of it like an old skin.

At work, Mother had a Moscow phone book. When she took me with her, I could open the book at random and plunge into the columns of Kuznetsovs, Matochkins, or Shimovs, forcing myself into the crowd; it was a pleasure to know how many surnames there were in the world and if one day everyone decided to change their names, no force could ever restore the original ones.

So, when they took me to the Alexander Garden to visit the Tomb of the Unknown Soldier, I felt that the highest award was permission to be unknown, and I understood that such an award was given to one person and there could be no others.

There was a second fear paradoxically associated with the first. I remember the creepy feeling of my own inauthenticity, which could not be overcome with a pinprick in my thumb or a look in the mirror; did I exist, was I someone if there were no papers about me? Was I protected, so to speak, from accidental disembodiment, of not being known as me, if my name was not attached to my being, and my inner being, by documents? My parents had passports, ID, passes—what about me?

I told my parents about this fear, and Mother, trying to reassure me, showed me my birth certificate, but the green booklet did not convince me. It certified the fact of birth but not the fact of my subsequent existence. I thought my parents were hiding something, there had to be a paper just about me, and they'd probably lost it or never got it in the first place, or there was something horrible about me written on it, some stamp of selection and rejection, a sign of unreliability.

My parents got sick of providing me with reassurance and explanations that there was no other document and ended up raising their voices. The next day, Grandmother Tanya gave me a passport, handmade from a notebook, with a photograph and a state symbol, copied in red pencil from a coin. Even though I understood that she made it for me the night before after overhearing the argument, the passport calmed me down instantly. I never even touched it again, did not take it out of the desk drawer—it was enough to know that it existed.

I could not have known about the anxieties of earlier years, of not having a passport, not being documented in life; having a passport back then meant the conferment of civilian personhood, when it was so important to have documents without any notations that restricted your rights; but my fear was real and so was being freed from it.

I imagined yet another, conclusive way to liberation from my fears: to follow Lenin and perform some exploit that would allow me to take on a new surname, a pseudonym; to be reborn and get a name given by history itself.

My question, would I be able to have my own surname when I grew up, ended in an expected scene. My parents brought up the business with my passport, they wanted to take me to a psychiatrist, but then changed their minds—apparently out of shame and embarrassment; they would have had to explain that the child did not want to carry the family name, and what would the doctor think of the parents, would he suspect them of something? Probably all I wanted was to certify the right to own myself, which I was denied—the right to my own self, my own life, my own destiny.

The word "owner," however, was a harsh rebuke, an accusation of a terrible sin.

I can't say that I wasn't allowed to own things. But as soon as the adults began to think that it was more than some object that tied itself to me, rather that I was starting to organize a close circle of objects, determining what was mine and what belonged to others and demanding that this division be recognized, thereby tracing an outline of myself—measures were taken.

"Oh, look at this owner growing here," they said with a grimace of scornful disapproval, as if they were talking about a pushy invasive weed, outpacing the docile useful plants.

"You must live for others," the grannies said. "You must live in their place," they said, meaning the victims of war. I imagined that someone was living for me and in my place; this formed a vicious circle of lives turned over to others; a chain of substitute existences that completely erased the individuality of man.

For me the scorn for the concept of "owner" also meant the invisible power of ancestors. Later, in the nineties, the word "ancestors" was used ironically for parents, stressing the newly discovered generation gap and the fundamental difference in approach to the new times. But back in the eighties the word "ancestors" still reeked of gunpowder, blood, and dirt, creating the sense that they were here with you, seeing right through you and able to pass on what they saw to Grandmother Tanya or Grandmother Mara as easily as handing over an X-ray.

Each grandmother tried to make me her grandson. Between them they had lost eleven brothers and sisters, two husbands, and an almost uncountable number of more distant relatives. As the only grandchild, the only one amid the dead, missing in action, and arrested, I was not just a child: I was a fantastic win in the lottery, a win in the game with the century; a justification for their suffering, deprivation, and losses; justification and meaning.

They both had grieved more than they had happily loved; they did not have a woman's life from youth to old age—they were more sisters of dead brothers and widows of dead husbands, and their love in terms of time was spent more in loving the dead than loving the living. So there was a fear that their love and hope would tilt the scales of fate, a suspicion that love was not always protective, that on the contrary it could send one on a dangerous path, to face a bullet, to die.

They both greatly pitied the men of their cohort, which made passion an insignificant particle in the face of history, sympathy for male weaknesses, and disbelief that a man can be fully trusted, since tomorrow a notice might come calling him away. Their lives were solitary and austere, as if they were widows of an entire generation, as if beside their own husbands, they had to mourn the men who died without families, the ones renounced by their families, and the ones who were never remembered on the day of the great victory.

They treated their children with hidden wariness, afraid to tempt fate with happiness; the children were accorded strictness, harshness, and even cruelty. But when a grandchild was born, born in another, less dangerous time, all the restrained feminine and maternal instincts awakened. I would even say that their love for me was a little like the love of a woman for a man—a passionate seriousness and a demanding delight. They both saw the first person in their life who was not under the heavy thumb of history, who could not be taken by the universal draft or a form warrant for arrest, and they decided to give him everything of which they had been deprived: joy, happiness, peace, confidence. But deprivation is not renewable, and they could only pass on longing, desire, thirst ...

They were jealous of each other, and they did not compete in generosity, love, or attention but in the solidity of their presence in my life. They often peered at me, looking for evidence of their husbands, brothers and sisters. The dead were resurrected in me—in pieces, individual features—and the grannies, each in her own way, reassembled me, reinterpreted me, yielding no ground to the other. If Grandmother Tanya said that my hair color was like her younger brother Alexei, who died without news in the Kharkov siege, it meant that Alexei was saved; while Grandmother Mara's older brother Pavel, also fair-haired, his blood had been shed in vain onto Finnish snow in the winter of 1939, melting in the spring, into the black peat flows of Karelian lakes, and he had vanished without a trace.

In the end, the grannies agreed: I had something of both Alexei and Pavel; better they had not agreed, for now I had to be responsible for two; eye color, shape of temples and mouth, form of nose—there was a line of men seeking salvation in me, and the grannies weighed and measured small bits of inheritance. I was supposed to take the best personal traits of each, for each one I had to live an unlived life, embody the unembodied.

The grannies saw and discussed some other me, an object of posthumous pride; and I was lost, wondering if I myself existed at all, or if I was just the sum of other people's features, an eternal debtor.

This burden throughout my childhood was latent; besides the power of my parents, my teachers and coaches, the requirements of kindergarten and school, there was also the power, the word and opinion of the dead, who in the afterlife seemed to be holding a continual family council, discussing and evaluating me, arguing over my fate.

LEGACY OF THE LIVING

Several times a year the living and dead met; that's how it felt to me, in any case. The main meeting point in time and space was my birthday.

The table, freed from daily trifles and opened to its full length, was covered with an ancient tablecloth, spectral as a shroud from a thousand washings.

Embroidered in red on the white cloth, proverbs unfolded in a spiral from the center. Like tree rings, they swirled in a single endless sentence, admonitions in thread. Measure seven times, cut once; When the cat's away, the mice will play; You can't catch fish without work. I saw the sententious simplicity of the proverbs and their similarity to contemporary slogans: Peace for the world; He who does not work does not eat; We are not slaves.

Usually, proverbs were spoken with a dash of irony, stressing their age and naive edification, but here I sensed that they were not harmless. The tablecloth turned into a short outline of the future; all the life coming to me was already predestined and planned in those simple phrases.

At last, the table was set. A festive landscape appeared, with culinary accents and hills and dales, and the tablecloth moved into the background; only the red letters refracted in the vodka glasses reminded us of its presence.

Grown-ups, mostly relatives, gathered and made toasts in my honor. This ritual was grandiloquent, serious, heavy. The toasts addressed to the future were like the instruments of a sculptor or orthopedist; they cut away the excess and added what was missing; it was all the worse that there was no sense of encroachment on their part, only love, goodwill, and wishes for a better life.

They drank vodka, and some had wine, not dry but sweet, fragrant, dark, intoxicated with itself. They brought gifts, wonderful presents, thoughtfully selected, useful; but the abundance of gifts, their significance, became too much by the end of the evening. The presents were put in my room, and I sensed the incursion of other people's wills, arguing not over my gratitude but my future.

Maybe I would have preferred something less dangerous and coercing than the books, periscope, globe, chunk of diamond-bearing kimberlite, bear tooth, case of drawing instruments—the presents which lay like a weight on my shoulders. Once again I was being reassembled, reinvented by people who thought they were fulfilling my dreams.

I would leave the room, come back to the festive table, and see the grown-ups holding old shot glasses, which just two months ago had been used for somebody's wake; now they were in the service of my birthday. A transparent terrible liquid glimmered dully in them; every glass drunk in my honor laid a debt on me, a promise made in my name, for the rest of my life.

Living water, dead water—when I was very sick, with my temperature at almost 104 ° F, and I lay there, disassociated from my body while my mind wandered in other worlds, my father would come in late at night, as if he knew the hour for these ministrations. I could smell the tickling, transparent scent of inert freshness—that was the vodka which he dipped gauze into and rubbed my body with, so that the fever would leave with the evaporating alcohol. The stinging icy touch on my skin was not like my father's hand but an otherworldly breath; that was how he returned me from the depths of illness, dragged me back to *this* world.

When the vodka was poured at the table, I thought the men were drinking it in order to open up a capacity for inner vision, like sorcerers and shamans who traveled between worlds. Words spoken with a shot glass in hand—unless it was a merry toast—had a special weight, a special ability to affect others, a special ability to come true; they were words spoken by the dead through the mouths of the living.

At the height of festivities a cold draft swept through the dishes, bottles, and glasses, the fringes of the tablecloth swayed, and the merriment leaned over an abyss, looking into it. Poses changed, speech grew more hushed, fingers moved thoughtfully, and someone would be the first to say: let's have a song.

The couches, cupboards, and chairs disappeared, the light of the chandelier became diffused; jackets, ties, and dress collars grew tight, as if people wanted to liberate themselves from images imposed upon them, as if inside each person there lived a tramp, a nomadic, homeless parasite, not a person but a persecuted spirit, the ghost of an exiled landowner—Decembrist—People's Will radical—politician—priest—prisoner; a figure shimmering and always moving north or east.

> They're taking our comrades away in chains
> They're taking them far away
> Our comrades groan in pain
> The chains rattle night and day.

I hid under the table, wanting to disappear before everyone was reborn. Above me, they were singing a different song; the song, like bad weather, came in bursts, intensifying, then simmering down, again and again. The voices of the singers resembled the sound of wind gusts, rolling over the field and bending the grass. Convulsions caused by the whipping wind keep nature from dissipating, from calming; the voices were like that, and along with my fear I was glad that I was below, under the table, seeing only feet, shoes that were not keeping time, since there was no rhythm in those songs, and not seeing the faces.

When I climbed out after the inundation of song, someone was weeping, allowing tears to roll down his cheeks, as if it were part of the ritual; the vodka gleamed dully in the glasses. The songs must have shaken up the molecules and the vodka had been transformed into tears.

They cried for me, about me, as if they could see a terrible, confused, and jagged prophetic dream. Then, awakened, they picked up knives and forks and returned to the mayonnaise salads, herring, sausages, and the overloaded table.

There was always an abundance of food, the *vinegret*, the Russian potato salad with vegetables and diced meat, mixed in a tub, and the table turned into a feasting vessel with barely enough space for knives and forks; but a special place was reserved for a plate of eggs stuffed with red caviar among the crowds of dishes, bottles, and fruit vases.

Grandmother Mara got caviar in gift boxes on holidays. Caviar on the table was evidence that everything was fine, a barometer of prosperity, more a signifier than actual food. You could not eat all you wanted, you could have one or two portions, but not three—that would earn you a frown of displeasure from Grandmother Mara who watched the whole table, noting who ate how much and making equalizing operations, moving bowls, platters, and decanters so that everyone could get some of everything. Grandmother's restriction told me that caviar had to be eaten with the eyes, which I could not yet understand, lacking the skill of feeding on pictures.

Besides which, the caviar on the table reminded me of sunny spring ponds, the weightless glowing bubbles of eggs with black dots in each. When we came to the dacha, I headed for the pond to see the roe grow murky, filling up with dirty juices, and the dots had turned into worms, and I sensed something just as murky, unsettled, and ripening in me.

As I thought about this, I noted people's teeth squashing the eggs, the shining steel crowns, the awfulness of a nicotine-stained tooth with a metal filling. I thought grown-ups ate caviar like predators who sensed the time of spawning, of fledging, and came to savor the delicacy, the childlike state of being alive, energetically charged for life, still close to the mystery of creation and birth, when the promise of the future already exists in a small particle. They devoured these fetuses of the future, munching on them with vodka, as if when the caviar came into contact with alcohol, its deathly taste was mitigated.

The wives watched their husbands, setting aside the shot glasses or covering them with a hand when another round was being poured. The men were not free; their wives' gazes kept them attached by a thread, anxious, worried, angry.

The party would start to fade, poisoned on itself, dissipating, people were tired and flabby, as if lightly touched by sleep. That was the only time when you could clearly see that both grandmothers—they were usually seated at opposite ends of the table—seemed to grow in significance, and looked at their adult children from the height of age, turning into statues, supports that held the vault of the table, the vault of life itself.

My father liked chess and we played often. At the end of the game, almost all the figures were dead, their lacquered bodies heaped up on both sides of the board, the black and white board a battlefield, with pawns fighting in the midst of wild cavalry assaults.

But my queen usually survived, and Father had to plan several moves ahead in order to corner her.

The dull rooks and bishops that could travel only straight or on the diagonal—Father usually traded the knights—surrounded my queen, pushing toward an attack. I was astonished by the survival of the queen, the most powerful figure on the board, who could not be taken one-on-one, who could slip out of traps that would kill rook, bishop, or king.

The two grannies at the table were like those queens. They underlined the tragic weakness and vulnerability of man, subject to typhus, drafts, blood poisoning, gingivitis, caught in a trap, cut off from family, forgotten; wounded, bearing the metal of war in the body, unable to reenter peaceful life, turning to drink; needing clothes mended and washed, to be fed, someone to deal with the thousands of details as persistent as lice and as constant as a child's sniffles. The providential nature of women was revealed in the grandmothers—woman as mourner, woman as widow from youth to old age. You could see woman's terrible inflexibility, the ability to survive, to build the universe so that it supports the man, for in it he is a transitory, flickering silhouette and the woman is like a caryatid, and their relationship is that of the eternal with the transitory.

For them, the people around the table at that moment weren't children or even grandchildren—they were distant descendants, and my parents were no different from the rest; the grandmothers were like right and left, alpha and omega, life and death.

I was between them, I belonged to them, as if my parents had performed the requisite physiological act, but the true right of parenthood belonged to Grandmother Tanya and Grandmother Mara.

FIELD OF SILENCE

The skill of dealing with time and darkness was given to me by my grandmother Tanya. Setting aside my homework, I sat with her at the kitchen table, picking through buckwheat, rice, and wheat; chaff to the left, grain to the right, separating the clean from the unclean. Sometimes she said, as if to herself, that with every year the grains were getting dirtier, and her fingers flew, accustomed to small work—darning, knitting, copyediting, and setting type.

Covered with blankets and cardboard, the radiators breathed hot wool, and the angled lamp shone brightly, as in an operating room. My attention, focused since morning on the rigor of notebook squares and lines, began to blur, and the concentration of school gave way to languor, the tiredness from running around after class, and the translucent filtered sadness in the remains of a frosty day.

Picking through grains seemed like fortune-telling to me. Cooked, the grains became mush, food, fit for humans; uncooked, it was the food of birds and animals, a memorial dish set on a grave. The hard, faceted, rustling grains belonged to the field, to the earth, they were connected to the underground, the posthumous kingdom, and picking through them was the same as dipping your fingers into that kingdom.

Grandmother receded from me, as if she were present in both worlds simultaneously; her graying hair and the brown spots on her skin were like signs from that other kingdom.

The grain was a kind of rosary; but she did not recite prayers, she called to the deceased. The ghost of the Leningrad blockade, which took her sisters, the ghost of battles where her brothers were lost without news, floated over the table; grain—the most important value of a hungry age, the measure of life and death—had turned into grains of memory. Grandmother did not throw away the damaged ones, she swept them up and put them in the bird feeder outside the window, as if she were watched by the shades of people who died of starvation, for whom even damaged grain was a treasure. Blue tits congregated at the feeder, but sometimes I wondered—were they really blue tits? Were they even birds at all? They looked into the apartment, hesitating, as if recalling something, and then it seemed to me that they found strange their own little bodies, feathers, beaks, pinpoint eyes, their twitters and bustling movements.

I both liked and feared helping grandmother: engrossed in the monotonous sorting, I lost a clear consciousness of myself, but I could feel some alertness, someone's invisible presence in the dark beyond the turn in the corridor.

There on the wall of grandmother's room was something akin to an iconostasis of photographs. Pictures in six rows, in old carved frames, in simpler new frames, big and small—the photos that survived; several dozen people, men and women, in groups and alone, in civilian clothing and military uniforms; a wall of black and white faces.

Grandmother neatly avoided explaining who was in the pictures. I did not press her, out of my hidden horror: all the faces belonged to people who had never known old age—otherwise I would have met at least some of them. These were all interrupted lives, how else to explain that they were gone?

In the evening, in the circle of the lamplight, I could sense that the unknown and hidden were awakening in the dark and moving toward the edge of the light, drawn by the rustle of the grains.

In my daytime life I gave little thought to who they were, taking their secrecy as a given, as a rule of life, even though I guessed that they were my relatives, my closest ancestors.

Their absence was so absolute that it stopped being a negative concept. The world was constructed as a system of deficits that through their constancy became a quality of presence.

Picking through the grains with numbing fingers, pondering the significance of Grandmother's silence, I would suddenly feel the weakness and baselessness of my own life, as if it were a random oversight of fate, and I wondered "Who am I? Who am I?"—testing the solidity of the silence.

"There once was a man in the land of Uz," Grandmother

Tanya would say, forgetting that she was talking to herself aloud, as if she were telling a fairy tale.

"There once was a man in the land of Uz" was her secret phrase, which she whispered when she was fighting an illness or her heart felt heavy. I looked for the land of Uz in encyclopedias, dictionaries, and atlases, I didn't find it and decided that Grandmother had invented it, a land of losses, a shard of a land, with only one syllable left of its name. Nothing was left whole in that land, and in it lived a fractional man, like two-fifths of an earth-mover, which happens if you do your math problem incorrectly in school. And this fractional man knows only the current name of the country, Uz, he doesn't remember that it once had been longer, and he is not afraid of the fractional things in it, nor is he afraid of himself, shattered into pieces.

Grandmother would scoop my unsorted pile over to herself, and sensing that I need cheering up, declaim from Pushkin's "Ruslan and Ludmila" with an ironic glance at the table with its mounds of buckwheat or wheat:

The stunned knight came upon a field
Where nothing lived, just scattered skulls and bones.
What battle had been fought, what did it yield?
No one remembered why the screams and groans.

Her voice would change and she'd always read the last lines gravely:

Why are you mute, field?
Why overgrown with grasses of oblivion?

"Why are you mute, field?" Grandmother would repeat, and I thought that she had in mind a specific field, but one that didn't exist anywhere upon the land.

The field of Pushkin's fairy tale with its severed heads, evil sorcerers in caves, dark rivers, traces of old battles, a field where everyone is alone—when Grandmother finished reciting, I imagined that I lived in that kind of field, the emotions were familiar, even though I couldn't say why I experienced it that way.

I was overwhelmed by a numbing sense of being an orphan. I had two grandmothers, I had a father and a mother—and yet I was an orphan. Yet how, and why, could that be? The answer was hidden in a field of silence.

We finished up the grains, I sat down to my homework, and everything that had occurred at the table became unreal and vanished. But a week later Grandmother would bring another few kilos of buckwheat—my parents chided her for her excessive purchases—and it would all repeat: the lamplight, the photographs awakened in the dark, the horror of losses, "There once was a man in the land of Uz," "Why are you mute, field," and once again I tried to control the feeling that I had approached a most important truth.

I imagined that every old thing had an empty space, like that within a porcelain statuette, filled with silence; every person had a space like that. Not swallowed words, not a secret, but silence; it was a silence that did not require the nominative case—who or what?—but the prepositional—about whom or what?

I started looking for evidence that my intuitions, which I felt deeply but could not express clearly, were not delusional. I became a detective of the unknown: there were some words or some object that would confirm that my feelings were not lying to me, that what everyone was being silent about actually existed. I did not expect instant and full revelation, I needed just a hint, a sign.

Where could I seek it? I lived in a one-bedroom apartment, went to school, spent the summer at the dacha, occasionally visited my parents' friends … I leafed through the books on our shelves: I might find a forgotten notation in the margins, an old note or receipt, a page from a calendar used as a bookmark; I pulled photos out of their frames, looking for a hidden second picture; since I was good at hiding places—I had several in the apartment—I looked for those that belonged to others, but found nothing more than presents bought ahead of time and money secreted away from burglars.

Actually, I didn't believe the find would be in a hidden place; I rather expected that in deference to my persistence, a second face, a second bottom would be revealed to me. And the more ordinary and unobtrusive the object would be, the more unexpectedly and obviously would its ability as shape-shifter appear.

Naturally, these searches were not all I lived for; they occurred like bouts of fever, and between them my existence was the ordinary existence of a schoolboy. But I can't remember anything about those long intervals, although I remember my desire to get evidence of the reality of the conspiracy of silence and the intensity of every moment of the search.

When I had searched the apartment and other accessible places many times without result, I almost lost faith in my suppositions. The world was so solidly constructed, so authentic in the poverty of its unambiguity that I grew depressed, sensing that my entire life was being decided, that if I gave up now and believed that there was no false bottom, then my guesses would retreat from me, choose another paladin, another detective.

Give up, all the circumstances, all my failed attempts, said: give up. And only the weakest, barely audible voice whispered: give up and you will be no more, because "you" are that inner ear and inner eye; you did not notice that each failure was a step; you are close, so very close to success, try again!

Try! And so one day when I was alone in the apartment I set the alarm clock in a visible place, marking time until Grandmother Tanya's return, and started a new search. Despair,

despair, I had fingered the lining of clothes in the wardrobe, removed books from the shelves, opened the forbidden drawers in the desk, discovered general and private secrets, learning who was hiding what from whom, opened jars of shoe polish, peeked behind mirrors, reached into the ventilator openings, studied the innards of the washing machine—despair, despair, despair, everything was empty and silent!

The minute hand was hurrying, catching up with the hour hand, I had fifteen minutes before Grandmother's return, I had to put everything back the way it was, lock all the cabinet doors the correct number of turns, line up the shoes in the entry, wipe away my fingerprints in the dust—I would have to lie and say I thought I would do a bit of housecleaning—move the hangers in the closet to the exact intervals at which they hung before my incursion. Neither my grandmother nor mother would notice anything unless I left obvious traces, but my father with his passion for order would be affected by the smallest, most insignificant change that occurred in his absence; he would feel the difference, so I had to use my fingertips to learn where a thing had *properly* lain and return it to that position.

Thirteen minutes, twelve, ten, nine, six—and suddenly in my rush to find clues I knew that grandmother would be late; she wasn't aware of my plans and likely wouldn't have approved but with blessed generosity she was giving me another half hour by walking from the metro.

And in that unaccounted-for half hour, when all signs of a search were removed, when the clock was ticking unhurriedly, I saw the apartment with new eyes, I saw that there were a few places, a few objects to which I had never paid attention, even though that seemed impossible.

For an instant it was like being inside a rebus or brain twister: a ray of light from the corridor pointed out the pier glass, which reflected the brass bell that Grandmother used to indicate the start or end of our games; I picked it up and rang it and the brass *ding-ding* began the countdown to a special time, when toys come alive.

They were right there, gathered in the corner of Grandmother's couch: a rag clown with hook-nosed plastic boots; Timka, a stuffed dog with button eyes; Mymrik, a rubber man with a hedgehog-sharp nose who carried a first-aid pouch sewn by Grandmother over his shoulder; Bunny, a white winter hare, synthetic and bedraggled; and a few others, secondary, unnamed. They formed a partisan unit, the underground anti-Nazi fighters. Grandmother and I usually played war, and it never occurred to me to ask why these completely unwarlike creatures became partisans.

Evening after evening they crept through ravines in the folds of the blanket toward the back of the couch, where the railroad tracks were, laid mines under an important German train carrying tanks or weapons, retreated, binding the wounded with bandages from Mymrik's pouch; the clown stayed behind to provide cover, led the Germans on a wild-goose chase, and died in the snow of the sheet billowing from beneath the blanket, only to be resurrected for the next day's foray.

That day my entire toy army, my comrades, whose imaginary wounds were as my own, real ones, sat leaning against the back of the couch as if it were a log, and looked at a single point; the trajectory of their gaze indicated the edge of the bookshelf. There was a book, a big book bound in dark brown leather that blended with the shelf; there was no title on its spine. That must be why I glanced right past it so many times, as if it were insignificant.

I immediately remembered that I had seen Grandmother sitting at the table with the book in front of her. She masked those moments so deftly, making them accidental, meaningless, transitional between two pastimes, say, reading and darning, that I was completely fooled.

27

I took the book down from the shelf; there was no name on the cover, either. Heavy, resembling a barnyard ledger, the book opened, revealing the glazed whiteness of empty pages.

Could I have known that this was the printing house mock-up of an important edition? No. Instead, I made another assumption based on all the stories about revolutionaries who wrote their missives from prison with milk or invisible ink. There was a text, it just had to be developed! Grandmother had saved this wordless tome for some reason, set it on her shelf so that it was unnoticeable to others but not to her, perhaps as a reminder of something, always in view.

I was impressed by the gracefulness with which the book was hidden in plain sight; as I turned the empty pages, my excitement and anticipation made me see faded letters. They combined into words, words into lines, the lines filled the pages; the book flickered spectrally, and dissimilar handwriting, various fonts, pictures, photographs, footnotes appeared—all unintelligible, vanishing, slipping away. This was the book of books, an ark of texts that never were, written in accordance with the grammar rules and orthography of various ages; the texts crowded one another, merging, disappearing.

I turned—behind me was the wall of photographs, of silent faces, and I thought I saw a very thin connection between the faces and the handwriting, the phantom bits of text. I did not know whether my desire had given rise to this or whether I was just delirious. I knew it depended on me whether the lines appeared on the white pages; it depended on how I lived, what I sought, what I believed. It would be an original source, a material truth, the answer to my questions; a reward for my loyalty to myself.

Thus my life, without losing its habitual flow, took on a dimension of expectation, an anticipatory spirit of the promised encounter. I hid my knowledge of the mysterious book without letters deep inside me, understanding that faith in its special qualities should not be tested often, was fragile; but I did not give up my efforts.

Amid the household objects, I looked for ones that would take me beyond the quotidian, would open the limits of current history, geography, and destiny. A bronze mortar, an antique microscope, a compass, a Solingen straight razor in a leather sheath, a boot tree, a silver teaspoon, a worn leather cigar case, a prerevolutionary pocket watch with crossed cannons on the lid, a rusty cabbage chopper, heavy green glass apothecary bottles with incomprehensible labels, a forged four-sided nail—they were a vanishing breed, they lived as hangers-on, souvenirs, meaningless trifles; but I, on the contrary, recognized their seniority and wisdom: in the easiest form for a child they taught me about time, about what was authentic and real and how to recognize it.

You could even say that I now had two lives. In one, I was son, grandson, schoolboy, October Scout, pal of my peers, a boy of my age. In the other, when I was alone, I was no one, I enjoyed a blessed anonymity, as if everyone in the world was recognized, defined, attributed, while I was superfluous, auxiliary, unexpected, no one's son and no one's grandson; I was frightened by the ease with which I moved into that state, by the strength of the sense of my separateness.

Left alone, I turned into a greedy, indiscriminate seeker of knowledge. My hunger for interests and desires, my search for the heights of impressions, for feeling the meaning of existence spurred by the dreariness of life around me gave my search a savagery.

I raced around the apartment, opening adult books at random, marauding through dictionaries, mastering mysterious-sounding terms and concepts, stealing art books, committing paintings to memory—without any idea of subject or meaning, like a nomad filling saddlebags with booty that seems valuable—things that might change him in the future. I was given a very small interval to create myself out of the only materials available to me; if I didn't manage it then, I never would.

LIFE WITHOUT SOUND

Grandmother Tanya was hard of hearing. She could hear only very loud sounds: breaking glass, sirens, locomotive whistles. You couldn't call her on the telephone, get her attention from the next room, make a comment across the table, or reply with your back to her. To have a conversation you had to put your arm around her and speak into her ear. Later, as an adult, I realized that my special attachment to her, aside from other reasons, was the result of those embraces as we talked.

Grandmother Tanya's deafness annoyed those around her, and she was often asked to use a hearing aid or an ear trumpet. There was a kind of envy in those requests, a secret wish for equality: the suspicion was that Grandmother Tanya, by not using a hearing aid, was making her life easier by excluding one of the most obnoxious components of Soviet reality—sound. Speeches on the radio and music from loudspeakers did not exist for her, and speeches on television and street conversation were nothing more than bare gesticulation.

The home radio was kept on, the old wartime habit, but muted. The television was for daily, ordinary news, but the radio muttered along just in case there was suddenly something incredibly important and fateful. I think the adults subconsciously trusted the radio more, it was older, and they thought that if war broke out, the television would present a soothing picture while the radio would "awaken" and start speaking in the old announcer Levitan's remembered voice. The radio, the one that had been wired into every apartment, was perceived as the voice of the communal unconscious, like the shared neuron network of all the apartments, which on its own, without a central control, would sense danger and warn us.

I thought that the radio not only broadcast programs but that it eavesdropped on us; it was part of the general conspiracy of vigilance. Grandmother Tanya had a friend who spent the war in the air defense corps charged with early plane detection. When she showed war photos, huge ear trumpets to detect the sound of plane engines, I saw an image of that universal listening, greater than necessary for everyday life, attention to words and sounds that saturated daily life like glue; the power of language, where every word contained a backward glance at itself. I sometimes wished that all the grown-ups would be like Grandmother Tanya; no, I did not wish them harm, I thought it would be better for them, too.

Grandmother Tanya could not hear me, and until my parents got home I had freedom that I didn't even think about; I took it as a given. Her deafness gave me an early independence, a window of a few hours a day when I was on my own. My inner biography grew out of those hours of solitude.

Not only deaf, Grandmother Tanya also could not see well without her glasses: her vision had been damaged by the strain of editorial work. She was a pensioner, but continued to work at *Politizdat*; I didn't know what the contraction stood for—Publishing House for Political Literature of the Central Committee of the Communist Party of the USSR—but I sensed the thrilling monumentality of the name.

I considered Soviet abbreviations and acronyms, offensive in their unnatural combinations of sounds and truncated syllables, as the names of beings that were part of the mysterious hierarchy of power, and Politizdat was, using Christian terms, an archangel, especially since it was located on no less than the Street of Truth, that is, Pravda Street.

One day, grandmother left her purse open; a shiny corner of some metal object was sticking out. Out of simple curiosity I pulled on it—and brought out a ruler without millimeters and centimeters, only unusual, nonexistent measures of length with carved names: Nonpareil, Cicero, Sanspareil, Mignon, Parangon.

Nonpareil; Cicero; Sanspareil; Mignon; Parangon—fright made me drop the ruler, for I had accidentally touched a thing from Politizdat, a magical artifact! What did those measures mean, those names, so like incantations? What sorcery took place there on Pravda Street?

Pravda Street, the name began to glow with awesome light; all my trifling transgressions, my searches of the apartment, my secret thoughts, everything I thought reliably hidden now lay before the six gigantic letters PRAVDA as if under a magnifying glass.

From then on, as soon as Grandmother Tanya said, "I'm going to Pravda Street," something hearkening back to olden times overwhelmed me with primal fear.

Grandmother Tanya was probably the only person with whom I used to feel spiritually safe. The feeling that she had suddenly acquired all my secrets—for I understood the real meaning of the adult threat "I can see right through you!"— undermined the very possibility of my existence.

So I decided to go to Pravda Street, to see it, to be assured of its supernatural powers; it was a desperate move.

I had no idea what was there, whether I would be able to even access the street (when Grandmother went there she took a red leather ID with gold letters), or how to find the building where she worked. But I set out without asking for permission, alone so far from home for the first time. When I turned onto Pravda Street from the big boulevard and saw the signs,

I thought I had the wrong street: there were ordinary houses, trees, courtyards, stores—nothing supernatural.

I thought perhaps the real Pravda Street could not even be found in ordinary topography, perhaps it was something hidden, with only one unobtrusive entrance. Could ordinary people even get in, the ones who don't know the secrets of Nonpareil and Cicero, who don't know the secret password? Was Politizdat in another world whose existence was proven by Grandmother's ruler without the usual centimeters?

I decided to walk to the end of the street. After a few blocks I was ready to turn back when far on the right I saw the corner of a building that seemed to come from another planet; aha, corner of Nonpareil, corner of Cicero, I recognize you, Politizdat!

The building was like a blueprint of itself: naked form stripped of ornamentation. It was a Constructivist crystal, the ideal of cutting up the universal into indivisible simple elements, the ideal of thinking with these elements, ready to be checked for correctness against an ideal. The building stood alone against chaos, against the bustle of the streets, against the city and its residents. It extended beyond its limits, as if the axes drawn on paper by the architect continued into the air along invisible lines of force; the building tried to even out the neighboring block, to straighten the line of the other buildings, and to organize the rhythm of pedestrians.

Across the street was a yolk-yellow culture club, framed by a colonnade, ornamented with plaster, bas-reliefs depicting the joy of Soviet people—marching off in columns, some waving banners, others sheaves of wheat, still others model airplanes.

The House of Culture with its plasterwork and columns, built much later than Politizdat, seemed like an artifact from the deep past, from Soviet antiquity. In the Soviet eighties the Constructivist architecture of the thirties looked like science fiction; the Futurism that projected the future still worked a half-century later. Constructivist design, which incorporated the complete cycle of *truth production*—from the editor's office to the printing press—bore the sense of a severe wholeness that subsequently fell apart, decayed, was replaced by an abundance of attributes and décor. I could not tie Constructivism to a certain era—there was very little of it left in Moscow—and so it seemed that the house was built outside of time, alien to everything and with power over everything.

I circled the building a few times. Politizdat was exactly what I had expected. But there was something that confused me. I looked through the spacious windows: huge paper cylinders turned and the printing presses tossed out reams of newspapers.

The day before, our school had announced another collection of wastepaper for recycling; the school was in the regional competition, and all pupils were instructed to show up with at least three kilograms, and if you brought in five, they would raise your grade in deportment.

The last collection was in the previous quarter, but the neighbors' apartments had filled up again with unneeded copies of *Izvestia, Pravda, Komsomolets*, and *Vecherka*. In the morning all the pupils showed up with piles of newspapers; the older ones hauled two or three piles, some helped by their parents, some using old people's satchels on wheels. Piles and piles, some still white, others yellowed—I don't think the school officials had expected so much, and now they were trying to reduce the paper overload, seeing something indecent and seditious in the haste to be rid of newspapers. Paper to be pulped kept increasing, no longer fitting in the cloakroom, and everyone who walked in froze at the sight of so many old words surrounding him.

The school porch was strewn with bits of paper; the remains of transcripts of Party congresses, editorials on international aid for Afghanistan, feuilletons on the American war machine, articles on record harvests and heroic tractor drivers.

The paper shreds and ashes made me recoil instinctively. On the school porch I recalled Grandmother's ruler, the names Nonpareil, Cicero, Sanspareil, Mignon, Parangon—scary but majestic and endless, and I thought proudly that through my grandmother I was in touch with the mystery of deathless words.

And now to see that Politizdat had something to do with newspapers! I took a very deep breath. Two men walked past, printer's ink spotting their clothes, and one held a sheaf of freshly printed pages and was declaring heatedly to the other: "I told them we needed Nonpareil here!"

Nonpareil, the incantation had been spoken on the street, anyone could hear, anyone could learn. It stopped being an incantation. The magic was gone.

Watching the ream of paper spinning in the pressroom, I experienced the deepest disillusionment and the deepest relief simultaneously. I was sorry about the self-deception that had made life profound and significant, but the joy of liberation was greater: I knew that I could feel completely safe with Grandmother Tanya.

Once again the days stretched out, the months of my existence near her; I went back to waiting, observing, spying, seeking the false bottom of life. I noticed that Grandmother Tanya treated old things with a hidden pity, she repaired and darned clothing, sent old books to be rebound, as if they had suffered from the cruelty of the age. But she never grew attached to anything, she did not accumulate souvenirs, the trifles to which people entrust part of their memory.

She had only one thing of that sort, a small porcelain figurine—three green-glazed frogs: one covered its eyes, the second its ears, and the third its mouth.

"See nothing, hear nothing, say nothing." Grandmother Tanya explained the meaning of the figures, which she kept on constant view.

Other people's possessions were separate and at a remove, by virtue of not belonging to you, but Grandmother Tanya seemed to have purposely placed the three frogs right on that very boundary separating me from "other people's possessions," as if to train me to notice them and understand their meaning.

At first I thought my grandmother was teaching me how not to live: the three frogs were a satire, a caricature like the ones that appeared on the back page of newspapers. But gradually I began to look deeper at the frogs and tried to grasp what set them apart from their surroundings in Grandmother's room.

The room had a large table with papers, a wooden darning mushroom over which a torn sock or stocking was stretched, a velvet pincushion, a basket with pieces of fabric, an old portable sewing machine, books, and table games always ready for me. It was all so well-studied, so reliable, always in the same place, determined long before my birth, and it seemed that life went on year after year, attaching objects and people ever more firmly to their place, gently and not quite really aging them.

Only the three frogs, as tiny as Japanese netsuke, meant something different. Sometimes, when no one was home, I sat and looked at them, trying to understand them whole, as a triple statuette, three syllables of a single word. I sensed an old suffering in them that was causing the glaze to gradually crack and chip.

Once during winter vacation, I was dying of boredom as I recuperated from a bad flu and high temperature. Still sensing the remains of the fever, I wandered the rooms agitatedly, looking for something, picking up and putting down objects, seeking a release from illness to freedom. I found nothing; tired, irritated, I turned on the television—at twilight during vacation they ran adventure movies for schoolchildren.

I don't remember the film, one of the many Soviet movies about our intelligence agents in the West, shot on pretty much the same streets of Tallinn or Vilnius. Fired up by the shooting and fighting, still reliving the chase and shoot-out at the end, I wandered around the apartment again, found myself in Grandmother's room, and my eyes were fixed on the three frogs at the edge of the table.

In spy movies a small detail—a beige handkerchief in a jacket pocket, a bottle of wine on a café table, the rear window lowered in the car—shows the invisible spectator that the surveillance has failed, the operation is off, connections have been figured out, and danger is all around, dissolved in the carefree day, for any passerby could be counterintelligence. But the sign has to be extremely natural, unobtrusive, so no one watching could guess it was a special signal.

Suddenly, with the same certainty as the movie's hero, I understood that the three frogs were such a signal. Grandmother Tanya decided to give it to me, to show how people really live— see nothing, hear nothing, say nothing. My intuitive guess about the vast expanses of silence had its second proof, after the book in the brown binding, the book without words.

I took the statuette and moved it under the lamp, to show (in the tradition of spy movies) that I had noticed it and got the message.

Grandmother Tanya came home. Awhile later she dropped into the room where I was reading and gave me a quick look. Then I walked down the hall past her room. The three frogs were still under the lamp, where I had moved them. The brown book lay before her on the table, opened to the first glossy white page. Grandmother was scribbling with a ballpoint pen on a scrap of paper in preparation for starting a line. There was no determination in her pose, she brought the pen to the top of the page and then put it away, picked up another pen that might not be as messy; it was as if she knew that the first word would inexorably oblige her to continue.

I understood that Grandmother had sat this way many times before, fighting with herself, remembering all the previous failed attempts, and that today the pen would not touch the page, either. But at the moment I sensed that my future had been born. I was prepared to wait.

THE POWER OF THE AX

My attachment to Grandmother Tanya weakened over the summer vacation, when Grandmother Mara took over—my summertime dacha grandmother; in the city she lived separately, but I spent the three summer months with her. Heavy, solid, and physically strong, she was a true dacha sovereign. Our small plot was filled with apple trees, plums, cherries, currants, gooseberries, sea buckthorn; we grew potatoes, cucumbers, onions, garlic, turnips, beets, squash, pumpkins, and herbs. Grandmother Mara would walk around the garden looking for a bit of space to plant something else. It seemed she lived from spring to fall, barely tolerating winter, waiting for the first warm sunlight to put seedlings in cans and milk cartons onto the windowsill next to the frosty glass.

She'd gone through many professions. She'd been a maid, a warehouse keeper, a seamstress, she worked the elevator in a clinical laboratory. When they showed me pictures of her in her twenties and thirties, I thought I was being fooled, for I had seen that woman in the mosaics at the Kiev metro station and in the sculptures on Revolution Square. I could not consider that young woman a relative any more than you can consider a figurative or architectural style a relative. At one with her generation, she was the embodiment of the era's heroine, "a simple Soviet girl," a peasant from a leading kolkhoz, a swimmer, veterinarian, or student.

They were women who had not acquired femininity, often not pretty, but even the pretty ones retained the soft dullness of peasant rag dolls; in astonishment at getting used to blouses, jackets, shoes, simple necklaces; joyous and inspired, dynamic in metro frescoes and static, caught by a camera; as accustomed as nudes in an artist's studio to seeing themselves depicted on gables and ceilings, to identifying with the great construction, with socialism, which had chosen them as heroines, or to use today's language, as top models, for just as today runways and magazines are used to display fashions, it was through their features and clothing that they portrayed the new times.

Her father gave his daughters peasant names as dowries: Mara was a family nickname for Marfa, and her sisters were called Fevronya, Pavlina, Agrippina, Felka, and Lukerya, old-fashioned village names. It was probably the only thing he could give them, sending them out into the world, before dying in the Civil War. She grew up in post-revolutionary orphanages, and for all her determination to have a family, she retained a sort of unease about her femininity, which apparently was taken as emancipation by the men who courted her.

In the photographs from the war years, of the sort that have vanished, a clearly feminine image appeared, as if the four-year wait for her husband and fear for her children had given her a face. Gradually, the individuality wore away; in the war years she approached the peak of self-awareness and then gave herself back to the era so it could fill her head with the appropriate thoughts, concepts, and ideas. Grandmother Mara enthusiastically gave herself up to this important work until there was an upheaval in her later years. She thought the world was broken, Communism was broken; bitterly she locked herself in her memories of the past. But then I was born, and she turned to me as passionately as she had welcomed the new future in the thirties.

She liked lipstick and kisses, she liked sweets. She always had candies in a bowl, chocolates and caramels with jam filling. My family considered sweets excessive, an indulgence that ruined not only teeth but character and attitude, the start of spiritual decay; they brought me up with ridiculous seriousness, unable to distinguish between the essential and the trifling, taking extreme positions on everything, as if it were party politics and not candy.

Only Grandmother Mara lived as if we had earned all this—chocolate, cake, candy, halvah, caramel, marmalade, meringue—just by surviving, by being born despite the war, destruction, and hunger, and therefore, we should celebrate and sweeten every day.

When she entered a room it felt as if several people had come in. Having grown up in horribly crowded peasant huts and workers' barracks, in the human rivers of trains and stations, she never could separate herself completely from the masses. She walked around the room, she gestured, as if trying to fill the space with people; every movement presumed the presence of someone else, a line, a parade, a meeting of party members, a crowd storming a store counter. Internally, I staggered, feeling the wave of her presence, intensified by the odor of her perfume that rolled over me.

She lightly sprayed her throat and neck, but in combination with her personality the already overwhelming fragrance of Red Moscow seemed incredibly cloying, sticking to everything, narcotic, as if she remembered a completely different smell—rot, smoke, decay—and was trying to kill it with this perfume, unconsciously adding more than necessary.

She had two lipsticks—crimson and purplish brown; her face powder was in a red compact; the bottle of Red Moscow perfume with its ruby top looked like the Kremlin towers and their stars; she managed to desacralize red, making it her own.

From the color of blood shed for the revolution that saturated the banners, red turned into the color of a vivacious blush that came from health, joy, and sensual appetite. In fact, all of Grandmother Mara's cosmetics created a range of blushes, as if she wanted to demonstrate her satisfaction with life under socialism.

Grandmother Mara's looks were clear evidence that she appreciated the material side of life. An inattentive observer might conclude that she was a loud, impulsive, bossy but essentially harmless pensioner.

Yet the first time I heard the word "ruthless," I intuitively understood its meaning through Grandmother Mara. No, she wasn't cruel, she knew how to be tender, and she loved sincerely and fully; ruthlessness is something else—it is the absence of intermediate states. Grandmother Mara did not know how to internalize an experience, she always overcame it—or solved it—in a single movement; therefore she could be ruthless even in kindness.

If a tree was not fruitful, she had it cut and dug out in order to plant a new one. I learned to use ax and shovel, to dig out and to chop clinging roots. I approached the task reluctantly, hoping that Grandmother Mara would change her mind and spare the tree, but the first chopped root unloosened the ties of pity, and I fiercely dug into the ground to find the main root that kept the apple tree firmly in the ground. I struggled like a fairy tale hero with the power of the tree, deep, dispersed, and intractable.

I think at times like that Grandmother Mara felt special pangs of love for me, certain that I was her grandson more than I was Grandmother Tanya's, or the son of my parents. My father would remove the cherry or apple tree three times faster, but he would do it without passion, just another job. Grandmother Mara kept the garden not out of love for gardening; the garden was her domain, her little empire, and she was using her Communist upbringing on the irrational plants, believing that a fruitless plum tree was setting a bad example for the others and therefore had to be destroyed before the others were tempted by the joy of fruitless growth.

She let me use Grandfather's ax—a terrible executioner's tool, which had somehow survived all the moves and the wartime evacuation, as if such objects do not vanish, as if they were more than things, with a fate and a soul; resembling a Scandinavian battle ax, it was an instrument and a weapon; life began with it in a bare spot, with no people; it gave birth to a house, utensils, fence; peasants fought with it against swords and rifles; a weapon of labor and a weapon of rebellion.

I felt it, I felt the power of that ax, which was still too big for me. I picked it up and the ax made me grow to match its size, taught me how to use its weight effortlessly to chop branches and wood. When a tree indicated by Grandmother Mara was turned into a pile of branches and a stump—an octopus-like shape, resembling a terrible animal—I looked in amazement at the emptiness cleared of trunk and branches. The space was a result of that ax, and the labor became profoundly justified, as if I were repeating the actions of many generations of peasant ancestors.

I dragged the green branches beyond the fence; a short breather. Grandmother Mara fed me like an adult worker, like a man, and then she handed me a matchbox to start the main part.

Grandmother Mara believed that the best ashes for fertilizing came from freshly sawn trees, burned while the leaves were still firm, while the foamy sap still dripped from the cuts. I made a big bonfire, putting old dry logs on the bottom, for a hot and long-lasting fire, and threw the fresh branches on top. They caught reluctantly, slowly drying on the fire of the bottom logs, so the burning lasted until twilight. I stood in the smoke and trembling air, amid the sparks and searching breaths of the flames, stunned by the heat, thinking of taking a rest but knowing that somewhere in the yard that had grown viscous in the heated air, Grandmother Mara was watching me work.

The next morning, tired, with aching muscles, I still rose early, for I had to see the culmination of my actions; Grandmother Mara, who never slept past seven and often rose with the sun, living in the ancient peasant rhythm imbued in her from childhood, came out to sift the ashes.

At the hour of thickening dew and the first sun rays, not so much warm as luminous, I could see her approaching frailty; her dress refused to fall smoothly and freely, keeping its angles, seams, and darts, as if her bulky body had weakened inside and the fabric hugged her like a sheet does a very ill patient, gathering the smell of unaired linen in the folds; in the hour of morning dew she came out like a witch, a sorceress, with a trough and an old sieve, as if she was going to cast a spell.

She used a trowel to gather the still hot ashes, putting portions into the sieve and sifting it over the trough; a mound of delicately gray ash, with darker flecks, grew in the trough; the finest dust that could not be held by the sieve flew in the air, settled on the grass, while the coals that did not burn fully rattled around, black bone trees, the broken joints of burned branches.

I was amazed that the apple or cherry trees that were alive and full of juice just yesterday, cracking under the blade of the ax, had been burned, and that the old woman was sifting their ashes; but it could be no other way because of all the grownups only Grandmother Mara was capable of deciding without a second thought what would live and what would die; she stood on the border of life and death, ordering one to be chopped and burned in order to fertilize another, more worthy tree.

Here I understood why some of the old men in the dacha compound called her (behind her back, of course) Soviet Power; "Has Soviet Power gone by yet?" "Have you seen Soviet Power?" Without mockery, half-jokingly, half-seriously. Grandmother

Mara had never held any official posts, had no titles or awards, not even the most trifling, merely nominal ones; but when she showed me which tree to destroy and I followed her orders, it seemed that we were serving something greater than concern over the harvest; Soviet Power was revealed to me as a life force and the mystery of annihilation simultaneously. Grandmother Mara, despite her lowly public position, was an apostle or at the very least a Soviet zealot in the true, invisible hierarchy.

There was only one circumstance which made me feel that Grandmother Mara knew much and had seen much that did not quite fit into the Soviet canon, but either hid it or forced herself not to remember it.

When we visited her in the winter at her Moscow apartment, she put a tablecloth on a big round table—we did not eat like that at home because of our cramped quarters and harried life—and set plates from a porcelain service that was kept in the sideboard.

Grandfather Trofim brought the service back from Germany after the war, along with the sewing machine and silk bedspreads in the Japanese style, embroidered with birds and dragons.

The bedspreads and sewing machine were almost never used; Grandmother Mara used a Soviet machine for sewing, the spreads were kept in the closet, but an exception was made for the porcelain service for certain family meals. These three things were metaphysical trophies, as if Grandfather Trofim had returned from a distant kingdom with three special objects.

The marvelous objects were equivalent—with adjustment for time and place—to family treasures, for which every generation had its own attitude. Paid for in blood, Grandfather Trofim's early death, they created the family, the community of people allowed to eat soup from German porcelain, admire the bedspreads, and appreciate the mechanical beauty and harmonious structure of the Singer sewing machine.

The bedspreads had a citrusy fragrance—Grandmother Mara saved the skin of oranges and tangerines and used the dry bits against moths; a repairman came once a year with tiny tools, like dental instruments, and a narrow-necked oil can, to tune up the Singer; we weren't allowed to scrape our spoons on the bottom of the plates so as not to scratch the enamel.

The service enchanted me with the sophistication of its creator's mind; five kinds of plates, three kinds of cups and saucers, tureen, salad bowls, cream pitcher and many others—with wide and narrow necks, with thin noses like a beak; pots, jugs, vases— nobody knew what they were really called or for which foods they were intended; no one could imagine a life where there was so much food that all these forms and shapes were needed.

"This must be for jam," Grandmother Mara said, and everyone carefully put jam in the thin dish, but no one was sure that it was intended for jam, and it seemed that the dishes that remained on the sideboard looked down on us with aristocratic displeasure.

The service was for twenty, and I kept wondering: Why so many? Were there families with so many close relatives? For a while I consoled myself with the guess that it had been made with extras, in case something was broken. But then one day I saw Grandmother Mara's gaze while she set the table, as she looked from the mountain of unneeded plates to the photograph of Grandfather Trofim. And I understood, I realized that Grandfather Trofim brought this service back from Germany in the hope that he would one day gather together the large prewar family, all the relatives. Maybe he even imagined them sitting at the table; having been separated by war, they would meet again, passing bread, serving one another, pouring vodka, and these gestures, arms crossing and fingers touching, would renew their family ties; the German service would stop being specifically German when the victors broke bread and raised glasses over it.

Grandmother Mara's eyes saw what I did not—the emptiness, the absence. For me, four people at the table was the norm, the maximum, while for Grandmother Mara it was the remains, a small part of something larger. She set out the service to remember, to count all the dishes and cups that did not appear, all the unneeded bowls of soup.

I pictured the wall of photographs in Grandmother Tanya's room; for a second I pitied both grandmothers, who were irreconcilable and so similar in their loneliness.

BETWEEN GRANDMOTHERS

It is both simple and difficult to compare my grandmothers; they were so different that each defined herself through negation—I am not her—which over time bound the two so tightly that one could not live without the other.

One could say that our family was the result of a historical misalliance; both grandmothers were born before the revolution, one a noblewoman of an ancient line, the other a peasant from recent serfs, and it is unlikely they would have had a grandson in common if not for 1917, the Civil War, and the establishment of Soviet rule.

For peasant Grandmother Mara everything beginning with 1917 was her history, her time. While Grandmother Tanya lived, perhaps without fully realizing it, in an alien time; it merely moved her inherent era farther and farther away. The two women could not have come together: time flowed differently for them. Their conflict could only grow.

Naturally, as a child I did not know that Grandmother Tanya belonged to the nobility, did not know that the family was divided by a temporal marker into "present people" and "former people"; that our family was in its essence not something finished but a continuing attempt to find a common tongue, to coexist, realized in the children and in the grandchild, that is, in me; that I was in effect something experimental, a child of two times.

Grandmother Mara, a Communist who did not belong to the Party, should have been impressed by non-Party Grandmother Tanya, an editor at Politizdat, a person with entrée to the ideological inner sanctum. But it seems that Grandmother Mara did not trust Grandmother Tanya, knowing her dubious social heritage, nor Politizdat itself or the very genre of ideological speech.

Lenin and Stalin were immutable for her; they *had said it all*, their speeches were no longer words, they were signs on tablets, and there was no need to say or write anything more; therefore the official language elicited an unrecognized protest in her that grew into a quiet war, an overthrow of grammar and orthography.

I think she found inexplicable bliss in talking about "communisum" and "socialisum," stretching out the terms, stomping tight shoes to fit the big clumsy feet of a peasant girl.

Saying "perscription" and "supposably" was not simply a vulgarization of awkward "intellectual" words to suit the speech of village, not a parody of buzzwords used in inaccessible spheres of culture.

No, she killed complex words just because, she was certain that words were not important, there was no ontological faith in them, they were to be mocked like the vanquished. She saw the future of communism as wordless somehow: the kingdom of the final truth would have no words.

Even in insignificant situations she spoke aggressively, pushing, harsh, trying to tear the words apart, use them all up so that the final silence could come.

For me, Grandmother Mara's aggressive speech merely epitomized what I sensed in the speech of all adults. Grandmother

Mara immediately invaded your side of the field with words, as if she used their meaning not for communicating but as bellicose weapons.

Grandmother Tanya spoke softly, both in intonation and in choice of words, her sentences always left space for a response. She used neutral language, and I always felt free with her, like a soldier during a truce, when you don't have to keep expecting shots and looking for the closest cover.

In every conversation, Grandmother Mara (no matter what was being discussed) tried to exact some special proof of the speaker's sincerity and existential attitude. She seemed to believe no one, and condemned herself for that lack of trust, but still attacked, insisted, as if she needed the person to tear his shirt, claw his chest to the flesh and blood, exposing the gaping flesh of feeling, even though they might be discussing ways of pickling cucumbers.

Her fixation turned Grandmother Mara into an investigator, a torturer: Is there truth in the person? The connection she had felt with you—was it still true? She perceived lying as absolute evil and would never admit it was a psychological mechanism that could perform, say, a defense function as well.

Grandmother Tanya allowed me to maintain some moral mystery inside me, a hidden moral life. Her principle was "just don't lie to yourself." But Grandmother Mara thought the more important principle was "don't lie to others." She demanded that I tell everything, as if cleansing from guilt could come only in confession, preferably before several people, not just one. The most ordinary formulas of apology in her presence took on the weight of repentance.

I have to mention here what I later called the metaphysics of remarking. The concept—remarking—was key in education; "I was given a remark," "You will get a remark," "I'm writing a remark in your notebook."

A remark is not just some words with moral content; the words are secondary, first comes the act of remarking, the act of a specifically organized seeing. This seeing is not neutral, it nearly unconsciously fixes on almost anything wrong, latches on to it, calculates, classifies, and only then do the clichéd words come.

Wherever you were, you were watched by the collective hundred-eyed Argus, the visual field of existence was not safe and free; it was bad enough that you practically had no private, personal space; intense moralizing held sway in the public domain; everyone watched everyone else, zealously hurrying to be the first to make a remark, to execute a microact of power.

This feeling—that every person is both policeman and judge, that you are surrounded by people without eyelids, who never blink—this very feeling is probably what I experienced, and Grandmother Mara was its most vivid personfication. Once, in a good mood because it was May Day and there was a parade of thousands, she explained to me, "Soviet power is you and me and we are all together, that's what this power is like, it is ours, it belongs to everyone." I understood what power Grandmother Mara had in mind—the power of remarks.

The difference in language and morality was the first distinction I made between the grandmothers; gradually, a few dropped words and details created other distinctions, deeper ones.

Grandmother Tanya sometimes spoke of her childhood, the most insignificant episodes that had no historical context, walks in a meadow or a trip to the sausage store. These episodes were an expression of her person; her recollections were detailed, extended, filled with moments of understanding, moments of revelation of her own individuality.

Grandmother Mara's recollections could not strictly be called recollections. Turning to the distant past, she wandered in twilight where vague visions appeared that did not seem to relate to her life; she could not clearly define where the existence of her brothers and sisters ended and her own began, she did not have a personal view of the world and therefore no personal memory.

But it all changed come the revolution; that and the establishment of Soviet power pulled her out of her former dissolution in everyone else, tore her out of the darkness of communal living where the concept of "individual" was rather vague.

So Grandmother Mara's creator was Stalin. Naturally, the social and psychological upheaval was done by the revolution, but that thought was too complex for Grandmother; she needed an "author," a demiurge, a "father" for her new personality, because attributing her second birth to historical events meant that she was both an orphan and vulnerable. A peasant daughter, her greatest and unacknowledged fear was being alone in history, without instruction and edification, without a leader's guidance.

Lenin merely "lit the way," he was a prophet, while "Stalin brought us up to be true to the people," as the 1943 anthem said, and for Grandmother Mara her birth as an individual was "registered" in Stalin's name. The name Stalin was not just a symbol of victory and faith and Communism. When she said "Stalin," she was giving a name to a complex and contradictory alloy of traits of her own personality and the qualities of an era.

Cruelty and the readiness to quash disagreement, to sacrifice herself and others, was what she called "Stalin," thereby justifying them and making them the necessary part of the whole. They were connected to honesty, concern, and sincerity—the bad and good in such a monstrous mix that "Stalin" was an incantation joining the incompatible and forbidding all attempts to understand oneself, which would have ended—given her meager intellectual means—in an inner tragedy.

For Grandmother Tanya the comparable character-forming concept was the blockade of Leningrad, or simply The Blockade.

Grandmother Tanya never spoke of her sisters who starved to death in Leningrad, and I heard her say the word "blockade" only two or three times; that evinced how deeply The Blockade had taken root inside her and become a way of being. Talk of the inhuman horrors of blockade life were not welcome; what was welcome were descriptions of heroic exploit, and Grandmother was left behind in the prison of silence that surrounded the death of her sisters, and she found in this the only correct and honest way of relating to life, history, and destiny.

Grandmother Mara never mentioned the siege of Leningrad as part of the war; this may be explained by the fact that she had no relatives there, that Grandfather Trofim had fought in the south, and her worry for family was tied to other points on the map.

The shadow of the blockade fell on Grandmother Tanya's everyday life; an old illness made her keep a strict diet: porridge, boiled vegetables, boiled fish, unsweetened tea, a bit of fruit. She probably did not need to be this inflexible, she could have spoiled herself a bit without worrying about her health; but people of her generation had difficulty giving into laxity, following their mood; they did not know how to handle it, they had been trained by an era that did not recognize intermediate states, vacillations, mutability. It was easier for Grandmother Tanya to deny herself all small culinary pleasures than to permit herself to enjoy them from time to time.

Grandmother Mara loved to eat and derived pleasure from feeding others: her cooking creations overwhelmed you not so much with their taste as their number, opulence, satisfaction, and Rabelaisian forms.

On the one hand, Grandmother Mara had great admiration for steadfastness. But on the other, she sensed something in Grandmother Tanya's behavior that in the thirties would have been called something like "counterrevolutionary lifestyle."

She probably saw it like this: she considered the culinary abundance that she created out of literally nothing, finding products in almost-empty stores, as an achievement of the Soviet regime. All those pies, soups, and blini were the substance of *Sovietness* for her; she did not simply cook, she participated in the shared celebration of food, bringing joy to the stomach; she created examples of the happiness and plenty promised under socialism.

Grandmother Tanya's refusal to try any of these dishes elicited suspicion. I think Grandmother Mara sometimes suspected that Grandmother Tanya was actually healthy and used a medical excuse to reject not the food but the regime, enacting a dietetic insurgency against the Soviets. I sometimes imagined that Grandmother Mara wanted to force-feed Grandmother Tanya to prove that normal, healthy, festive food would not harm her, and expose her deceit to the world.

At the table Grandmother Mara kept a close eye on us to make sure everything was eaten, and no excuse or trick could spare you. You had to overeat to the point where you couldn't swallow the tiniest bite, and only then did she smile in satisfaction.

Her treats were sometimes a torture, I could not eat the most wonderful, freshest, finger-licking, meat pies; my revulsion went far beyond children's sudden food antipathies.

I wasn't frightened by the overflowing affection—essentially all the manifestations of care were excessive in both grandmothers, as if they should have been shared among five grandchildren; I feared not the care but what was inside it, like a blade in a sheath.

"Then why did I cook all this?" she would exclaim rhetorically and with great pathos if you refused another helping or asked her to pack less for home (this was a mandatory part of the ritual, the food made its own kind of intervention into other kitchens and tables).

"Then why did I cook all this?" Grandmother Mara would exclaim. And there was a whole philosophy in it: create such a profusion—of food, feelings, instructions, intentions—that the addressee had to accept, with no chance of refusing without hurting the giver's feelings or questioning the kindness of the gesture.

In just the same way, she imposed her opinions, her understanding of the world, and established her power in relationships. Your wishes—actually the wishes ascribed to you—were always *already* fulfilled, and you had no space for maneuver, for acting on your own.

I think it was Grandmother Tanya's tact, verging on dissembling, that bothered Grandmother Mara the most. Almost unconsciously, Grandmother Mara embodied the hungry dreams in hundreds of wartime diaries, which listed the foods that would appear on the table in peacetime and described how mindfully and plentifully people would eat. She sensed that she had the right of the victors on her side, that true generosity obviated tact, but she still knew that Grandmother Tanya was more strict; and that drove her mad.

But Grandmother Mara could not control herself, and over and over stacks of blini would appear, too many to fit in a bucket; sometimes I thought that everything she touched turned to food, as if a genie had played a joke on her.

Even stranger was the other side of her "cooking persona," which many people considered eccentric.

In the spring, on the eve of blossoming, Grandmother Mara would become agitated, worried by a premonition. And then one day she would say, "The sap is running!" and send me for grandfather's ax, as if she could feel what was happening inside the birch trees without going into the woods.

I entered the grove cautiously, the ground made sucking noises from the recent melt, branches knocked down by winter winds were strewn everywhere, young tree trunks bearing the teeth marks of hares and elk, and the usual paths were lost under last year's fallen leaves. The forest, which had restored its wildness over the winter, was alien to me, still in my city mode. I would have preferred to wait for the paths to be trampled once again, for foliage to hide the traces of winter, and the fallen trees and branches taken away for firewood. But Grandmother Mara brought me to help her chop through the thick birch bark, and watched with inexplicable excitement as the first drop dripped into the three-liter jar. The desire to animate herself after a long winter with sap coming from the earth turned Grandmother Mara into part-spirit, part-animal, and I avoided drinking that liquid seething from the tree. I believed it would make wood goblin fur grow between my toes.

Also in the spring, when the earth was still a mass of dried blades of grass and last year's leaves—it all lay as it had fallen in December, squashed by the wet and heavy snow—but the mean sharp teeth of nettles were breaking through the old grass on sunny hillocks, Grandmother Mara went with a sack to collect the nettles. When she had picked all the young nettle leaves in the closest hillocks, she came back to make soup, meatless nettle soup, which was merely "whitened" with flour.

I watched her pick the nettles, and she seemed like a persistent herbivore who would outlive any predator, because predators cannot live without meat, while herbivores can get by on twigs, leaves, and buds. She was performing a ritual, feeding us food from the kingdom of the dead, where translucent shadows of those who died of hunger flitter around meadows and gather edible herbs, the first spring greenery, still as weak and thin as themselves. Once a year Grandmother Mara reminded us who we were and where we came from, which vegetative root was ours, for she, our ancestor, ate soup in the thirties that did not even have sorrel but only coltsfoot and birch bark.

Spring passed, and I forgot these thoughts; but in summer the wallpaper had to be changed in the dacha rooms. Grandmother Mara mixed flour in warm water to get a white, bubbling, slurping glue. She said there was a time when she would never have thought of using flour to make glue ; she and grandfather would have sat by the kettle of glue mix, taking turns with spoons, and they wouldn't have needed anything else, not even bread, just a pinch of salt.

Once, when she was busy, I took a spoonful of the mix and tried to swallow it; I threw up behind the shed. Maybe in other circumstances, I would have felt pity, thinking about her hungry past—but all I felt was her conviction that people should consume with joy the inedible, getting calories from glue, shoe leather, and bark, and I was inadequate, a pathetically weak descendant of real people.

I tried eating the soft inner bark of birches; I stole a leather belt and hid in the woods, trying to boil it in a tin can, waiting for it to soften, but I was unable to chew a tiny bit. I was hounded by the fear that in case of real starvation, there would be no gradation; I would immediately fall to the very bottom, would be forced to boil insoles of shoes, to catch rats.

My grandfathers could have taught me to retain my dignity, not fear hunger or war, live openly and boldly; but they were gone so long and so definitively, that I could only guess, catch fleeting accidental glimpses of what I had lost.

STOLEN GRANDFATHERS

My grandfathers were taken by the war: one died from his wounds ten years after the victory, the other was lost, missing in action. They were both absent from my time, each in his own way: one had been dead a long time ago although he had been alive, the other seemed to have never existed at all.

I am sure that my grandmothers and parents remembered

the grandfathers and spoke with them in their heads. But they never told me their biographies, never talked about them with me at all. If they had talked about one, who died, they would have had to talk about the other, who was lost, and for some reason they didn't want to do that. So they preferred to keep both cloaked in silence. I reassembled my grandfathers in pieces, fragments of random recollections, the few remaining objects, without finding anything abnormal about it, thinking that everyone lived this way.

Our dacha was in a place where battles were fought in the winter of '41. The Germans took the neighboring village, but not ours. The former line of the front split the dacha region in half. The trenches and foxholes of the frontline were filled in, but in the field and woods where the Germans had stood the grass and trees grew a little differently, a shadow fell on nature even on the sunniest days. I understood how dangerously close it was to Moscow: an hour on the commuter train.

There were still dozens of old blinds in the woods, big trenches for tanks. Kids weren't allowed to play around them, for there were rumors that decades ago someone was blown up by a mine. But the trenches and foxholes didn't elicit any desire to crawl through them, they were blurred holes filled with black rotting water that digested fallen leaves year after year.

Every little village in the area had an obelisk with a list of names and an inscription like "They Passed Into Immortality." An artillery captain was buried near a local pond—either his unit had been stationed there or he had died on the spot. The grave was tended by the dacha residents and the villagers, but it was as if they were fixing something in their yard, so the repairs made it resemble more a rural sanctuary than a military memorial. A quiet neo-paganism arose in the region, a weakly pulsating cult of *departed ancestors*—"They Passed Into Immortality." Essentially, the cult was very distantly tied to official events, fireworks, parades, gigantic monuments, and eternal flames; as if the universal sacrifice was so great that any memorial was rendered insignificant. Gradually all the ground that held the dead turned into a memorial and took on features of sanctity, blessed by sacrifice and blood.

In this cult my warrior grandfathers had become nature: a birch, bird, brook, grass in a meadow. The phantom shadow of the German presence, the trace of the extreme edge the Germans reached in their attack on Moscow, was stronger than the imaginary presence of the grandfathers. I tried many times to imagine that maybe one grandfather had hidden in this pit from gunfire and the other's tank stood here, but I felt nothing. Without the support of real memory, it was just a failed attempt at self-deception.

But everything German attracted me. I had a morbid interest as one sometimes does in relation to something extremely repulsive: sores on a beggar's leg or a dog hit by a car and smeared into a red spot on the asphalt.

Besides which, the symbols of the Third Reich, which were unceasingly preserved and refreshed for propaganda purposes in the Soviet Union, did not go through the stages of aging and decay that the Soviet military symbols, images, and heroes had experienced.

Soviet art had played itself out, the content was gone, leaving only the form. In some sense, what their soldier husbands had been like had already been told on behalf of my grandmothers; in any case, a solidly established canon had been imposed on us.

Grandfathers—all the dead—had been appropriated by the state and returned in the form of ideologically laden images; their death turned out to be the main justification for the regime.

Grandmothers might have risked going against the canon. But they could not go against themselves.

The men's lot was to act, the women's, to wait; men got

arrests, battles, and death, women got suffering and the passive portion of existence. Naturally, this is an arbitrary distinction, but it makes something a little more clear.

The female line continued, through the grandmothers, while the male line was cut off with the death of the grandfathers. The grandmothers passed on only their views and understanding to their grandchild. They were afraid of history: involvement in history killed their husbands and brothers; you have to hide from history, snuggle deeper into the family circle.

Only the grandfathers could have given an example of historical courage, historical action, historical duty—but the grandmothers, I think, were afraid that such an example could be fateful, could push me toward a dangerous path, and unconsciously they tried to protect me from the grandfathers, to hide them and keep them away from the house, the family circle, which they might destroy accidentally. The grandfathers were turned into restless ghosts who came home to the wives but were not allowed through the door and given a corner in the barn, where the women slipped out to see them, keeping their presence a secret from the family.

I tried to imagine what my grandfathers would be like now, in my time. I went to the "Generals' Building" on Sokol, whose terra-cotta bricks seemed to have been fired in a special flame so fierce that a fire truck had to be kept handy as part of the guardhouse. The walls displayed memorial plaques, with military leaders armored by rows of medals, and bas-reliefs of banners, weapons, laurel leaves, bayonets, funereal ribbons sprinkled with five-pointed stars; old men in uniform often strolled in its rectangular courtyard defended from the street by bastion walls, as if protecting the building from the winds of new times.

One time I saw two old men come out the heavy doors with cream-colored curtains, one in navy black and the other in blue summer uniform, four or five rows of medals and ribbons on their chests. They must have been an admiral and a general, both around seventy, they had started in the war as lieutenants, and now maybe they were friends, married to sisters, or maybe one had saved the other on the Black Sea or the Barents Sea, during the defense of Sebastopol or in military convoys; their highly polished shoes gleamed and the old men were smiling.

A Chaika limousine was waiting at the steps, it belonged to the admiral, I thought, and a boy a little younger than I in the backseat looked at them with longing and adoration. The admiral greeted his grandson with a smile, a squint, and a salute, while the pilot general spread his arms, long thin fingers stretching out of the sleeves—he was missing two fingers on his right hand—and pretended to be flying right from the steps to the car.

How I wanted to be in that boy's place! I thought my desire was so strong that like a cuckoo I could push the boy out of his body and the old aviator would come down the steps pretending to be a plane for me. But with that feeling I realized that I would be betraying my grandfathers, denying them for the sake of inner well-being, and I turned away, bitterly leaving the boy in the Chaika his old men.

Grandfather Trofim was my mother's father; I had seen pictures of him, heard a few stories, rather sketchy; I knew he was an officer, served in tanks, fought the whole war, and died in the mid-1950s from his old wounds.

In fact we were separated by only three decades. But a prehistoric man looked out at me from the photographs; his features and his uniform said that he had lived in some distant time of which there were very few remnants, things made solidly and out of indestructible material—cast-iron doorstops and irons, sewing machines on cast-iron pedestals, heavy nickel silver spoons.

Grandmother Mara kept his decorations in a candy box hidden under the linens in the closet. They were rarely taken out or shown to me, I think I saw them only two or three times, so I have no visual memory of them; I remember the weight of the box, which I was allowed to hold, and the feeling that Grandfather Trofim would not have permitted keeping his medals in a box with the word "Assortment" in gold letters.

There was an Order of the Red Star, the Order of the Red Banner, other orders, and a dozen medals. No one really knew how he earned them or where he had fought.

I imagined the orders and medals in rows on his chest, enveloping him with their golden glow; but each order meant a lot, "weighed" too much, and this excess of meaning that intensified the complex hierarchy of awards erected a solid wall between me and my late Grandfather Trofim.

Once I decided to steal the medals and hide them in a place known only to me, to bury them, because they outweighed the cemetery urn with light ashes, outweighed the fleeting memory of family, as if the medals acted in their own self-interest. On the death of their bearer, they became his executors, so to speak, acquired the right to speak on his behalf, and the other material evidence of his life—papers, clothing, personal trifles—lost out to the heraldic symbols. The medals wanted to be remembered, they stole Grandfather Trofim from me, they did not steal my memory but were the key to remembering him.

On our dacha plot, which Grandfather Trofim received from the government a few years before his death, he had time just to build the summerhouse and leave some symbolic objects, seemingly from a fairy tale.

Grandfather Trofim transplanted this oak from the woods, they told me, pointing to a big tree whose roots had spread to a third of the plot and suffocated the roots of other trees. The apple trees were being killed by the oak, but no one would consider sawing down this memory of Grandfather.

Grandfather Trofim dragged this stone from the woods, they

told me, pointing to the enormous glacial boulder that looked as if it wouldn't budge without a crowbar.

The oak and stone—Grandfather must have been bored in civilian life, performing these inexplicable exploits, measuring his strength against stones and trees, capturing them, moving them onto his land. He finally died of ennui, oppressed by this great weight, the weight of former feats; he wanted to be cremated. What he sought perhaps, in his weariness, was a definitive death.

I studied the statutes engraved on the decorations, which order was given for what; I fought the orders and medals in my imagination, forcing them to speak, trying to imagine the enamel Red Banner fluttering, how the soldier etched on the Order of the Red Star grabs my rifle and turns to me to tell me at last how my grandfather had fought. But the orders did not come to life and I just wasted paper by drawing battles. The grown-ups were touched by my dedication to Grandfather, while I suffered attacks of despair that increased on days commemorating military achievements: the same orders were depicted on posters, glowed in lightbulbs on lampposts, and gazed at me from postcards; silent and oppressive, they were given to me as coins in place of a monetary note, instead of memories of my grandfather, as if there had been an exchange of a person for awards at some unknown rate.

Grandfather Mikhail; no one ever mentioned his surname, I never saw any photographs or heard any talk of him; his name existed only in my father's patronymic. It was as if he had never lived, had never met Grandmother Tanya, had no face, character, or habits, and existed only in documents, a ghost of the civil state. "Grandfather vanished without a trace" my parents replied curtly. It seemed that Grandfather Mikhail did not vanish in some specific albeit unknown part of the country, of the planet, but simply fell into another dimension.

Gradually I pictured a vicious circle of losses: the sergeant who buried the lieutenant on the battlefield died, along with the secret of his grave; in the hospital a private who remembered the village where the sergeant was buried also died, and so entire chains of human names died off; one, two, dozens, hundreds, and Grandfather Mikhail was there among them, on the dark side of memory.

The only object I knew for sure belonged to him was the medal "For Bravery" on a worn, shiny ribbon, alone, as if lost. It contrasted strangely with the box of orders and medals belonging to Grandfather Trofim, as if he had possessed numerous qualities that turned into awards, while Grandfather Mikhail had only one, irrational and infinite bravery, which led him too far, to the place from which no one returns, where people die without a trace; beyond the limits of the universe, where death is not an event that can reach the living.

As a child, I probably rarely noticed that I had absolutely no grandfathers. It had always been that way, and it did not seem strange; Father was born during the war, and in some sense he was its son, as if in the war a woman could become pregnant, as in myths and fairy tales, from a military wind, the stamp of a boot, the gleam of bayonets, from the stormy, tense atmosphere.

My father was born when all the men had gone off to war, and this collective departure of men and the subsequent return of the few somehow obviated the question of paternity, made it pointless. The boy was born into a circle of women, righting the deathly absence of men, equalizing the balance, as if life could not stand it and boys started being born on their own. What had been before the war was gone like burned archives, like the state of paradise, and there was no way back there even mentally.

I sometimes thought that my father's patronymic was not real, it was simply that people had to have one. My father could have been Petrovich, Sidorovich, Ivanovich, Alexeevich, as if some office had supplied the patronymics to restore the proportional relations of names in the generation lost in war. He was registered in the name of the Mikhails who had died, in a redistribution of newborns among the dead soldiers, like posthumous rations, perhaps taking children away from living fathers for the benefit of dead ones, because the dead need descendants more than the living, they have no other way of perpetuating themselves. The silence of my grandmother and my parents was a sign to me that they knew about this government operation that changed the familial ties of the whole country.

Sometimes I thought that Mikhailovich was code, a cipher, a pseudonym; that Grandfather had existed, but lived the life of a secret agent, a spy, about whom one could not say that he existed; someone who worked for decades under a cover in a foreign land, who was anonymous even for those who worked with him.

Grandfather Mikhail was in army communications; that was all I knew about him, but I couldn't tell if that was true or part of his cover story. There was a huge, nonworking radio receiver on legs at home; it had broken long ago, and the tuner moved the indicator to different marks for wavelengths and names of cities without effect. Father had wanted to bring the receiver to the dacha, set it up in the attic as a retro ornament, but Grandmother Tanya always stopped him gently. I thought this was a special receiver, that it had never gotten ordinary radio stations with music and news; it served another purpose—Grandmother Tanya was waiting for a signal from Grandfather Mikhail which had been delayed for decades, lost in atmospheric distortions.

I did not notice the exact moment when I started inventing Grandfather Mikhail the spy. The USSR was a joint creation of millions of nameless "authors" who spent a lifetime making this imaginary space, starting with children's games of war versus the Germans or the Reds against the Whites; I made up Grandfather

Mikhail because it was my obligation as a person entering the world of a certain culture. The culture had a ready-made plot of espionage as the search for the secret causes of the world, the revelation of the true face of reality; there already was the figure of the spy, the man who went abroad, beyond the known, into the transcendental.

In trying to find the truth, to understand the past of my grandfathers, I merely immersed myself deeper into the mythological sphere that had taken them from me; I was creating it myself.

I also did not realize that both grandfathers, while called that, were not grandfathers in age or spirit. How could they be grandfathers when they were only approaching middle age when they died, when they were young fathers? There was a generational gap, as if a scythe had swept away a certain age range.

This optical defect of generations must have been obvious to the sculptors who filled the country with huge figures of soldiers and goddesses of victory; having died young, these grandfathers were unsuitable for grandfathers; the further back in time their death retreated, the less power they had over our memories of them. And the greater the ease with which the place they should have held in history and the consciousness of their descendants was filled with phantoms, created by indifference to individual destinies, by the dark, earthy pathos of fraternal graves.

When I was still in kindergarten, one spring evening the teacher told some of us that we would be picked up by our fathers, and later than usual.

We were brought out after dinner to the playground. There was a truck and our fathers were unloading huge logs, bigger than they could embrace. It was almost dark but the sky still had the bloodred, troubling sunset, like a sign whose power was longer than a single day; it extended into the future. It was no longer the sky of a bedroom suburb of Moscow, it was the sky of a fairy tale, with endless fields with the severed heads of heroes and viburnum bridges, where the sources of living and dead water flowed, where the swift falcon flew beneath the clouds and the gray wolf leaped over ravines; the sky over the field in the stories that Grandmother Tanya read to me as she picked over the grains on winter evenings.

I quoted them, surprised that I had memorized them without even trying:

The stunned knight came upon a field
Where nothing lived, just scattered skulls and bones.
What battle had been fought, what did it yield?
No one remembered why the screams and groans.

Why are you mute, field?
Why overgrown with grasses of oblivion?

I quoted them and suddenly saw that the logs being unloaded and set down on the ground were fairy tale warrior *bogatyr* figures carved in wood. They were set up in lots of playgrounds, used as supports for swings, huts, and wooden slides. But with the approach of nightfall and the silent labor of men— the fathers were digging deep holes and mounds of dirt piled up, as if they were digging graves—the wooden fairy tale heroes looked like ancestor idols.

We children stared in confusion; that day we had been rehearsing for the Victory Day celebrations. We were given costumes—national costumes of all the republics of the USSR; each was symbolized by a single child, but the Russian Republic had several; the most fair-haired boys and girls were dressed in embroidered red shirts and long pseudonational skirts and headdresses.

We were supposed to sing the anthem lyrics, "Arise, enormous country," and a few military songs. To help us learn them, they played records over and over, and by the end of the day I was full of the refrain "Let noble anger boil up like a wave, it is a people's war, a holy war."

This was not a song. The chorus voices grew stronger and crossed the limit beyond which the choir and the audience disappeared, leaving only the all-penetrating, earthshaking sound: "Arise, enormous country," said the internal voice of the rampant universe.

When the wooden idol-knights were dug in, I realized that they could have sung "Arise, enormous country": they grew on the field of oblivion, and no power on earth could save them from their spell, turn them back into living people.

I touched the closest statue and felt the firm dry wood; suddenly I understood that my father had never known his father and grandfather. For an instant under the crimson, dangerously open spring sky his drama, his double orphanhood was revealed to me.

MY PARENTS: ORDER AND PAIN

Father was hypersensitive about order. Every item on his desk at home looked as if it had been placed there by someone obsessed by geometry, a paranoiac of right angles, who could detect even one degree of misalignment. It was the ultimate arrangement, as if each time he left he might not come back and therefore assembled his things so that he might remember them forever.

I never saw Father arrange anything on purpose or expend any effort to maintain that order; but I couldn't say that it happened on its own. Without effort and without spontaneity, he created order by his very existence. When I was at home, alone at his desk, I lay in wait for the moment a book would be crookedly poised, hanging over the edge of the desk, as if I hoped to get through to my father via that gap of a few degrees.

Father probably became a brilliant specialist in catastrophe theory because of this sensitivity. I think that he "got" the world only in static forms; the fear of shifts, spasms, and drift made him a marvelous "earphone," a human radar. I sometimes saw huge graphs on millimeter-squared paper on his desk, the teeth and dips of extremes, I saw Father bent over them, and I could sense that those teeth were digging into him, wounding him, and that he was suffering; as if an ancient chthonic creature, the god of chaos, had dug its claws or fangs into him.

He sought order, and not in the police sense of enforced regulation. Rather, he wanted the world to be fixed, once and for all. He spent a lot of time with maps, the principles of cartography, the compilation of map legends, the signs for depicting objects for seismically unstable regions. I think that unconsciously he thought of the world as a map on a scale of one-to-one. A map is a special kind of cultural object, in which reality is given in an ideal state, which can be imagined but never occurs in reality. Every map is a utopia and an anachronism, a moment of fixed time, it becomes obsolete the moment it is created, and in using maps we deal with a past that is specially organized so that it names and reveals itself.

He had the personality of a collector, a seeker of causal relationships that can be laid out on a baize-covered surface; minerals, shells, plants, stamps—he collected a bit of everything. The collecting could not become a passion because I don't think he had any passion in him; a collection was the model of an arrested, compartmentalized universe—there's a reason those drawers with sections resemble prison cells. The world as it is did not suit him, the world had to be repacked, made transparent, reduced to museum methodology.

Order was not merely observed at home; it was simply an expression of his figure, his character, his will. The collections—from badges to stamp albums—were external bastions, defensive walls protecting him from the unpredictable world around him.

As a development of his desire for order, he had an almost painful preference for symmetry. He kept trying to restore a disturbed inner balance, placing spoon and fork equidistant from his plate, setting the toothbrush mugs in the corners of the bathroom shelf, putting books in piles, performing numerous tiny operations with objects according to unknown principles—color? form? weight? application?—setting them up in pairs, one balancing the other to achieve a harmonic state known only to him.

He sought stability, steadfastness in daily life, sought it with such force that you guessed an unconscious fear behind it. Born in the war and four years old when it ended with Japan's capitulation, Father must have developed a fear of history's catastrophic nature, preferring times with no extreme characteristics, either positive or negative. After all, the period that was called "stagnation" in the history of the USSR was actually the realization of very definite hopes of the grown generation of children of the forties. And the generation of their parents.

I think that Grandmother Tanya, who lost almost all her brothers and sisters in the war, a widow, unconsciously brought up her son to be unobtrusive, even unnoticeable. I don't mean she wanted him to hide from everything or become a gray creature no one was interested in. Grandmother wanted him to have a glorious fate and success; but a fate and a success that were providentially safe, the kind that were not entirely real.

I think that when he was born, she begged—this is a story for a Greek myth or a sermon—that her son never be noticed by the gods, neither with evil intentions nor with good ones. Her wish came true—the man instinctively avoided extreme situations that would bring him to the fore; a man of the firm middle ground.

She must have been horrified by her wish come true; but the gods could not intervene a second time, even if she asked—it would contradict the first, strict condition of their agreement.

I would think she was not the only woman to request that her child be saved from fate, that her child not be seen as a target for the forces of historical destiny hovering over continents and oceans; and she was not the only one who was heard after the great and terrible war.

In some sense (higher than the juxtaposition of faith and atheism) they were prayer-saved children. But who knows what such children miss, if this apparent protection they allegedly received meant being left alone, left behind, separated from life.

Not a Party member, not an activist, not a former adept of Communism, Father nevertheless accepted the USSR as an adequate form for his existence. The cumbersome state, historical, and cultural construct, incapable of development despite its progressive rhetoric, suited his profound need for stopped time, and the rest—the absurd ideology, the inconveniences of daily life, the absence of freedom—was a heavy but not impossible price to pay for that deep and crucial correlation.

Of course, there were times when the price was unbearable and to accommodate it, to survive, he created—and imposed—crazy ideas.

He had a central concept from which came his perceptions of people and his attitude toward life. I may be exaggerating by picking out only one aspect of a complex, but I remember the paralyzing effect that the word "willpower" had on me.

When I did not want to do something, did not understand why it was necessary, did not want to accept something imposed upon me as my own idea, could not allow someone else's opinion of me to become mine, did not want to give up my sensation, feeling, mood, or thought, Father would say that I lacked willpower, and said it as if my very existence was a violation of a universal agreement and I was an indecent and shameful figure.

Willpower was an instrument of self-coercion that helped you survive in a place where your wishes and intentions were meaningless. Obstacles, barriers, and violence caused by injustice, stupidity, lies, and the absurdity of circumstances were seen out of any context that required a definite moral reaction: just a dynamic phenomenon, a useful piece of exercise equipment for that willpower.

Thus, a person could avoid protest and rebellion and accept all the circumstances and still preserve his dignity by the thought that he had overcome private difficulties, when in fact it was the monstrous way of life that had to be overcome. Rejecting it would have shown real willpower.

I believe it was academician Lysenko's theory that cells are born out of unstructured "living matter." He rejected the role of genes and DNA; his invented "living matter" was a tabula rasa in which external influences did not meet an invariant component, the conditional "selfness."

Father's "willpower" was like Lysenko's "living matter," presuming a person's continual ability to mentally mutate and forget oneself.

With that, Father imagined "willpower" in purely inherited images of resoluteness picked up from industry, from metal work and turning lathes. The way to develop it was "working on oneself": self-trimming, self-sawing with screeching metal and showers of sparks.

Only in Mother did I encounter the flexibility I so needed, the smooth transitions from approval to disapproval, a wealth of semitones in relations. She seemed to be made of a different material than everyone else—and I sensed that this was the source of her suffering, what made her vulnerable.

Mother often suffered from headaches. Today headaches are

not perceived in the same way; advertisements offering healing fizzy tablets have done their hypnotic work. Back in the eighties, with scant medications available, a headache did not seem like an easy opponent. People talked about them constantly, shared home remedies, compresses, massages; it seemed that every-one—the schoolteacher, the old man in the bus, the woman in line, the barber, the doctor—all had a headache, and the pain sometimes subsided, allowing a few days of normal life.

It was the era of the headache, the pain was the sediment, the reflux of all feelings and thoughts.

But Mother had a particularly fierce pain that would last several days; the attack came unexpectedly, unpredictably. This suddenness and inability to determine the cause (the doctors could not give a reliable diagnosis) gave aesthetic meaning to Mother's suffering; this was not an illness, it was pain—pure suffering situated in the head.

Neither coffee nor pills helped; she held her head with her hands, as if it had grown heavy; she moved through the room as if some power were twisting her muscles; she whispered in a changed voice, as if someone had possessed her.

I thought that someone else's old pain, wandering the world, seeking a head in which to ache, was entering her. At one point I decided to track the pain and understand how it got into the apartment: Did it seep in through a door or window left ajar, did it sneak into her purse at work or the store?

I set traps for the pain, imagining it to be like a draft, and I hid behind the shoe rack when my parents came home in the evening, watching for a dense stream of air slipping over the threshold, moving the dust on the floor or the nap of an over-coat. While the grown-ups changed into house clothes, I looked through the grocery bag—would there be a strange object, would I notice something odd about a package of grain?

When the attack reached its peak, Mother, who was usually

very controlled and unremarkable, suddenly was emancipated in her movements and revealed herself deeply and powerfully; she tolerated the pain without tears, moans, or complaint, but the pain removed the bonds of habit and seemed to reassemble her beauty, dispersed by every-dayness, and her nonmaternal femininity. One time I saw her holding her head with both hands, as elegant as a narrow pitcher, a *sealed* pitcher—the pain was not penetrating from outside, the pain was always inside Mother, in the vessel of her head.

During the attacks Father's voice was subdued. And things felt freer, I guess; and I sensed and remembered that difference—it was supposed to just be quieter, but it became freer. I'm ashamed to say it, but sometimes I wanted Mother to have a headache because it gave a rest to feelings that were imperceptibly suppressed; the house grew calmer, gentler, there was a mysterious fragrance of carnation from the pungent Vietnamese salve that Mother rubbed into her temples, and her light wool blanket radiated warm, electrified waves that hushed street noises; the universe of the house changed orbit and revolved around Mother's head. Hoping to reduce the pain, I would ask for it to be passed to me, but it would not, as if it could not go beyond Mother in a generational sense and stopped with her.

Grandmother Mara never had headaches, and I don't think she ever pitied her daughter in her pain; there was only one time when I saw Grandmother with her during one of those attacks: she reluctantly embraced her and started reciting words, an ancient, flowing abracadabra about stones-oaks-winds-seas-tears-clouds.

The old woman was a whisperer and she was "whispering" the young woman; thanks to the ancient rhythms of the spell, I saw the female body as an entity made by nature for suffering. Grandmother Mara leaned toward my mother, embraced her, whispered conspiratorial words, ran her palms soothingly over her head, and you could no longer tell which hand was Mother's and which Grandmother's, they had melted into each other; Mother moaned weakly, and Grandmother Mara repeated the moan, wove it into the incantation. The outlines of the two bodies formed a lump of flesh, breathing clay.

Grandmother Mara broke off the whispering, pulled away, broke the clay body into two figures and, with regret and slight disappointment, regarded her daughter. Mother felt better, her face brightened, and her body seemed lighter, as if suffering was no longer weighing her down and had finally found a comfortable place inside her, free of everything that had resisted it. And now Grandmother Mara looked at her daughter with approval.

Order and pain—those were the family principles; I protected myself as I could from my father's will, for he wanted to organize my life and make me like him, and I felt compassion for my mother. Naturally, my parents were the most important and closest people in the world for me, but with one exception—in the everyday moment, in measuring time. As soon as I began thinking of my grandfathers and feeling I was their descendant, the grandson in me started arguing with the son.

On those rare occasions when the grandson won wholly and fully, when I heard the tense silence of the wall of photographs in Grandmother Tanya's room, when we picked through the grains and I thought every grain in Grandmother's fingers was telling her something, my parents—as if an invisible power were transforming them—became strangers; the ones on the side of silence; my foes.

They had shut the door to the past and limited themselves to this day. There is probably a reason why the clearest memories I have are the winter weekend evenings devoted to laundry, the washed sheets hanging in the kitchen, dimming the already weak light; it was stuffy, and the stuffiness was made thicker by the darkness outside. The kitchen window was covered in steam, and I could spend hours wiping an opening in the condensation. It would cover over instantly, and I would clear it again.

It seemed as if nothing existed in the world besides the kitchen, the smell of soup, laundry, and burned matches. Everyone, I thought, lives this way—scraping a small hole to see a little bit. It never occurred to me to take a rag and clean the window.

My parents' life appeared to have an abundance of desires; much later, as an adult, I understood that what I had taken to be the grown-ups' desires was not that at all.

The substitute for desire was necessity; the necessity of finding food, buying clothing, getting me into Pioneer summer camp; necessity and not desire was the spur to action. When, for example, there is an inescapable task—you must buy oil whether you want to or not—and there is a total deficit of everything that could be of any value, desires fade and are replaced by needs.

Another factor that was exhausting and stripped life of any profundity was the petty and absurd tyranny of necessities; there are shoes but you can't find spare shoelaces anywhere, there are five pots of different sizes on the shop counter—what luck!— but not a single frying pan ...

Whatever difficulties my grandmothers and grandfathers suffered in the thirties and forties, whatever deprivations befell them, the nature of those difficulties and deprivations were different. They could come in an endless succession, they could destroy you or break you, but they were serious, threatening, large-scale, directly linked to the historical fate of the country and the world, they bore personal and general meaning.

The quiet absurdity of life, on the contrary, destroyed destiny and grandeur, mocked steadfastness and courage, and demanded that you make yourself commensurate to it, reduce your dreams and become one with hard-to-get items. The world of needs and deficits spun a tiny web of the power of circumstances, in which people got trapped.

Deficit does not only mean a constant sensation of the absence of something. It creates a complex system of the ersatz, mandatory substitutions, a system of switching and redistributing functions and meanings. It makes every life situation chronically difficult, like a disease without a disease, which consists of intertwining and multiplying complications, because, in the final analysis, every thing and every phenomenon is not in its own place, its own niche, but is displaced to replace something missing.

This is the world in which my parents lived; I existed in this world as their son. And as a son I felt things I did not feel as a grandson.

Probably every Soviet family put their name on a list "to increase living space," and they waited for decades, without a clear idea of what was happening at the head of the line. We were registered in a line like that. I sensed that we were links in a chain; someone was waiting for us to move so they could occupy our apartment, someone else had to move so we could obtain a new home. Our place in the world was defined by the line that lived its own life, simultaneously inexplicable and powerful.

At some point we began a countdown marked by the phrase "So when we move," a countdown of postponed intentions, delayed plans, and we began living in the nonexistent new apartment we'd moved into, like furniture and objects, the best features of the present; but the line did not budge, and our hopes and dreams remained on the dubious shore of the future.

As a son I was also part of the line, sensing the pressure of its slow movement; our apartment belonged to the line, we were temporary tenants. I thought that my grandfathers would have found a different way to live, although I saw the neighboring old men who were certainly also in line. From my parents I could take only a lesson in tolerating this kind of life.

Some evenings—because meat patties, *kotlety*, were always cooked for dinner—Father took out the heavy meat grinder and attached it firmly to the table edge. Mother pushed the meat, thoroughly cleaned, through the neck. But it got stuck anyway, tendons wrapping around the blades, stalling the mechanism. Father took it apart and rinsed it, and then they started again; the ground meat was passed through a second time, and sometimes even a third.

There was something unbearably dreary in this struggle with the meat, which seemed to be taking posthumous revenge. Second-grade, and not very fresh, the beef set an example: the thick strong sinews were able to stop the blades—so one must grow sinews instead of muscles. That was more reliable than counting on spirit and heroism. You need the sinewy strength of a dying man, whom torturers will tire of beating, they will scrape their knuckles on him and give up. You have to grow up like that, not so much brave or strong as tough and unsuitable for dividing up, sinewy and cartilaginous so that your meat blocks the knives; so that life struggles with you and finally leaves you alone.

I imagined that my grandfathers had a different strength that allowed them to maintain dignity, and the grandmothers retained some reflections of it. Father and Mother had no strength of their own, but the powers of a great order, which I could only intuit, moved through them. That was another reason they were my foes; if my thoughts and strivings were revealed, my parents would make every effort to make me only a son and not a grandson; if they learned what I felt picking through the grains with Grandmother Tanya, how I waited for her to write the first line in the wordless book dressed in a brown cover, our evenings at the kitchen table would be banned and the book would vanish as if it never had existed.

THE PLASTIC HORSEMAN

I often sensed my parents distancing themselves from me, I saw that they were not with me in some situations; they handed me over to people or circumstances, transmitting someone else's will, like puppets.

Kindergarten, school, hospital, Pioneer camp—they literally handed me over, silently acknowledging the right to *take me*. I'm not talking about a child's experience of the alien and unfamiliar; this was a guess about the all-encompassing power of the state with its national anthem on school notebooks, October badges, Pioneer pledges of allegiance, friendship of the peoples, and concern for the health of Soviet children; a guess about the forms this took, forms that did not recognize the private yet could be softened through personal relations, but still powerful.

My parents sent me to school not only because they wanted me to study; it was as if another will was added to theirs, one that did not coerce them as much as paralyze their ability to even consider any other possibility, say, homeschooling me; that they, like me, were part of some universal obedience class.

In addition, the grown-ups talked about resolute action, self-reliance, and independence. But I knew, my sixth sense told me, that one day something would happen and my parents, who kept telling me that you have to stand firm and achieve your goals, would submit to someone else's will, as if they had never lectured me at all.

There was another power to which my parents gave me up as well, perhaps without understanding it, a power as palpable as it was faceless, without a single specific source. It was like being left in a labyrinth and exposed to radioactivity without a mask, or special clothes, or a Geiger counter, or even a warning. It was a mythical labyrinth, a forest of signs, and you were forced to comprehend them on your own, for no one ever talked to you—either at home or at school—about the nature of the symbolic.

My parents worked for two years in Egypt on the Aswan Dam; they were taken on excursions to temples and burial sites closed to the public, to the pyramids and necropolises of animals. They had a crate of slides they brought back from there.

Sometimes on weekends they hung a sheet on the wall and turned on the projector, which smelled of ozone and the dust burning on the hot lens; and on the sheet appeared vanished yellow sands, the ancient god Horus carved of granite, the sarcophagus of Tutankhamen, the Temple of Karnak, the sphinx alley, Luxor, Amenhotep's columned hall, walls covered in ash from the bonfires of Napoleon's soldiers; and most important, the hieroglyphs, everywhere, as if all the surfaces were covered with a single, endless text.

The hieroglyphs and statues of Egyptian rulers, impossibly far from me in time and space, did not elicit intellectual curiosity but a profound interest and equally profound anxiety; I somehow knew their oppressive presence, their dead mysteriousness; I felt closeness rather than alienation.

But all my attempts to understand where that sense of recognition came from were in vain; sometimes I almost reached understanding by a physical effort—but each time I fell short by a step, a millimeter, a second.

Yet understanding did come.

The Pioneer camp where I was sent had a big storage area, a windowless cellar, where they kept bugles, flags, drums, banners, posters, and costumes. It was a big camp, with probably a thousand children; these props had been kept since the camp's founding, it seemed—the administrators were probably afraid to throw them out or burn them, since someone could write an anonymous letter revealing that Soviet symbols were being destroyed at Camp X. The job of camp director must have been a highly desirable one; it was a good location, high on a bank of the Oka River, with a view of the flood-meadows, and so the administration preferred to save this arsenal of propaganda assets for an eventual inspection.

I was sent to help the cleaning woman sweep the storeroom;

she gave me a broom and dustpan and went off somewhere. I was left alone in the dark space with burned-out lightbulbs; it was filled with cupboards, shelves, and boxes, the ones that might come in handy placed closer to the door, and farther back the old and dusty ones that were never touched.

The particularly disorderly disorder that comes about when various people use things only from time to time was rampant in there; small poles without banners, piles of gold fringe, spools of gold braid, rolls of faded red bunting, rolled-up banners, tarnished bugles, broken drums, hundreds of small flags with stars, tattered songbooks, white belts with star buckles, scattered cockades, plastic emblems of the USSR, and costumes—moth-eaten fur hats with red ribbons, a cloak à la Chapayev. The mess formed a shipwrecked mass. Drawings from camp contests were stuffed into various cracks, and they protruded like giant cabbage leaves, always with the same elements—red stars, Pioneers, flags, tanks, foxholes, hammers and sickles.

A spacious and innocent sunny day awaited outside, while here, in the musty cramped dark there reigned the senile promiscuity of things, the trash heap orgy of obsolete symbols. If there had been just one ordinary object, say a soup pot or an oar, the room would have resembled a storeroom, a collection of junk like the ones I've seen in dachas. But no—here there were only the tools of symbolism, abandoned, touched by the beginnings of corruption, when an object begins to fall apart but still maintains its form.

I suddenly realized that for each child in the camp there were three caps, one-and-a-half bugles, two drums, two banners, five flags, and fifteen posters; they manufactured them faster than they were used up, and they didn't wear out, just got old and accumulated. You could explode trying to blow the bugle, hold a banner, wave a flag, carry a big sign, and play the drum at the same time.

"It would be fun to play grave robbers here," an inner voice prompted; of course, my parents had told me about thieves in the Valley of the Kings who went down into the stone labyrinths, avoiding traps, and I often imagined myself as one—for I looked for secret places in my parents' apartment, finding other people's secrets, intruding on forbidden territory.

I had just decided to play at being a robber of subterranean Egypt when I bumped into something, and the whole edifice of things reaching to the ceiling made a cracking sound and began to list. It was enough to touch one thing for the rest to fall, held by nothing. A bank of shelves fell on me, and with it a mountain of emblems, banners, and drums along with folders of rules for Pioneer games and packets of pennants. They tipped me over softly and stiflingly, pressing me onto the floor, squashing me. I tried to climb out, then laughed: how ridiculous to be buried under this! But after three minutes my arms started going numb under the shelves, I was dizzy from the heat and dust, and most important, I didn't feel like calling for help, not out of shame or embarrassment but from a worrying, unhealthy lassitude.

In a desperate need to free myself from the pile of dead things, I fought my way out, covered in dust and flakes of gilt paint, and ran to the river to let the flowing water wash away the decay of paper and fabric. Now I did feel like a thief who had made his way into an Egyptian tomb and was caught by dead watchmen; a thief who had not believed the stories of ghostly guardians and who then felt their spectral and yet fully real power.

Another event at the camp advanced my understanding even more.

In a playground surrounded by tall, dark firs stood an enormous portrait of Lenin.

I had seen many different depictions of Lenin, some I liked, some elicited no response. But the camp portrait was special. Triple the height of a man, it stood behind us during morning roll call; you sensed his gaze on the back of your head, pushing you down into the ground. I felt that the Lenin in the portrait knew I thought something about him that the others did not and he wouldn't stop until he squashed me some day.

Lenin's face—lips, cheeks, eyes—had melted downward and the forehead, huge, convex, filled with petrified thoughts, took up more than half of the head. The exposed gigantic forehead was horrifying, as if a great and terrible idea was pushing out the skull from within. When we were lined up under that portrait, I thought that Lenin's head would burst any minute, and something bloody that had been living inside him, like a tapeworm, would crawl out; Lenin would die, but that *thing* would live.

Around that time, my parents gave me Nikolai Kun's *Legends and Myths of Ancient Greece,* probably for the pictures rather than the text; once again, as with the Egyptian slides, I sensed that this was something familiar and once again could not understand why I had these feelings.

Lenin on the poster reminded me of someone or something; I imagined that once I figured it out, I would be safe; the very fact of comparison, recognition, would save me.

Enlightenment came unexpectedly; there must have been some preliminary hint, but I don't remember it, I remember only how I understood, and gloried in the risky accuracy of the comparison, that Lenin was giving birth to the *revolution* the way Zeus gave birth to Athena!

I sensed instantly that I had performed an action for which my upbringing, education, and general life conditions had not prepared me; like a cosmonaut, I went out into space, a place where few venture.

The ancient Greek myth and the portrait at the Pioneer camp were one and the same. This was a powerful breakthrough; I was no longer defenseless before Zeus-Lenin, I knew what he was made of, I grasped the matter of his image, I had power over him; of course, not absolute power, but enough to protect me from his pursuing gaze from the poster.

The case with Lenin was more of an exception; more often my feeling about Soviet symbols was what I had experienced in the camp storeroom—lifelessness. I regretted that I had not lived in the times when the heroic legends were created, before there were children's red flags and pins.

Every year my parents took me to the photographer's studio near our house, where they had a small pink plastic horse, a toy Red Army stallion. It came with a yellow plastic saber in a blue sheath—the random motley colors proved that the toy was fake even as a toy—and a knit wool cap with an October star and a pointy top, a fake Budyonny broadcloth helmet.

Sitting in the plastic saddle you were supposed to raise the plastic saber over your head, as if riding to the attack; the photographer commanded "Flash!" with an important air and my parents squinted and smiled in satisfaction. For them, this was fun and the props seemed appropriate for my age. Maybe they wanted to even give me some historical images, a sense of connection to the past, in safe form. But for me, this was painful and insulting nonsense, as if they were intentionally mocking me.

Exposing me with plastic saber to the camera, showing the photos to friends—the shots were a guaranteed success and people always said that I would grow up a "real Budyonnovite"—my parents always hit me in my sorest spot, my secret desire to be someone's heir, to take on a great fate, exploits, and glory; they stressed that this was a childish and insignificant game.

The plastic horse was popular at the photographer's studio, because all the parents wanted to capture their sons on it, with the saber; while I was being photographed, someone was waiting his turn, hat-flattened hair being combed. But I was the only one of the kids to have seen a real saber!

One of my parents' friends had a saber in a scabbard hanging on the wall; it belonged to his uncle, a Red Army commander who had started fighting back in World War I.

The scabbard was beaten up and scratched, as unattractive as the legs of our old dacha table that had been scuffed by boots for a century. At first I even pitied it, as if it had outlived its usefulness and had wandered around, falling on hard times, and it was kept out of kindness on the wall instead of in a trunk.

But once—Father was sick and stayed home while Mother and I went to visit—they took the saber down and let me hold it. I almost dropped it, it was so heavy. They took it out of the scabbard and it scraped the trim around the throat—and showed itself all at once, more than a meter long, with a lengthy groove in the blade, from the guard to the tip, tempered, with a violet-blue sheen and a patina of hardening.

The handle was at my eye level, and I imagined what that sharpened steel does to a body, how a single blow at a third of one's power would cut me in half, vertically or diagonally. I understood the mechanics of a cavalryman, borne forward by the raised weight of the saber, the horse's legs in unison with the chopping blows. I pictured clearly—as if someone else's blood had come to play in my veins—that I could have been a soldier in the Civil War, a Red horseman.

"Born in the saddle," "one with the horse," they traveled through books and films. The best fighters of the Red Army, the spirit of the Civil War, warriors without front, rear, or flank, creatures covering forest and steppe in their maneuvers, appearing where least expected, turning upside down all the planned dispositions of troops; strange immortal creatures who cared nothing for time and space!

They forced me to sit on a factory-made plastic horsy on wheels, while I wholeheartedly wished for real things that could pass something along to me, without realizing that I sought them in a very contradictory way.

I was capable of simultaneously desiring my grandmother's secret book and penetrating the space of silence, and also wanting to become a hero in a Soviet epic—a horseman from Budyonny's army, a partisan of the Great Patriotic War, son of the regiment, the boy who handled the shells, the messenger for the underground who never named names when arrested.

The pendulum swayed continually, and I swung one way and then the other, living in two registers of perception, two planes of existence.

In one, the reality around me was a cardboard shell hiding the entrance to the real past; the cardboard did not protect from the terrible icy winds.

In the second, the secret of the past was not horrible, but entertaining; reality was a landscape of boredom and longing for great events, for exploits, as if our ancestors had performed them all, leaving nothing for their descendants to do. These two layers occasionally intersected, interacting in a strange way, but they still followed different paths.

The USSR, continually editing and reshaping its mythological past, was essentially a matryoshka doll of images and myths that sprouted from one into another; some formed cause-and-effect connections, others were pushed aside; inside each construction you could endlessly search for the truth, accepting the legends of the previous era which became the "real past" by virtue of seniority.

You could climb into a pit, descending deeper and deeper, without realizing that the entire construction was artificial; that was why you didn't know where to put the spaces of silence, areas that were forced outside the limits of the Soviet universe.

The temptation was always there to admit that those spaces were nonexistent, that they were the fruit of my imagination; to seek myself only within the Soviet historical myths, to consider them as having a real existence.

In choosing myth, you acquired the richest milieu for self-definition, self-construction, for fantasy; in admitting the veracity of the spaces of silence, you found yourself alone, in a bare, viewless place. That choice was a constant motif throughout your life: constantly balancing on the edge, leaning one way then the other, flickering, living in incompleteness, rechecking your feelings: Who are you, a lonely, impotent spy or a rightful heir to the past, a Soviet Theseus who will find his sandals and sword under a rock?

The former demanded patience and the ability to live without hope, the latter, bravery and desperate belief; and so I took both paths, thinking I was taking one, unable to distinguish the obstacles along different roads.

IN SEARCH OF WHOLENESS

By now there was a hint of the collapse, a brink-of-war disorder in daily life; things were definitely vanishing from hardware stores. The first to go were items that fasten—nails, screws, wire, cement, glue, without which boards and bricks are useless and pointless.

Father had a small shed at the dacha for his tools; there were also jars and tins with nuts and bolts. They were picked up on the side of the road or taken from things in the dump; every nut found on a dacha path, perhaps fallen off a bicycle, was examined for its thread, cleaned, soaked in kerosene, and then put in the appropriate jar. Bent lengths of wire, aluminum, copper, steel, of varying diameters and sizes, hung from long nails in the shed; wire was not bought, either, but found somehow. Going through an old structure, Father pulled out all the nails with a claw bar, straightened them with a hammer, and diligently saved them.

Of course, we collected old boards, planks from vegetable and fruit crates, pieces of baseboard—they could come in handy for the never-ending dacha repairs. But a quiet abnormality appeared only in the collection of things that could be called connective material; there was a huge shortage, as if the material world reflected the changes in the nation, in the political object called the USSR.

Grandmother Tanya also participated in the gathering of fasteners: she kept various buttons in round candy tins. Hundreds of buttons, matched and unmatched, cut from our own clothing or of unknown provenance; buttons from a military uniform, buttons with British lions, pretty mother-of-pearl buttons from a blouse, wooden toggles and huge plastic buttons from a fashionable ladies' coat. You could probably use them to re-create the history of clothing for several decades or write dozens of novels—for example, a meeting between a man in a jacket with British lions on the buttons and a lady in a jacket with bronze clasps. I used to go through the buttons and try to imagine the fate of the people who had worn them, as if they were all gone and only their buttons survived them, hard, resilient, and huddling together.

Zippers, of various lengths, colors, and teeth, had their own place; together, there were enough buttons and zippers for a hundred articles of clothing. Grandmother Tanya, who had spent a lifetime working with paper and did not tolerate a casual attitude toward it, who knew the value of paperweights that protected sheets of paper from drafts and clumsy people and affirmed the fact that any movement of paper as document could be fateful—Grandmother Tanya kept stores of paper clips and paste.

All the grown-ups at home saved connective material as if it were part of a secret universal undertaking. But I, led by a different feeling, suffered in several ways over the diffusion and decay, the loss of wholeness.

At school, we also collected scrap metal; every quarter all the classes, including the lowest ones, went out to scour the neighborhood for lost metal—and always found some, even though just a few months prior, at the last hunt, we'd thought we'd cleared out every corner. But no, metal appeared out of somewhere, as if a huge mechanism had just fallen apart midoperation, with nuts and bolts and springs bursting from of its belly, ruining some of the mechanical connections, but the machine kept working without knowing that some essential parts were lost and no longer functioning. We went through yards, back lots of garages, collecting the remains of the machine's self-destruction, so they could be melted down and made into new parts that would not repair the machine but could cobble it together enough to keep it going.

There was a political map of the USSR on the wall—I guess my parents wanted me to learn geography as well while I played with my grandmother. She was starting a quilt and had settled into an armchair beneath the map with all the pieces of fabric, scissors, needles and thread.

I had always seen the USSR as a whole. The rest of the world was fragmented, but our one-sixth of the world could not be separated; it was like an ingot.

Of course, the union republics were shown in different colors on the map. I had never paid any attention to their differences, it had never occurred to me to look at the map from that point of view; the Union as a whole absolutely predominated over the particulars, whatever colors and names they had.

But now—horrors!—I fell into a different dimension in which the USSR looked like the quilt Grandmother Tanya was sewing.

I was being cruelly mocked, given for an instant a jester's vision that turned concepts into their exact opposites. The USSR could not, did not have the right, to look like a quilt!

The Union, "the indissoluble Union" of the anthem, was a guarantor of the dependability of the world in its everyday minutia: light in bulbs, beets in the store, ink in my pen, bus at the stop, tea in the pot, the postman's ring at the door, a new coat for school—all that was the Union. Its existence affirmed that water would run, snow would melt, and sugar dissolve, as if without it, without its indefinable power, even simple physical processes would cease.

Yes, I did sense that an unknown force had cut short the life of my ancestors, had stolen the memory of them, that the three frogs "see nothing, hear nothing, say nothing" on Grandmother's table showed how we really lived. But that was weakly related to my concept of the USSR; if the Union could be imagined as a person, I would have said that the USSR-man did not know what strange things were happening inside him.

I would have been happy to forget the image of the quilt Union, but I could not; it was deeply ensconced and periodically returned in waves of fear. The more I chased it away, the more clearly I saw that my usual picture of the world had developed a crack and that this was only the beginning.

The only domestic space I had not studied thoroughly was Grandmother Mara's apartment. I visited only with my parents and I was always supervised, so even if I had a few minutes of solitude, what could I do in that time, especially when the adults were in the next room and could come in at any moment?

But Mother got a bad flu and I was sent to spend my fall holiday with Grandmother Mara. She was rarely home, it turned out, taking walks, visiting friends, and she did not insist that I accompany her.

At first, I was uncomfortable in her house—there was no place for books, neither shelves nor cupboard; only the book she was reading at a given time lay on her nightstand. I was surrounded by a world of fabrics—drapes, runners, tablecloths, napkins, antimacassars; the mass of her dresses, entangled and resembling a bud, pushed against the closet door.

Naturally, I searched her two rooms very quickly, but it was a disappointment. Besides the war trophy porcelain set, silk bedspreads, and sewing machine, the rest of the things were like idiot servants: stupid cups, stupid combs, stupid mirrors, stupid marking pencils, some of them old but still like newborns, without memories, unable to tell me anything.

I started watching Grandmother Mara; at home both my parents and Grandmother Tanya were beginning to suspect that I was getting into the wrong places, but they explained it as searching for sweets. Grandmother Mara didn't know this, so if I watched her closely, she could lead me to the hiding place or the object that I did not suspect. To tell the truth, I wasn't certain of success—Grandmother Mara's straightforward nature did not give me much hope that she had a "false bottom."

There was a storeroom near the toilet that served as a kind of Siberian exile. Things that survived from the past were kept there: a bag of bluing, a kerosene lantern, a suitcase of household soap, cast-iron irons, washtubs, dried up washboards, cabbage cutter, cleaver, spinning wheel, laundry baskets, lengths of unbleached linen. She forbade me to go in there—without explanation, just "no."

Of course, one more ban when I had violated so many meant nothing. But when I approached the door in her absence, I remembered Blue Beard's secret room. My hand froze as I reached for the doorknob.

I had peeked into the storeroom beneath her arm and it did not seem scary. But now alone in the apartment, where water coughed in the old pipes, I grew uneasy.

Back in the living room, I found the candy box with Grandfather Trofim's medals, and I attached the Red Star to my shirt. I would not have done that before, but I needed support and security, and I was not usurping his award but using it as a sign of his protection.

With the star tugging at the fabric of my shirt and a flashlight in my hand, I entered the storeroom. There was a weak scent of dried-out soap and aging wood and metal. Empty jars filled the shelves, ready for summer canning, and they reflected the flashlight in dozens of flickers.

What was there to fear here, what should I be looking for? I was ready to leave, ashamed of my fear, ashamed that I needed to put on the star, when I noticed that the washtub seemed to be covering something.

Beneath was a large square object wrapped in worn oilcloth and tied with string. Grandmother Mara knew how to make clever, complicated knots, she said Grandfather Trofim taught her when they had to move and pack up; Grandfather Trofim was a soldier and he probably knew how to tie up a prisoner and join two steel ropes to pull a truck out of a ditch; a genius of the small skills that evince human reliability.

It was a difficult knot that showed she used what she learned from Grandfather Trofim. I knew I would not be able to duplicate it, my fingers would get lost in the loops, forget which end of the string went where. The knot would give me away—if I tied it my way, Grandmother would know that someone had been in the secret place under the washtub. But I also knew: if what I was seeking, what I needed, was there, then I would be able to re-create the knot. I didn't know the way now, but afterward I would. I pulled on it.

Under the oilcloth was a row of dark burgundy volumes with gold inscription, obviously old, overly large, as if books had degenerated since then.

With the tenacity of Egyptian hieroglyphs or Hittite cuneiform writing, the gibberish abracadabra, the deepest secret transcribed into ordinary letters struck my eyes: A to ACON-

EUS, ACONITE to ANT, ANTARCTICA to BACON, BAR-
BARIAN to BEDLAM, BOREDOM to CANADA, DELHI to
DYNASTY, and so on to HINDI to IMPERIALISM. Here the
row of leather-bound books, ornamented in gold letters, stars,
sheaves, and machine gears, broke off.

My soul heard the echo of the words Nonpareil and Cicero,
the ghost of my previous self-deception.

I could not resist those consonances, I could not get enough,
and my recent disillusionment had not been a lesson.

This was the GSE, the *Great Soviet Encyclopedia*, in the
1920s-1930s edition. I perceived the GSE as a great book of
spells fallen into the hands of an underage ignoramus; there were
missing volumes, as if someone tried to destroy them. Who?
People? Time?

I was not bothered that among the unfamiliar and clearly
magical, unreal, secret words, there were familiar ones like Germany and Iron. I understood—discovered—the real setup of the
world, where Germany or Iron, the names of countries, things,
and actions, were merely a small part of the truly real, where
iron is connected to imperialism (a connection it was possible to
imagine), deficit with Donetsk, and Germany with the mysterious Gerhardt.

The encyclopedia contained names of vanished things and
like the International, its language was the language of ancient
magic, but power had deserted these words. Not knowing how
many more of these books remained, I assumed that perhaps I
was seeing the only extant copy in the world, a gift from the gods
of the past to me.

Comprehending nothing, incapable of figuring anything
out, I spent the remaining days at Grandmother Mara's reading
the GSE the minute she stepped out the door, intoxicated by the
smell of old yellow paper. I had stepped on the Atlantis of books,
the continent of the past that had floated up from the ocean

depths. Gradually there appeared a world about which I knew nothing. Those names, phenomena, and events did not exist in my time, or if they did, I intuitively sensed that they were presented in a completely different way.

At home with my parents, I often read the SSE, the *Small Soviet Encyclopedia* published in the 1960s, primarily out of a superficial curiosity, the empty passion of an erudite. And that helped me so much; numerous people the GSE wrote about with a view to eternity did not figure at all in the SSE. Geographic and scientific concepts were the only things the encyclopedias had in common.

I thought that if one were to read the entire GSE, aloud, like a prayer, even without understanding the meaning, the reading would give birth to, create the USSR, the forgotten Soviet Union of the twenties and thirties, gone into the past.

In one of the volumes I found a dry maple leaf, and lazily wondered what happened to the tree from which it fell; I doubt it survived. I shivered with foreboding; what if the past that gave rise to the encyclopedia does not exist at all? What if it wasn't preserved at all except in this one book?

It didn't give me pause that Grandmother Mara, who didn't like to read and would have trouble with encyclopedia articles, had the GSE. An encyclopedia that survived by accident should be kept by a person who would never be considered a Guardian. Maybe Grandmother Mara didn't even know what was in the package, maybe she'd never looked, following Grandfather Trofim's orders.

The flyleaf of each volume was the color of dark straw, like the soldiers' uniforms in the 1940s. Against that background, bright crimson thorny vines twisted into a single pattern, looking both like branches of a prickly shrub and barbed wire; not an abstract design or an ornamental element, it was a naturalistic depiction, a martyr's epigraph to the book, doubling, tripling its weight and significance, as if the knowledge it contained had been paid for in blood.

In the list of editors, I knew only two names: Kuibyshev, also the name of a city, and Schmidt, who gave his name to an iceberg—a polar explorer, organizer of all the northern expeditions, conqueror of the Arctic, and creator of the drifting North Pole Station. I remembered that when the volume I held in my hands was published, Schmidt was in the Arctic, exploring the Northern Sea Route, and could not have worked on the encyclopedia, where he was listed as editor in chief. I knew that for certain, because I had read a lot of books on polar explorers— the Arctic, the great white "nowhere," was a blank page perfect for manufacturing ideal exploits and heroic figures, and those figures, without an ideological sell-by date, were still featured in books and films in my day.

That meant the GSE had been made by the rest, the unknown people whose names were preceded by the red thorns on the flyleaf. I reread the list twice, and I found two names—Bukharin and Piatakov; I couldn't remember how I knew them, but they must have slipped through the conversations of adults, flickered like ghosts, outside time or context; ghosts surrounded by an aura of greatness, or significance, or tragic death, or betrayal and villainy, or maybe all of the above.

Juxtaposing the celebrated fate of Schmidt and Kuibyshev with the silence and obscurity surrounding the others, I began to understand that the USSR I knew and inhabited was just a copy, a piece of the other, earlier one. I set my flashlight on the floor and on the very first try I replicated Grandmother's tricky knot on the package. I was right, it was intended for me.

When I returned home after my school holidays at Grandmother Mara's, I went to the *Small Soviet Encyclopedia* and I did not find Bukharin or Piatakov; instead, there were articles on Bukhara and Piatigorsk where their names should have been.

The inviolably singular USSR was shaken; I had never heard the Soviet Union used in the plural, it was impossible, contradicted the dependence of the world upon the singularity of the USSR; but I risked it—slowly, with difficulty, as if pushing those gigantic stone letters, I said to myself: USSRs. Two USSRs. That USSR. Today's USSR.

USSRs.

Now I kept asking to visit Grandmother Mara. My parents were happy, they thought I had gotten over my dislike of her. What I cared about was being near the secret books hidden in the storeroom and watching Grandmother Mara: Had she guessed I had been in there? Did she know what she was concealing? Grandmother continued her everyday life, so ordinary that I wondered if I had dreamed up the hidden ancient encyclopedia.

I was counting on spending the winter holidays at Grandmother Mara's so I could get back to the GSE. To keep my parents from denying my as-yet unvoiced request, I worked on my studies and ended the quarter with excellent grades. But the night I brought home my report card and was about to ask at dinner to stay at Grandmother Mara's, my parents beat me to the punch, exchanged a cheerful look and announced that because I had done so well at school they booked us a stay at a boarding-house and the school had awarded me an invitation to the New Year's celebration at the Kremlin.

I don't think they understood my disappointment, which I was unable to hide, and I explained it as the result of being overworked at school, but they were hurt I didn't appreciate the gift. I was in their power, and I reflected sadly that this must be how it is—a secret book is opened only once, and whatever you did not have time to learn from its pages is gone forever. How angry I was at them, unwitting accomplices of a life arranged to hide secrets! I meekly agreed to go on vacation and to the Kremlin party; I was even forced to pretend to want to go so my parents wouldn't start wondering why I was so eager to spend the holidays at Grandmother Mara's, which I'd never wanted to do before.

In the final days of December, Mother and I moved into the vacation boardinghouse, planning to return to Moscow for one day, for the party. Snowy woods, early dark, cartoons in the hall, and other children to play with—Grandmother's storeroom was shunted aside, disappeared, the great GSE volumes vanished, leaving only the role of child enjoying the holidays, which I grew into.

I did not want to go to the Kremlin but was afraid to say so, for the party at the Palace of Congresses was a kind of unmatched peak in a Soviet childhood, the highest recognition of achievements and reliability.

I had never understood the festive crowds on Red Square gathered for the fireworks; the space was dangerously exposed to the winds of ancient times. O, how empty and terrible it was in early morning bad weather, the navel of the earth from the ascent to the Museum of the Revolution down to the Vasilyevsky Slope, a place where the curvature of the globe is clearly visible! The body of the square looked to me like the squashed chest of a bogatyr, the scales of his armor the cobblestones, and in the corner lay his chopped off head, the round Execution Place. Saint Basil's Cathedral blazed like a funeral pyre, the spiral designs on its domes combining war helmets and the multiple heads of a dragon; a place of ancient battles, a place of executions, its cobbles buckled by the wild forces of the earth beneath it; a place of victims and funeral feasts. Across the square, by the wall, stood the Mausoleum ziggurat; the tense diagonal between Execution Place and the Mausoleum burst open the square, turning it into a parallelogram, making an already distorted space even more lopsided. How could anyone stroll around Red Square without anxiety?

SERGEI LEBEDEV

From the warmth and light of the boardinghouse Mother and I stepped into the frosty early twilight, the icy dark hole of December, and took the long walk to the train. Snow-filled forests and fields surrounded us, we saw only occasional lights, and it was hard to believe that a big city was only a dozen stations away. Time did not exist for these woods and fields, they were the same as they had been centuries ago. Daylight made them charming, they were suburban, filled with vacationers, but in the evenings, when the last skiers hurried to the train, they became wild again, lost in snowy expanses, stolen by the dark.

The day before we had gone on an excursion to an old nearby estate, the mansion yellow and white, with columns at the main entrance and sculptures in the parkland, but now I thought that the estate was gone, the trees visible in the daytime were gone, and we were walking on a road from nowhere to no place. We might run into horse-drawn sleighs from the last century, and so we had to firmly believe that a railroad station awaited us at the end of the road and that we had left the boardinghouse behind us. Otherwise we might not reach our goal or find our way back.

We reached the station, Mother led me by the hand confidently. The commuter train, covered in frost and battling dirty winds, rattled along, its irrational mechanical heart beating in the engine car, while the darkness beyond the frosty windows gathered, turning into corners of buildings, platforms, and people in the light of streetlamps.

The noise, crowds, and marble of the metro closed in on us and then threw us out near the Kutafya Tower by the Troitsky Gates of the Kremlin.

We passed through the Kremlin walls. I had been transported from the rarefied air and timeless darkness of the forests outside Moscow and now I was immured in stone—the towers, walls, crenellations, chimes, the brick ensemble of the Kremlin oppressed me. The sight of the Ivan the Great bell tower, the

96

towers and cathedrals floodlit by klieg lights against the sky was so powerful I thought my ears would ring and my nose would bleed. It was impossible to breathe there, impossible to feel, because my feelings were in spasm.

One sensation did get past the spasms—the Kremlin could see me, even though it was incredibly large and I was insignificantly tiny; it was indifferent to the other people walking next to me, but I had a flaw which the citadel could sense.

At the time, I was sure that the Kremlin had been built in the Soviet era; this belief coexisted without contradiction with the knowledge that the chief architectural symbol of the Soviet Union was much older. The red brick walls and ruby stars made the Kremlin an incarnation of the Union, the chimes on Spassky Tower counted out the hour in the enormous country; it wasn't the symbol of Soviet power, it was simply *power*.

I realized what the Kremlin knew about me; it knew about my vision of the patchwork quilt Union, it knew I had opened the secret, banned book of the GSE and had spoken the impossible word "USSRs"; it exposed me—How could I have not foreseen it, how self-reliantly and forgetfully had I risked venturing inside its walls!

For an instant I thought guards would ask us to show our tickets again and they would find a problem; we would be separated and led away. I thought back to the guesthouse where our clothes were drying on the radiator and suddenly saw other people in our room, other clothes drying after a ski outing.

The hallucination passed but the Kremlin's gaze remained.

In the lobby of the Palace of Congresses teenagers were helping the arrivals; they were dressed in Pioneer uniforms even though they were too old to be Pioneers.

One of them, tall, handsome, wearing the Pioneer outfit as if it were a military uniform—I even thought he might have had it made in some expensive shop, otherwise the baggy trousers and too-short jacket would never have fit that way—pointed out our section of the coat check and turned away, as if we were bothering him with trifles and had called him away from his important post. The white wavy curtains on the huge windows, the immaculately clean collar of his white shirt, the dashing drape of the red tie, the crease in his trousers and his pointy shoes—the Palace would have made him the gatekeeper, and he liked being in the Palace, he liked telling people where to go. This was his party, his evening, and for a second I wanted to be him, to feel as comfortable and confident in the Kremlin.

We were seated close to the stage. The performance began. Snegurochka, the Snow Maiden, was kidnapped by a villain, the usual plot, and all the children screamed: "Come out, Grandfather Frost!" clutching our cardboard gift boxes with the sticky smell of chocolate. I had an acute sense of the meaninglessness of the party, the play, Grandfather Frost, the costumed actors, fake beards, confetti and paper spirals, the shiny tree ornaments; I had aged in minutes and was weary with monstrous adult ennui.

My childhood was over—I had dreamed of it so often, but now I sat, deafened, confused, feeling the unwavering gaze of the Kremlin, practically hoping they would take me away and lock me up with others like me.

My childhood was over; still, I did not regret opening the forbidden book—if they did not take me from the concert hall, did not lead me by the elbow as we were leaving, there would be events arising from my contact with the book, and those events were near! The new year was coming, and for the first time it would truly be new, not like the previous ones that followed the same pattern.

Discoveries and unknown sacrifices awaited me, perhaps the sacrifice of my life—the gaze of the Kremlin supported that possibility—but I was naively prepared to make sacrifices, even wanted them, delighted that this desire found approval from the Kremlin.

Two days later, when the television showed the chimes of the Kremlin marking the last minute of last year, I no longer felt its gaze. A blizzard raged around us, I slipped away from my mother to run outside, to touch, to hold the first snow of the new year. Cold penetrated my hand, I heard the thrum of guesthouse residents behind me, and I stood looking out onto the illuminated emptiness of the tree-lined lanes.

My time had come.

PART TWO

Great events sometimes send messengers, a sign: be alert, be open and sensitive, don't miss it, don't interfere by deed or feeling, or it will not happen!

Almost nothing remains in my memory of the long winters of childhood except sledding down an icy hill and skiing; I remember only the moments of movement. Flying on a big piece of fraying cardboard along icy ruts, rusty whorls of last year's grass in the ice, always with spots of blood—because someone smashed his face or cut his hand—flying to the deep garbage ravine filled with old tires. Two skis before your eyes as they pass each other, intersecting and separating tracks. The creak of the snow, the scuffle of ski poles on the ice crust, sliding, sliding, coming home, hot tea with cranberries, a heavy meal, and a heavy, dreamless sleep.

Only one winter left a long memory; the winter in which my awakening to my own life began with the Kremlin New Year's party.

The weather was good, vacation's end still far away, Father came to visit us at the boardinghouse, and I demanded we go skiing every day—everything in me demanded action, apparently senseless movement and quests.

The embankment of the narrow gauge train line that joined the railroad from the opposite side of the station had pieces of colored glass, light blue, violet, lilac, blue, and green, looking like shards of ingots. I was not allowed to collect the glass, I was told it could contain dangerous chemicals; I would have believed them, but there was another condition—I was not allowed to cross over to the side with the narrow gauge line. I think the first ban was merely a consequence of the second.

Gradually I learned from phrases not intended for me that the glass was being carried from a place that had, or used to have, a testing ground. There were few words which could excite as much, except for "airport," "military unit," and "secret laboratory."

One day, getting permission to play at the nearby ponds, I crossed the tracks and headed along the narrow gauge line. Pieces of colored glass glittered in the embankment gravel, and I could follow the trail endlessly. But a growing unease made me uncomfortable: the pieces of glass, iridescent, smoky, colored, were luring me, long warehouses and dumps stood on either side, but I could not see a testing ground, a big, wide space.

Two men came toward me, fishermen; dressed in cotton batting jackets with waterproof covers on their felt boots, with icebreakers and short winter fishing poles, they were headed to the ponds I had allegedly gone to see.

I cautiously asked them where the testing ground was. One man, round-faced, with silly, droopy ears, still shiny-faced from his wife's blini or waffles, looked at me in confusion, preparing to say, "What testing ground?" The other, almost an old man, with a narrow face marked with swollen red capillaries, tall, the icebreaker slung over his shoulder like a rifle, blocked my way, pulled a huge fur mitten from his right hand and took me by the shoulder, his fingers on a vulnerable bone. I sensed that if he pushed, pain would shoot through my shoulder. I had noticed that inside the fur mitten, his wool glove, mended many times, had three fingers; I knew it was an army glove for winter shoot-ing, leaving the index finger free to pull the trigger.

"How do you know about the testing ground?" the old man asked, not joking, as a man who had the right to pose such ques-tions. "Who told you? Why are you here?"

I looked down at my feet, saw a bluish-white piece of glass, and realized that there was no point in a story about looking for colored glass. The second fisherman moved away, while the old man let go of my shoulder but put his hands on my cheeks and drew my face closer to his, his eyes pressing on me.

A train came round the sharp bend, the engineer blew the whistle, and the old man let me go with a rasping, "Go away, pup." The locomotive and its chain of cars hauling gravel left us on opposite sides of the track.

I scrambled down the embankment and ran for it. I realized the adults knew something was wrong with this place, for we'd picked mushrooms on the testing ground for tanks near the dacha, but this was a different kind of testing ground, and the old man with the glove like the ones guards wear in winter may have even saved me. He obviously had worked there, and even in retirement he continued his vigilant watch.

Two or three days later we skied particularly far from the house. Crossing a long field, with the occasional tufts of grass, we could see a village of a dozen houses and a wooden church in the distance. We entered a bright birch grove with a glade. The glade was slightly raised above the road, as if dirt had been added to it; I was just thinking about that when my ski hit something metallic.

"Come on," my father said, noticing that I had stopped. "Let's go! We'll be late for lunch!"

I nodded, but as soon as he turned, I cleared the snow away with my ski. I saw a rusted track of a narrow gauge railroad. While we skied along the path, I saw among the trees a few old poles, rotting and gray with age, pieces of barbed wire on the insulators.

That evening I asked Father what railroad we had crossed.

"It's the old road to the Kommunarka *sovkhoz*," he replied instantly, as if he had been expecting the question. He replied in a way that stopped me from asking why a communal state farm needed a railroad and why they didn't use it anymore.

On the next to last day of my vacation, I was allowed to ski on my own. It goes without saying that I followed the familiar route past the village and the black wooden church to the glade in the birch forest.

The scary old man with the carriage of a watchman, the narrow gauge railroad to the testing ground, the abandoned railroad in the forest, the strange, sidelined, unknown roads—I had found the remains of the lost country, the Atlantis I learned of thanks to the *Great Soviet Encyclopedia*.

Here I was at the spot where I'd found the railroad tracks under the snow. I brought a small shovel and dug around as much as I could until I found the stamp: 1931.

Which way, right or left? The gray cloudy day gave no hint, there was no wind. Left? I thought I could see something in the distance, either a house or a gate or a watchman's hut. But once you go a hundred, two hundred meters, you realize that even though there is no one and nothing in the woods, you are distraught by the thin twigs, like bird feet, in the snow, by the crunch of the ice crust under your skis. Don't go left or right, the gray cloudy day tells you, go back to the guesthouse, they're putting the soup on the stove, forget these homely birches, last year's crows' nests falling apart in the wind, the rusty rails under the snow and the rotting poles with tin signs no longer legible.

I went back, not risking to go farther. But they stayed in my memory, a sleeping seed, those nameless railroads, abandoned trails of unknown things. One day I would find the explanation, I promised myself, not knowing that in five or six years I would read a newspaper article about the mass graves at the Butovo firing range, the firing trenches at the Kommunarka sovkhoz, illustrated by a photo of the narrow gauge railroad headed nowhere in the white winter space filled with the black spots of birch bark.

Standing there in the glade, for the first time I realized that life was a chain of events elicited by my actions, I saw how one inevitably prompts the next: GSE, New Year's party, firing range. I even smiled at how I had resisted going to the guesthouse, now understanding that events would find me, and I should trust them rather than my own intentions. The important thing was not to give up my search.

CLUSTERS OF
WHITE LOCUST BLOSSOMS

Back in Moscow, I took up and dropped various things, unable to concentrate, behaving like a dog that lost a scent. My parents soon brought news: Grandmother Mara was getting married. They were embarrassed, they thought she had lost her mind, it wasn't done to consider a second marriage at her age; they had gotten used to her loneliness, to the absence of older men in the family.

But Grandmother Tanya accepted the news easily, with a light sadness; unexpectedly, she was firm about not letting my parents interfere. I couldn't bear the thought of Grandmother Mara's betrayal of Grandfather Trofim, which distanced me even more from him, until I learned who the prospective bridegroom was.

Even in her late years she had several admirers, very different old men, and as a rule, significant people. The former head of a trust, a former weapons designer, the former chief engineer of an energy plant, the former director of a model kolkhoz—all were widowers and they swarmed around Grandmother Mara, sensing that they would live longer and better with her. She accepted their friendship, understood their intentions, and kept them close without putting anyone in an awkward or painful situation; this lasted for years, and they were all her husbands slightly. She took only one man seriously, the one who proposed to her.

He was the only one I thought had the right to be in a relationship with my grandmother, the widow of Grandfather Trofim—they were both soldiers, "brothers in arms," as they wrote in books, and there was no betrayal here. Besides which, the man embodied one of my dreams from the past.

Pilots and submariners, two Soviet castes of free-spirited heroes; not part of the group, not in a unit, but one-on-one with the enemy, with the sky, with the water.

Pokryshkin and Kozhedub, two fighter pilot aces whose planes were covered with stars for shot-down enemies and whose uniforms bore starred medals, were solitary men in the land of collectivism, aluminum angels of the Soviet skies; at first my heart belonged to them.

But later, in the middle of the 1980s, living and dead submariners began floating up from the weight of the archives, the commanders of Shchuka-class and Malyutka-class ships. They had lain on the bottom for a long time, engines off; now the pressures of the depths were tossing them to the surface, the fetid air conserved in the submarines escaped from the portholes with a whistle.

Suddenly their exploits and service were revealed; my heart switched from pilots, the geniuses of speed and maneuver, to the hidden men of the sea, geniuses of patience and obscurity.

In the Kuzminki neighborhood of Moscow, on the lane that led to the park and ponds, there was a game arcade I liked to play at, and I saved fifteen kopeks all week before the walk to the park. And then—Oh joy!—I put my eyes to the periscope, my fingers held the triggers for the torpedo launchers, and the dark silhouettes of enemy cruisers and destroyers moved along the sea drawn on glass.

Shoot—the torpedo makes the water foam and an orange light shines on the horizon. If you miss, the black German cruiser sails off into open sea to attack a Soviet convoy. I forgot I was in the middle of wintry Moscow, that I had never seen the sea; my fingers pulled the triggers, the torpedoes left their trail, and with ferocious glee I was blown up along with the enemy ships.

Grandmother Mara's fiancé was a submariner, a retired commander. He sometimes visited the dacha wearing a black uniform jacket with planks of decorations and a cap; I knew where his house was, in the village near the market: an old wooden house, an *izba*, with age-darkened gingerbread window carvings, with random-seeming additions, patched many times, and sinking into the ground.

It had a huge cellar: there was a hatch with a heavy ring beneath one of the rugs in the house, and when it opened, the earth breathed damply into your face. The innumerable supplies had an earthy smell—beets, carrots, onions (the cellar was rented to the market traders). How could I connect this house, permeated with heavy human smells, smoke, the sour stink of pickling, this house where grandfathers and great-grandfathers had lived and died, this house raised on a foundation of grub, on cool darkness where potato eyes grew blindly, how could I connect it to the sea?

I saw that Grandmother, clearly caring about the commander, still resisted a final connection with him; she had buried her husband, and the next one—husband or companion—had to be a man with a clear and simple fate, unburdened by old wounds and memory of the war; wounds and memory were identical here. I, on the other hand, kept waiting for him to talk about the war when he visited the dacha; to explain how he, a peasant son, became a man of the sea.

That winter I came upon the commander at Grandmother Mara's house. My parents had taken me to the dolphinarium near her apartment, and as I watched the pool with the bluish-gray glossy sea creatures, I thought of him, the commander, his habitual silence, his incredible sensitivity to sound—I think he could hear mice scrambling in the next room—the trained wariness of navigating a submarine that operated in the shallow Baltic Sea, where submarines were frequently discovered by destroyers or planes; the only story he told was about the ship getting wrapped in antisubmarine netting and how they escaped with just a half hour of air left; his ability to move silently, placing his cup on the saucer without a sound, eating without once clinking the plate with a fork, as if he was still waging his war; the dolphins, perceptive and agile, speedy, flying through a ring above the water, reminded me of him—and that very day he was visiting Grandmother Mara.

My parents had gone, they hadn't expected Grandmother to have company, but they left me, at her request. I had always known that people were divided into summer folk, the ones we saw at the dacha, and winter city friends, and it was strange to see this shift in calendar, seeing the old submariner in the seriousness of his feelings for Grandmother Mara; and seeing her, heavy, suddenly aged by another's love; she must have thought that acoustically the submariner sensed her better than she did herself, heard all the creaks and groans of her weary body.

The commander, his hair pure white, chatted politely and easily with me about insignificant things—cross-country skiing, school, what books I was reading. I almost told him about the narrow gauge lines, almost asked him what they were, but stopped in time—I thought he would politely laugh it off and then joke forever, no matter what I wanted to learn from him.

I sensed that Grandmother was slightly unhappy with her decision to keep me overnight, so I asked to go to bed, earning an appreciative look from the commander. She made up a bed for me, I turned a few times for show, and then was still, feigning sleep. A half hour later, Grandmother opened the door, came over, listened to my breathing, and quietly returned to the commander. I waited a minute and then moved to the door just as quietly.

Glasses clinked a few times, I could hear quiet conversation—the old man did most of the talking, recalling how he had seen Grandmother Mara at the dacha station with two pails of strawberries. She seemed uncomfortable and she began softly singing, hitting false notes, the song "The Fragrant Clusters of White Locust," which she loved.

I sensed the commander putting his hand on hers, asking her to stop. I suspected that Grandmother, knowing him well, sang a song he didn't like to get something out of him. The shot glasses clinked again, and she asked him why he didn't like the love song, he had promised to tell her a long time ago and still had not.

The commander replied: at first I did not understand what he was talking about, what events he was describing, they were impossible to imagine—but then I felt like a submariner whose damaged ship was sinking helplessly into the pressing depths.

In the spring of 1932 the black locust tree bloomed in the Ukrainian village where he lived as a youth; by then the starving villagers had eaten the first grass, and stray refugees lay dying in the streets devoid of birds, dogs, and cats.

The commander tenderly described the creamy white blossoms that he and his friend ate, bending the branches to the ground with their remaining strength. There were bugs in some of the flowers, and they ate the bugs, sour and crunchy; the two friends knew the flowers would make them sick, but their fragrance was so appetizing they couldn't resist; once they fell into a dream state and started retching they would stop.

The commander weakened first, the sweet toxic petals sickened him; "the fragrant clusters" had a fragrance that was too thick, luring him into dizziness, sleepiness, a deadly, starving

111

sleep; "The night drove us mad"—the locust flowers literally did, and he got up to eat a few more petals.

Other people came, breaking the branches and carrying them off to eat without sharing. The weakest, little children, who died first, crawled underfoot, licking the dusty clusters on the ground. A fight broke out—an impossible fight among weakened men who could not even make a fist or hold down a rival.

A bee stung the commander, the sting as painful as a bayonet wound; his face swelled up, turning watery and soft, and he crawled home without noticing where his friend was, crawling for several hours, slinking along the fences. His friend vanished—someone saw him being taken away by two women, to the hospital they said, where there was quarantine for people with dystrophy. If we had not eaten the locust, he said, Kolya would be alive today, he was still agile, he would have gotten away, not given up.

I had once tried the poisonous water hemlock whose umbrella heads wave in the ditches along the road, and I remembered my consciousness dissolving, I could feel what the commander had been through. My consciousness was gone now, too, I did not hear his last words, except for one phrase that sounded like a bell tolling: "Human meat in aspic does not jell."

They sat at the table, drinking a bitter liqueur, uncleared dishes before them; the commander was talking about the unimaginable, and Grandmother Mara did not respond to his story with surprise or indignation.

I sensed that he was not lying, but in my system of coordinates, what he was saying could not be true—it was delirium, phantasmagoria.

Commander, commander, why did you answer Grandmother's question, why didn't you tell instead of torpedoing a transport ship and hiding from powerboats, naval hunters? "If this did happen, it was only in a single place," I told myself, "only in that tiny town; human meat in aspic does not jell."

But why was Grandmother quiet? Suddenly I realized why she was marrying him, what it was that united them in the past, what he and she remembered.

There was only one salvation: to believe that both of them had been victims of monstrous circumstances, that they were exceptions. That's what I decided.

In the morning I no longer remembered the commander's story accurately, it had been distorted by my febrile dreams. But I had the feeling that somewhere inside me, in the rooms of my mind there was now a hole, a well that could not be closed, into which one might fall, and from its depths came the sweet fragrance of locust blossoms.

LIGHTS IN THE FIRMAMENT

I returned home happily, trying not to recall what had happened at Grandmother Mara's; I clung to Grandmother Tanya, so that when I talked or played with her, I could banish the vision of the deadly white petals at least for a time.

That winter Grandmother Tanya, as if sensing the changes within me, started teaching me to draw. I copied postcards or drew our dacha, but neither gouache, nor watercolor, nor pencils obeyed me, and my work was poor, but this did not worry Grandmother; in exchange for my picture, she gave me one of hers. That was the point of her new game: she was surreptitiously introducing me into the circle of her memories.

The first night battle over Moscow—the orange lines of tracers in the dark blue sky, the ghostly columns of searchlights, German planes falling like swatted midges; Stalin's funeral—a whirlpool of bodies, people trapped in the swirling masses on the street; the German dirigible Zeppelin flying to the Arctic in 1930, a gigantic silvery cigar above the Kremlin; the autumn parade in 1941 on Red Square—gray figures with vertical strokes of rifles appearing out of the snow and marching back into it.

I saw her pencil and pastel sketches done when she was young—pitchers, plaster heads, abstract compositions; I couldn't say that the hand of a strong artist was visible, but the precision and solidity of the lines revealed an artist for whom the world was clear, transparent, and safe.

But now many decades later, her style had changed completely; her drawings resembled *lubok*, the pictures on the walls of peasant huts. Her style became more childlike in execution, with extended captions; the drawings were turning into a home-made filmstrip.

Later, as an adult, I saw the drawings made by prisoners in death camps, the drawings of people sent to distant penal colonies beyond the Arctic Circle, I recognized the style—childlike, as if the mind was protecting itself from the experience, translating it to the safest forms of comprehension, separating it in time, moving it back to fairy tale days, and at the same time, taming it, bringing it into the composition of memory.

Back in that year, there was a lot of talk about Haley's Comet approaching earth. The newspapers and television said that it would be studied with telescopes, that a space probe would be sent out to meet it; the comet was a free gift to popularizers of astronomy, a new holiday on the boring calendar. I didn't know that Haley was the astronomer's name, I thought it was the name of the comet.

I noticed that both grandmothers, who rarely took an interest in that sort of news—a new nebula discovered, another spaceship launched—knew about the comet, as if there were some special reason for them to remember when it was due, the way they remembered birthdays and anniversaries.

They were preparing for the comet's arrival, and while the

preparations were not manifest in action, they were palpable. Grandmother Mara softened, and contrary to her personality she let go of her old feuds and worried that she would not be able to forgive everything in time. Grandmother Tanya, an incredible tranquil person, became calmer still, more tactful, as if apologizing even to the dust she wiped away or the salt she tossed into the soup.

It seemed that they wanted to talk about something, to tell us something, but were afraid of being misunderstood, that their statements would be taken with a condescending smile, and they kept silent, as if they knew that the mockery might later make trouble for the one who dismissed their warning so lightly.

I sensed the aura of mystery that surrounded the comet and tried to stick closer to the grannies, in case their anxiety would make them careless and they'd inadvertently say something that explained their strange anticipation.

Comet, comet, comet—I went to school, did my homework, made snow forts, but it was inside me, invading my dreams as the source of tormenting fears, like sounds that humans cannot hear but which resound in the body as confusion and horror. The comet was already there, it was constantly hanging over my head, and the nearness of the comet to the earth hinted at some future event, an exceedingly rare moment in time, when the veils are lifted and the invisible becomes visible.

One afternoon I came home early—they had canceled the final class.

Grandmother Tanya was sitting at the table, with a news-paper spread before her, open to an article about Haley's Comet with a bold and clumsy headline referring to the "celestial guest."

Grandmother had removed her glasses—even though she read with them on—and seemed to be holding an invisible book before her eyes, for which glasses were unnecessary. Softly, with a cautious step, feeling the way through the path of memory, overgrown and nearly gone, she whispered words, repeating them more confidently, with fewer hesitations, each time: "And God said, Let there be lights in the firmament of the heaven to divide the day from the night; and let them be for signs, and for seasons, and for days, and years.

"And God said, Let there be lights in the firmament of the heaven to divide the day from the night; and let them be for signs, and for seasons, and for days, and years," she repeated. "And for signs."

I had never heard words of such high seriousness; I understood right away their gravity, that they were but a small part of something whole, and that whole, existing higher than me, than Grandmother, higher than everything in the world, had suddenly touched me.

Were these the words that were supposed to appear in Grandmother's wordless book, dressed in a brown leather cover? No, I thought, no, this is yet another book I do not know, perhaps even the book of books. They surround me, secret or even nonexistent, and how many more of them will I encounter?

I naturally knew the origins of the planet, the appearance of life, fish climbing onto land, man developing from apes, the beginning of history which led to the birth of the USSR. That picture had no place for God, the firmament of heaven, or lights for signs. But with the same certainty I now knew that the world was arranged differently: another key to it had appeared on my chain.

It did not occur to me to ask about the provenance of the text; it could not have come from a book, it did not have details like a title or an author. I did not reveal my presence, did not ask Grandmother to continue, to say another few lines—those phrases were enough, they contained everything, and I still had to master them.

Unable to maintain this elevated sensation, as if I had climbed too high, I fell back into the winter evening after school, finding myself again in familiar circumstances. I retained only the word "sign," linked to the newspaper on the table, with its blurry black-and-white photo of the comet, flying like a bright, extended shuttlecock in the obscurity of the cosmos. I understood that the comet would find something, reveal something related to me, my parents, grandmothers, the past, the present, and I could not miss it, I had to read the sign—I used it in relation to myself for the first time.

Days passed, the date named by astronomers was approaching when the comet would be closest to the earth, but nothing happened. I despaired in anticipation. Every day I checked that Father's telescope was in place, every night when they were all asleep I hid behind the curtains and looked at the sky, waiting, not so much for the comet as for changes in the skies, for example, in the movement of clouds, the glow of stars, but I found nothing.

I made a decision and asked Grandmother Tanya to tell me what she knew about the comet. She seemed to have been waiting for the question and said I should come to her room that evening, and she opened her album of drawings. A few hours later I was looking at them.

A large mansion on a hill, almost hidden by twilight, windows reflecting light. A waist-high picket fence, with two dozen people gathered by it looking up at the sky—white, old-fashioned dresses, white summer jackets and trousers. Above, in the blue-black sky, dimming the stars, spread the yellow comet, curved like a scorpion's tail, spitting orange from its inflated head.

Who were all those people standing like friends or relatives, why were they frozen in the light of the comet? What sign were they reading in the sky, what were they learning of their destiny?

This time Grandmother had employed all her skill, and I recognized her, a little girl pressed close to a man in an old-fashioned military cap, as well as other faces from the wall of photographs in her room. I turned to the photographs, and Grandmother, noticing my gaze, gave me a look that told me I had understood the picture.

Twilight, field, fence, house, distant forest—they were all painted in dark blue tones. I realized that here blue was a synonym for the remoteness of the past, that with this drawing Grandmother was looking so deeply into her own memory, beyond any temporal magnitude I had ever known.

"What year was this?" I asked, as if inquiring about the depth of a crevasse.

"It's now 1986," Grandmother Tanya said, happy for the opportunity to give me a math problem. "Subtract 76 years and you will know when the comet came the last time."

I subtracted.

"I must be wrong," I told her. "I get 1910."

"You're right!" she said with a smile. "You figured it correctly. World War I started four years later. Back then everyone thought that the comet was an omen of great misfortune, and so it was. Of course, then came the revolution," Grandmother went on, correcting herself. "And the revolution made people joyful."

I froze. I had never known exactly how old Grandmother was, I knew she had lived a long time and that she remembered the Great Patriotic War as an adult. But 1910?

"Grandmother, you mean you were born before the revolution?" I asked, hoping that there was an explanation, a miscalculation in subtraction.

"Yes," she replied, without a smile this time and uncertainly, catching the tone of my question.

My world was crushed by her reply. I had been certain that everyone alive was a child of the USSR. All the elderly, no matter how old, were the old people of a new time begun by the revolution and aged by that time.

Of course I knew that people born before the revolution did not die in 1917, but what happened to them later? The question never came up—they dissolved, scattered, vanished. It was not hard to calculate that they were alive in the seventies and eighties, but it never occurred to me to do the math.

Grandmother was born before the revolution; she could have said before the Ice Age or before the Cretaceous period. I studied history, I knew about the Battle of Kulikovo, about Ivan the Terrible, and the abdication of Nicholas II, but that had nothing to do with me. It was prehistoric history; real history, my history and the history of my family, began in 1917.

Grandmother Tanya suddenly became a prehistoric creature, as if she were a Neanderthal. Like the submarine commander, I was submerged too deep; I didn't have enough breath for 1910.

Yet the picture attracted me, the comet in the drawing and the comet somewhere in the sky above the city moved closer to each other, and I was caught as if in a vise. I put my head in my hands, seeking to answer the question: Who were my ancestors, who were those twenty people in the drawing? The mansion and clothing prompted me; but my conscientious naiveté, brought up on stories of workers and peasants, resisted the reply.

Those twenty people had also had fathers and grandfathers and great-grandfathers; that obvious thought stunned me. I ran from Grandmother's room, threw on coat and hat and hurried outside; I ran without thinking until I reached the empty lot near school. I was ready to learn that the Soviet Union had a hidden past, that was part of the pain of being a detective. But I could not connect myself with someone *before* the Union; that was a forbidden activity like dividing by zero, the mind refused to do it.

But the historical shell had cracked and there I sat, pathetic chick, enviously watching the older boys as they played soccer on the icy snow, caught up in the simple joys of the game.

I wept, and tears blurred my vision. But then they ran off, the world began to clear up, I could judge distance again—and I experienced a sense of historical scale, historical distance, for the first time, as if I had been living in a floating indefinite moment. My year of birth, my age, the years of my parents' birth, 1917, 1910, when the comet had come, the year Grandmother Tanya was born—they all fell into place, a network of coordinates. I had acquired a field of vision.

Walking home slowly, I imagined what I would find. Grand-mother Tanya had been feeling ill for the last week. I could see through a crack in the door how she sat in an armchair, put on an eye mask, and turned on a lamp with a long black handle, and how the darkened room would fill with a chemical blue other-worldly light—the night light of hospitals and barracks, the light of bomb shelters, the posthumous light of blockaded Leningrad.

Grandmother exposed herself to that light; I was told it was a treatment, but I suspected that was just a pretense, not very convincing.

After sitting motionless for the requisite time, Grandmother would turn off the lamp, remove the cloth from her eyes, and get ready for bed.

But the day we drew the comet, she did not go to sleep—she opened the wordless book in brown leather binding and began to write.

I guessed—nothing was stronger than this certainty—that the blue lamp was a medium, an apparatus without which Grand-mother could not write what she was writing; the blue colors of the drawing, the blue light of the lamp, it all came together.

I understood that the manuscript was her memoirs; special reminiscences that could be hailed, recalled, translated into heavy violet ink only after special preparation, the ritual of self-blinding.

The blindness was in the burgeoning buds of cloth over her eyes, the blue light enveloped her face, absorbed by the pores of her skin, sensed by nostrils, ears, and hair, making her face visible to the dead with whom Grandmother could speak—her lips often moved, speaking words I could not hear—but whom she was not allowed to see, that was forbidden.

I contrived to be by her door every night, to catch a quick glimpse of the blue glow, but I did not yet consider asking her what she was writing or to open the book without permission. If I asked, Grandmother would not answer, or tell me I had to grow a little older. But if I read it myself, deceiving her, then I would end up reading some other, fake, superficial text, since I had no access or key.

Perhaps if Grandmother had typed her text, the standard font would have deprived the book of its power; but even though she knew how to type and enjoyed doing so, she wrote by hand in the abrupt penmanship of an editor used to correcting other people's writing instead of creating her own. In fact the text was an editing of myself, a rewriting of a random draft filled with inaccuracies and omissions.

A text about the past that has power over the future; I could feel almost physically that postponed power, the changes happening here and now.

As far as I know, Grandmother Tanya did not show her book to Father or Mother; they silently acquiesced to her right to solitude, or perhaps they were in no hurry to learn something new about the past, wisely delaying that moment. It's possible that they might have asked about the manuscript, if not for the events which pushed all texts into the background.

UPBRINGING BY THE ESTATE

The telephone rang just before morning, Father walked across the room using his flashlight, and through the partly open door strange, unfamiliar words came from the hallway—reactor, isotopes, radiation sickness. Half-asleep, still sensing the light from Father's flashlight through my lids, lulled by the slow sway of the birches outside my window, I dreamed about radiation sickness, imagining that it emanated from the body, so unbearable that it blinded other people, while the person whose body was radiating light did not suffer at all, but turned into a gas, a part of the sun, retaining mind and language. Father was still on the phone and seemed to be speaking even more softly, then hung up and went to the kitchen, where he sat immobile in the dark, but for how long, I did not know, for I fell back to sleep.

In the morning I was told not to go to school—an extremely rare event—and not to leave the house. My parents left, Grandmother Tanya knew nothing, and I sat in the apartment listening to the radio—I knew that if Father got a call in the night, in the next day or two there might be news on radio and television about an earthquake or railroad accident, but you had to be vigilant to notice it, because it would flash by, reported calmly, lost in the midst of humorous stories, hockey match results, and lottery numbers. But there was nothing on the radio, the television, or the newspapers.

Nothing the next day, either. My parents did not sleep at home, I did not go to school, and it was only on the third day that the word Chernobyl appeared.

On the third day, my mother came home, and soon after so did my father, to pack; he was headed to Chernobyl.

Accustomed to Father's trips, the anxieties of Mother and Grandmother Tanya, the names of unfamiliar places which because they were the location of train collisions, earthquakes, chemical spills, suddenly became the names of disasters, I usually tried to visualize the catastrophe: buildings in ruins, burned metal, corroded soil—my imagination could manage that.

But try as I might, I could not imagine Chernobyl, the danger was invisible, death flowed along with water, flew with the wind, fell in the rain, grew in the grass and leaves, penetrated objects; Father went off to an otherworldly realm, the kingdom of the dead.

I was sent back to school; there were lots of conflicting stories told in the school yard—it wasn't a power plant that blew up, but a rocket; war had broken out, there was a nuclear strike, but the public was not being told; no, others said, it was a power plant and now we have to wait for the next accidents, all the reactors have a built-in flaw; not so, others countered, a secret military plant in Zheltye Vody blew up, and they're covering it up by talking of Chernobyl; a bomber crashed, the plane had nuclear weapons, and no one wants to admit it.

Nuclear explosion, atom bomb, "peaceful atom"—all the concepts were muddled, leading to an explosion of false information, the radiation of rumors, a vague and therefore even more frightening sign of the end.

"The energy released by a single hydrogen bomb is greater than the energy of all the explosives used in World War II," I read in my *Book for a Young Commander*. "If the capitalists provoke us into a third world war, our goal will be noble and beautiful—to make that war the last in the history of humanity."

The last in history—the echo of those words resounded in me as if I were an old man who had lived his life wasting it on nonsense or difficult and useless efforts, leaving an aftertaste of spiritual exhaustion that reduces both joy and sorrow. I could give myself up to the idea of the bomb that would put an end to everything, obviate the complex questions of daily life, spare me from the emptiness of prospects, giving the future a single, dramatic, and fateful meaning.

I had seen photographs of Kurchatov, the director of the Soviet atomic bomb project, with his long black beard; I think my father told me that he had vowed not to shave until the war was over, and then, until the bomb was made. His beard, long black tufts with gray, scared me; the smoothly shaven rocket engineers Korolev and Keldysh looked like scientists to me, and Kurchatov like a black wizard; his face, slightly Eastern, confirmed my guess. I thought they had brought in Korolev and Keldysh as a screen, to make people believe that the atom bomb was being developed by scientists, when in fact it was created by Kurchatov alone, a sorcerer who knew the dark secrets of things, who knew the real human fears.

At the Red Square parade, trucks transported intercontinental missiles, dark green cylinders with pointy red noses, which did not look like weapons. Rifles, cannons, and tanks presupposed a concrete enemy and their construction had a definite aim. Ballistic missiles were abstract in form and target; they negated the geography of war in its concreteness, in its small-scale thinking, and the figure of the enemy as such. They required an enemy as abstract as they were—alien, unknown, without characteristics—an enemy in which there is almost no trace of enemy.

War, the war has begun, I thought. I had dreamed so often of becoming a soldier, running away to fight, and I suddenly realized that my dreams were no longer valid.

We had been brought up with terms like bullet, fragment, and shell, on the idea that a soldier can play with fate, one will find a bullet and another won't, and that maybe by behaving in a certain way, performing a heroic exploit, you can earn a reprieve from your bullet; the nuclear bomb did away with all of that.

There would never be soldiers like my grandfathers again and it was useless to think about being like them; the photographs on Grandmother Tanya's wall were useless, so was her manuscript book, Grandmother Mara's trophy dinner service, and the *Great Soviet Encyclopedia* in the storeroom; one day they would all be gone in a nuclear blast.

THE ETERNAL BULLET

When Father came back from Chernobyl and crossed the threshold into our apartment, he kept me, Mother, and Grandmother away from him, would not let us touch him. He knew he was clean in terms of radiation, but his caution was strong; for a few days we lived as if he had the plague. Grandmother Tanya, who usually did not show maternal sentiment, became more attentive toward him, looking at him sadly, regretting something undone, something she had wanted to tell him but for which she could not find the words or did not know how to begin.

On the third day, Konstantin Alexandrovich came to visit, he was Mother's cousin, a detective, a police major general, the highest-ranking man I saw during my childhood. Apparently he wanted to hear firsthand what was going on in Chernobyl; even he, one of the main officials in the capital's criminal investigation department, was not getting the whole truth.

We rarely saw him, he would come for an hour or an hour and half, then a telephone call would make him rush off; a black Volga with a radio antenna awaited in the courtyard.

Gray-haired, tall, broad-shouldered, he looked as if built for the expanses of gigantic construction projects, for enormous work that would cease without his efforts, he seemed to regard himself sometimes with hidden surprise, a general, a detective of the finest caliber: How did I find the time to become a man like this?

He looked at the world from two points of view, that of citizens and that of criminals. He incarnated a certain type of the era, a person who fights universal evil, not just anti-Soviet evil, and thus becomes a major figure.

Father told him they'd laid sheets of lead on the floor of the helicopter for protection from the radiation as they surveyed the exploded reactor. Konstantin Alexandrovich said something like "Yes, it's a well-known method." Father was interested, because he thought they'd come up with the idea at Chernobyl.

"When we flew to Checheno-Ingushetia, we also laid sheets of metal on the floor, not lead, though, steel," the general explained reluctantly. "They didn't have armored helicopters back then, and when they use machine guns from below, from a crevasse …"

I repeated the story to Grandmother Tanya close to her ear; two or three years earlier the police had undertaken raids in the mountains of the Caucasus, looking for caches of gold; it all began with large thefts of gold from the Kolyma mines, traced to Checheno-Ingushetia.

What the general described was war, even though neither he nor my father used the word; ambushes, shootouts, and so many bandits it was more accurate to call them partisans. I couldn't understand: What about the peaceful Caucasus, the *djigit* in his turban on the Kazbek cigarette pack, the Narzan mineral water Father was drinking after Chernobyl? Grandmother Tanya looked as if the general's story was not news to her. He seemed a bit irritated, rummaged in the right pocket of his uniform jacket and laid a piece of chewed-up metal on the table.

"Look, a bullet pierced the metal," Konstantin Alexandrovich spoke into Grandmother Tanya's ear. "It went through and then struck me beneath my heart, leaving only a bruise. I carry it with me now."

Grandmother rose swiftly, went to her room, and started rummaging in the round woven sewing and knitting boxes. She came back and placed a small piece of cloth on the table, about the size of a quarter of a handkerchief, uniform fabric with a hole torn in the center.

Like a bit of a mosaic, a fragment from which one could reconstitute a larger image in various directions, rough, stained with mud, blood, and gunpowder. A whole world, a soldier's world, fastened with the straps of a soldier's pack, squashed by the heavy rim of a cannon wheel, unfurled from the remnant of an old uniform. The hole in the center wrapped it up, swallowed it; it seemed that the entire universe could be pulled into that hole like a fine shawl through a ring.

They lay next to each other, the piece of cloth and the bullet that struck Konstantin Alexandrovich in the chest; they suited each other, like a lock and key. I desperately wanted—oh, how I later understood Saint Thomas's desire—I wanted to push the bullet through the hole in the old cloth.

"My great-grandfather's uniform," Grandmother said to the stunned general. "All that's left. He died in the Caucasus. In the last century. He was also a general." Grandmother gave a thin, apologetic smile. "Slain by a Chechen bullet, as they told us when I was a child. 'Slain'; we were brought up poetically. His uniform was burned later, the epaulettes, the old officer class, that was not approved. My sister and I cut out this piece and kept it. She gave it to someone being evacuated from the siege of Leningrad. They found me in 1947. She didn't pass along or save anything of her own, only this ill-fated piece of fabric."

Father and the general looked at them with distrust and a childish horror; I think they wanted to do the same thing I wanted—to combine the bullet and the hole in the cloth.

"A tsarist general," Konstantin Alexandrovich said. "Tsarist."

He pushed the bullet through the hole in the uniform fabric as if in slow motion. Father was embarrassed, for he had not known about his ancestor who'd been a general, and like me, had never peeked beyond the border of 1917, even though he was born in 1941. I think he was planning to have a serious talk with Grandmother Tanya after Konstantin Alexandrovich left, to explain that you can't come out with family secrets just like that, it's embarrassing, uncomfortable … Grandmother did not notice Father's reaction and gently smiled at her thought, happy that she had finally shared the family secret with him, as if he had become another person after Chernobyl, one with the right to know.

Amazed by the ease with which Grandmother revealed the secret, I took it to mean something else. I did not know how long it takes to write a book so I was certain that Grandmother had completed her memoirs—how else to explain the opening of the curtain of silence?

She had spent a month on them; I thought a month was plenty to tell everything completely, to climb into all the cubbyholes of memory, it would take a few days, no more than that. Excited and confused, I wanted to know everything about the general killed in the Caucasus, I could not wait, afraid that Grandmother would take out only pieces of the past from her hiding places, like a magician, without showing me the whole picture; she would torment me with sudden revelations, like inoculations or electric shocks.

Having convinced myself that Grandmother wanted to show me her manuscript but did not know how to give me a sign, I boldly went to her before bed and asked, May I read it? She pretended not to understand, adjusted her spectacles and gave me a disappointed look: Don't you understand … Stubborn in my stupid certainty that the book was now completely written, I asked again: May I or not?

Grandmother shook her head: No. She was uncomfortable, sorry she had shown me the secret of the book, sorry that now everyone in the apartment seemed united against her, and she wanted to hide, vanish, but had nowhere to go and nowhere to take the book.

But my desire and hurt were too great; instead of apologizing, I turned and left. It's for me, for me, whispered the petty demon awakened inside me, why won't she show it to me?

The next day I waited for Grandmother to go to the kitchen and I crept into her room. The book in the brown cover lay on the desk, with a bookmark—very close, too close to the beginning. I noticed this, realized that she was only starting, but my hands opened the book by themselves.

"For my dear grandson," I read the inscription. "For my dear grandson, when I am gone." Shame burned my heart; I turned, Grandmother was in the doorway.

Without a word she took the book from me, put it in a drawer with her papers and locked it with a key that she wore around her neck like a cross. She picked up the pen, tightened the cap, and put it in the glass with pencils. The pen jangled against the glass bottom, and it was irreversibly clear: there would be no book. I had ruined everything, cut it off at the very beginning. There would be no book. Grandmother sat down, picked up the newspaper crossword—which she never did—and picked up the same pen, then changed her mind, and took a pencil and moved the three frogs to the edge of the table.

See nothing.

Hear nothing.

Say nothing.

I should have fallen to my knees and begged for forgiveness. But the pain of shattered hopes was too deep, and so my thoughts ran in the opposite direction. I didn't need any stupid book! I didn't need to wait! I renounced Grandmother Tanya and became the grandson of Grandmother Mara, who would have been horrified by the news that I—the grandson of Grandfather Trofim, the brave tank soldier, and of Grandfather Mikhail, the imaginary spy—had a tsarist general ancestor.

It will be summer in a month, I kept telling myself, I'll be sent to the dacha, away from Grandmother Tanya, and there

I'll … I didn't know what I would do, but my despair told me I had to undertake a risk, like in the story about the son of the regiment who drew artillery fire to save the men.

That day the book in the brown cover vanished and no longer appeared on Grandmother's desk. She continued to study and play with me, but treated me as a child whose interests were the playground and school; there were no more picture memories in the album, no more poetry; and she never again invited me to sort grains with her.

RUN IN FRONT OF THE BLACK CAR

If parents only knew what ideas they accidentally give their children!

Sometimes my mother took me to the medical clinic near the Kiev Station. She had lived there with Grandmother Mara and Grandfather Trofim before and after the war, so revisiting her childhood places, she grew younger, cheerful and free, liberated from Father and Grandmother Tanya, and happily told me stories: how they made a special hook to steal bread from the downstairs bakery's truck; how in winter bandits used to throw dead bodies into the warm water seeping from the local steam baths; how German prisoners of war built houses and how they frightened her, she worried about who would live in them, who would be punished by being forced to move there. And at the same she wondered how Germans, who only killed and destroyed, knew how to build so neatly and deftly—maybe they weren't Germans at all?

I liked being in that neighborhood; the huge glass canopy over the platforms was like a magnet—you could be pulled in under the canopy, to the ticket office, and then onto a commuter or long-distance train, even though you weren't planning on a

trip. Buses and trolleys pulled up and drove off, river ferries were
docked at the landing, and Mother was energized by the hustle
and bustle, she bought me ice cream and let me eat as we walked;
we entered into a wordless conspiracy and didn't tell anyone at
home how good it was, just the two of us.

Soon after my falling out with Grandmother Tanya, Mother
took me to the clinic. We were crossing the bridge over the
Moskva River while a motorcade, surrounded by motorcycles,
passed us on the embankment in the direction of Leninsky Pros-
pect and Vnukovo Airport: three shiny black Chaika limousines
with opaque windows. Traffic had been stopped and the Chaikas
raced along the empty street, led by a highway patrol Volga, siren
blaring, showering puddles and store windows with flashes of
blue light.

I stopped, thinking that Mother would go on while I
watched the motorcade and then caught up with her. The cars
reached Sparrow Hills and I discovered that Mother, who was
not interested in cars or privileged persons, was also staring helplessly at the now-invisible motorcade.

I wanted to go on, but she stood still, in the grip of some
emotion. Down under the bridge at the corner by a traffic light a
boy my age stood with his mother, impatiently stamping his feet,
while his mother held his hand, pulling him away from the curb.

My mother was looking back and forth at the asphalt, the
double white lines dividing traffic, and at the boy who was obviously chafing at the delay and would have run across against the
light had he been alone. He would probably have pulled a prank
trying to scare an inexperienced driver by pretending to run in
front of the car. Coming closer I saw that Mother was crying,
but only her left eye was tearing up, as if, being a righty, she
had more control over that side. Slow tears accumulated in the
eye's corner, and she wiped them away, pretending to be dabbing
some speck with her hankie.

I could not remember my mother ever crying out of the blue like that. My mother was lighthearted; she could be sentimental, but in a fierce way, not weepy; at a moment of separation, a moment of fear, she always smiled encouragingly. But now she was crying with pity for herself, and I sensed that the cause of her tears was somewhere in the past of the girl who had yet to meet my father and become my mother. I realized that she had spent most of her life without me and a significant part without my father. Stunned by the unexpected separateness of a person I had always considered an immutable part of my world, I stepped away to give her privacy.

Later, as we sat in the clinic corridor, Mother talked—into space, to the side—about a boy she liked when she was at school not far from the train station, and how when she was twelve, she decided to marry him when they grew up, but then disaster struck.

Daily, at a certain hour, Stalin's motorcade of several identical black cars flew down Bolshaya Dorogomilovskaya thoroughfare to the Kremlin. The local boys came up with a game: they tied their hands together with a clothesline and ran across the street right in front of the cars. Why did they do that? Mother did not say.

The police and secret service did not try to stop the children, even though they ran across the street more than once. The guards seemed to be spellbound by this strange behavior, they, too, wanted to see if the boys would succeed and to experience those moments of delight, horror, and delicious fear that someone dared to play this game with the Leader, teasing the tiger in dangerous proximity to his whiskers. Probably no orders came from Stalin's bodyguards, the ones in the cars, as if they knew that their boss liked it; they had developed an animal sense for approval and disapproval, they must have perceived the impulses of his will directed at the backs of their shaved heads.

The cars hurtled past the children without reducing speed.

One day two of the boys, one of whom was my mother's crush, decided to run extremely close, so close that Stalin would be able to see their faces. They ran, but a policeman blew his whistle—they said he was new, his first day on the job, and didn't know this game. The whistle violated the general pact of noninterference, the secret service agents ran onto the sidewalk, but it was too late to catch the boys. The black cars were racing down Dorogomilovskaya, hubcaps gleaming, parting space, sending everyone—pedestrians, police, guards—reeling back toward the walls. Only the two boys raced across the street; the policeman blew the whistle again, and one boy lost his stride, tripped on the line, and knocked over his friend. They tried to get up, the rope stretched out and the nickel-plated fangs of the front car's bumper caught it, dragging the children. About one hundred meters later, right by the bridge, it stopped, and against all regulations, so did the whole motorcade.

It's most likely that Stalin wasn't in it, otherwise the cars would have continued on. But no one was thinking about that then. A great and total silence ensued, so quiet you could hear the ticking of the black cars' cooling engines. No one rushed to help or to call an ambulance, everyone froze in place waiting for Stalin to open the door to see who dared play this outrageous and delightful game. Maybe only a boot would appear, the boot would touch the ground but the Leader would stay inside. The boot would be even more threatening and majestic than Stalin whole—no one would have any doubts about whose boot it was—the boot would be Stalin.

No one remembered how long the silence lasted. Mother said the trains at Kiev Station seemed to have stopped too. The two boys, tied by the clothesline, their skin scraped to the flesh by the asphalt, with twisted joints and broken bones, also lay there in silence, trying to move but not moaning, for a moan could change the balance in the scale of punishment and clemency.

Guards came out of the black car, picked up the children and loaded them into the vehicle. They headed in the direction of the closest hospital, while the motorcade went to the Kremlin, and the crowd broke up, people trying to forget what they saw, erasing the boys from their memory until their fate was resolved.

The boy my mother had liked returned a month later from the hospital: against all expectations, there was no punishment. The absence of penalty and its anticipation destroyed the boy. The broken bones knitted properly, the wounds healed, but he never got over it; he hanged himself in the woodshed, with a clothesline.

I took the story in a different way than Mother intended. She was protecting and warning me, surely aware that bad things were brewing in me.

But I heard something else: a child can perform a deed that adults fear, he can throw himself in the path of a black car and stare into its headlights. I understood the spirit, the mood, of the boys; I realized that my mother was afraid of that—that one day either accidentally or intentionally, now or twenty years from now, as an adult, I would do something similar; run out, leap, rush headlong where I should not go.

I did not yet know *what* I would do, what I would achieve, but I absolutely knew *how*—like those two boys who dared to run across the road in front of a black motorcade that never stops.

THE RIVER OF HISTORY

As a reward for his trip to Chernobyl, Father was given a union-paid holiday—a few days aboard an excursion cruise on the Volga. It was May, navigation season was just beginning, it was practically the first voyage, which usually went half-full, but the ship was completely booked.

No one knew where the fallout would spread, where the radioactive rains had fallen; there were rumors that Western countries had registered higher radiation and people were guessing how bad it was in Russia.

A lot of people tried to send their wives and children wherever they could as long as it was far from the reactor. These were primarily scientists and military men who understood what danger radiation posed; in Moscow the first pre-evacuation whispers circulated.

The cruise ship left in the evening, and we would go through the locks of the Moscow-Volga Canal at night. We arrived at the Northern River Station, that relic of the 1930s, where plaster volleyball players eternally fly up over an imaginary net and plaster female swimmers dry themselves with towels. Parts of the sculpted images had fallen off, the athletes stood on rusty rebar stubs like prostheses, as if they were crumbling, dematerializing, vanishing into thin air with each new navigation, which for them meant time passing.

In a landlocked capital, the river station gathered five seas under a five-pointed star on a spire, which had once twinkled on a Kremlin tower; I sensed that this was not the feckless dock for quick ferry rides but a more important place.

In ring-encircled Moscow, here was the secret exit, a river road. Yet Russian history flowed along rivers, the rivers grew cities on themselves, dictated the geography of principalities—and the echo of that was palpable there: the station for ships bound for Yaroslavl, Uglich, Kostroma, the forests beyond the Volga, and the very word Volga, which was spoken more frequently than others at the station, with its deep and rolling *o*, ready to spill out of the word like a gemstone from a setting.

It so happened that my parents had traveled in all directions out of Moscow but never north. In childhood, that kind of randomness is perceived as a deeply-reasoned principle. Therefore, in my personal topography, the North was the land of fairy tales and historical legends. The mysterious city of Kitezh, vanished principalities, extinct nomadic tribes, the Polish regiment that seventeenth-century martyr Ivan Susanin lured into the swamp, Tsarevich Dmitri, exiled to Uglich, where he died—these stories were all jumbled into a narrative about extreme lands where people perish, vanish, get lost, a narrative about enchanted, unstable places that can open up and swallow, as if history had not yet "set" there, but was still a thin and spotty film of rust on the surface of swamps.

Mother and I settled into the cabin while the boat left the dock and moved into the night. She promised to show me the locks; I had drifted off to sleep and she woke me when the ship had passed the watershed and started going down the lock ladder to the Volga. Bright violet-white lights hit our portholes, and we went out on deck with the crowd of passengers.

Above us rose the locks, looking like churches, with colonnades and porticos, yellow and white, illuminated in the night. Between them, down in the channel, were the heavy black gates, slippery with water and seaweed. Other gates shut behind the stern, and the boat slowly sank into the lock pit. A rotten river stench emanated from the walls covered with grasses and shells; the grasses moved like worms, black moisture streaming down; I thought we were being lowered into a bottomless well.

The big river's water, agitated by the pumps, revealed its secrets; its smell—the smell of silt, crayfish, and leeches, the spirit of pike and burbot—precipitated like water on the skin. I thought that if we rose up again—there beyond the black gates—we would surface in a world like that of the fairy tale river king, where the lower edge of a fishnet sometimes floats in the foggy sky.

The boat stopped descending; the gates began to open silently. The boat started forward, and we sailed past the water-corroded walls; their fishy smell, the weeds, cartilaginous lumps and declivities—they were like walls of an enormous stomach.

In the morning I resisted leaving our cabin for breakfast, for I did not want to discover that my foreboding had come to pass—that we had sailed into an underwater kingdom; but Mother did manage to talk me into going upstairs for lunch.

The places along the walls were taken, but in the middle of the restaurant, beneath a glass cupola that collected the sun's rays like a lens, stood several tables placed together and formally set; the head of a sturgeon looked at me from a silver tray with its boiled eye. The head, as big as a teapot, with splayed gills revealing its jellied innards; a jaw half-open as if it would speak; the eye, dead but still seeing, the size of a coat button, perfectly round, with a black pupil in the center.

The sturgeon's body—from the first fins to the tail—was cut into even slices and laid out around the head. The funereal tray gleamed; the head, blanched in boiling water, was dull silver; its shape, like a pointy helmet, made it look like the head of a slain fish knight—or a knight who was transformed into a fish, slain and chopped into thirty-three pieces. The sturgeon looked out with an empty and terrible gaze—not food, not a dish, not a treat but a natural corpse, served up to the table of those who vanquished and killed it.

Now, I assume that it was the birthday of an important boss on the fleet; the ordinary passengers did not approach the center table, edging away from the party for high-ranking bosses, and that is why the sturgeon head stuck out in the white starched emptiness.

Then I saw what I had guessed correctly—here he was, the dead king of fish, and we were in his otherworldly realm. I twisted out of Mother's grasp and ran up onto the deck to see what I had been hiding from and to throw myself into the water, since we were already in it, anyway.

The Volga attacked me; I saw a mighty flow of water that could no longer be called a river. The centripetal force of the gigantic plain had collected innumerable streams, brooks, and rivers, with names in dozens of languages, mossy, woodsy languages in which forest spirits laugh and sprites giggle; the Volga was a continent of moving water, raised above the low lost land, above the distant lines of shores.

My entire life seemed a glacial, frozen existence. In delight, I sensed that it was not only the Volga moving, but my fate, too; the source and force of that movement were in me.

I ran to the stern, when the roiling water splashed out from the propellers, and threw the word "Fate!" into the watery furrow like a seed, I threw it endlessly, and I thought that the waves grew more powerful and violent upon hearing it. Fate! Fate! Fate! I shouted until I was hoarse and no longer knew why I was shouting, why I was facing down the water spraying from the propellers.

Catching my breath and stepping away from the rail, I sensed that something had changed. Wherever I had gone, wherever I was, I always knew where my parents and grandmothers were, no matter how near or far; they were orientation points, a lighthouse.

The lighthouse went dark, and that feeling was gone.

I was alone.

THE SIGN OF THE DEAD TSAREVICH

Mother caught a chill looking all over the boat for me, and she did not go ashore at Uglich, the last stop, but sent me along with a friend of hers.

The friend was one of those women who bring discomfort wherever they go—as if they worked as funeral mourners and everyone knew. Bustling, sharp-angled, she led me by the hand, but since she was childless she didn't lead me in a maternal way but as if she were planning to turn me over to an orphanage. Her gait and behavior, the wharf and gangplanks, and the expanse of the Volga behind me brought to mind Grandmother Mara's long-ago talks about being evacuated near Engels on the Volga, images taken from someone else's memory—satchels, sacks, a desert of water, wailing infants, inhospitable houses.

I didn't want to go anywhere, pleaded to be left on the boat, but my escort was implacable in executing my mother's request.

There were not many men on the boat, and they headed off to find a liquor store; the excursion consisted entirely of women. The noisy crowding on the wharf, the hurried descent on the gangplank, and the wind that prompted them to put on scarves, somehow turned them into peasant women, homeless, evacu-ated; there was a readiness for transfers, negotiations and strug-gles for seats, rather than a quiet trip; the women were nervous and agreed to split up—one would go for groceries, the other would fill her in on the sights.

The tour guide was a young woman of thirty or so, red-haired, narrow-hipped, ungainly; it seemed that she had lost the equilibrium of her life and stressed the instability, the readiness to fall, by wearing high-heeled shoes.

She wore a necklace of large amber beads, big earrings of landscape agate framed in silver, heavy rings on her narrow fin-gers, handmade by a jeweler but still ready to slide off. I don't think she wore them for beauty and charm, the ornaments were for someone who could no longer see them, a dead husband or fiancé, perhaps a young officer who died in Afghanistan—hence the slight air of mourning about her, the shadow of an imaginary veil over her face.

Every day she met cruise tourists, led them down the same routes, and she would have been better off in jeans and sneakers rather than shoes and a dress beneath a raincoat that was long and a bit old-fashioned, setting her apart from the provincial crowd. A personal tragedy had hardened her heart, left her here, tied her to this city. The expectation of revenge, something that did not happen, kept her here. The force of the hidden emotion made her the medium of the place, the voice of its silent land.

The city, museum-like and overvisited, abundantly gifted with churches and monasteries, waited with bated breath. There were too many churches and monasteries, they had been placed intentionally: they held down, contained, and soothed the unstable land.

The convulsions of the Time of Troubles, which had come from here, from Uglich, from the moist soil washed by the Volga, had been too terrible and powerful. Generation after generation built up this place in a special way. That's why the city felt heavy, overloaded, not a city at all but an outpost with a border within its very self, a city padlock enclosing the abyss that had once opened here; a city of silence, of muteness, for a word spoken here could reawaken the Time of Troubles.

My presence here was a hindrance, an insignificant one. I had the same feeling at the Eternal Flame at the Kremlin: separated by an invisible line, the soldiers stood on guard, and the people on this side of the line, dressed up, falling silent before the memorial, were trifling compared to the perfection and severity of the guards' silent vigilance, by the flame that seemed to come from the bowels of the earth, from magma. The soldiers guarded not the memory of war so much as this dangerously open place; and so Uglich stood still on watch, forced to allow everyday life into the city, the chatter of lines for food and excursions from tourist boats.

The guide told us about the life of Tsarevich Dmitri, and the cold spring wind from the Volga, blowing dusty swirls on the streets, fluttered red hair around her face. The strands of hair rose up like snakes, surrounded her face like a glowing halo.

She did not talk, she almost sang the words; the dead Tsarevich Dmitri, the dead husband, perhaps the unborn child—the female and maternal in her merged into a single passion, a single desire.

Before her eyes stood the boy tsarevich, the imagined fruit of her womb and the adolescent tsar, already estranged, born again in the womb of the land in order to rule. She spoke of the exile of the Nagikh family to Uglich, and each word had a sensual form like that of an auricle, of lips; the fire of obsession was in every word. Thank God no one was listening, they were busy with their own thoughts about the stores and what they saw in the windows—I thought.

The guide brought us to the place where Tsarevich Dmitri died, in the red and white church with lapis lazuli domes—clots of heavenly blue ornamented with stars; the Church of St. Dmitri on the Blood above the Volga, on a promontory cliff. I've been there since and saw that the promontory is small, just a slight headland of the shore on a low cliff. But as a child I felt the nakedness of the promontory, sharpened like a compass needle; invisible arrows of events still looked down from the air onto the spot where Dmitri, who wounded himself, had fallen.

The church was rather childlike, not grown-up; the domes seemed like toys—blue glowing bulbs dusted with gold stars, toys for a dead tsarevich; if you touched them they would tinkle, like fresh new ice; church as cradle, church as crib.

The guide recounted the story of how he died, playing with friends and falling onto a knife. Now her words were crowded, jumbled, radiating a female heat ready to escalate into hysterics.

The words pushed and shoved like fleshy large-bodied peasant women, hot from the kitchen and laundry, sweating, smelling of fried potatoes, onion skin and fish scales, ashes and dirty sour water. The guide did not lose herself in the speech, remaining lofty in gestures and pose, but the words were older and stronger than her. In her spoken intonations the drama played out: the people running from their houses, the alarm bells, the tsarevich's body crumpled in an epileptic fit, the bloodied throat—and the primordial power of the female element, which comes not from heart or head but belly, womb; the element that combines lust and birth pangs, in which a panting woman is half mad with passion or hatred, in hot armpits, below the belly, in the very roots of her hair.

The women, it was the women who tore apart the tsarevich's friends accused of murder; they did not allow the tsarevich to really die, to the end, they did not allow death to occur—with the power of the passion they resurrected the nine-year-old boy and turned him into an adolescent, handsome and innocent. From mud and blood, bits of human flesh and scraps of skin, squeezed-out eyes, torn entrails, mucus, urine, and feces, the true heir to the throne was born.

I listened and watched the women give in to the guide's words; they adjusted their scarves, drew their children closer, started rummaging in their purses without knowing what exactly they were looking for, leaning forward, greedily looking at the church and the ground around them. A distant, weak echo of what had happened here enflamed them. It was a cloudy gray day—as it had been hundreds of years ago in May; a tugboat dragged a barge of timber along the Volga past the church, a radio played in the distance, but the guide's voice was floating, we were all floating somewhere, as if the Volga were moving the shore with the church.

Now the women stood in a circle, listening closely, crowding one another, pulling back hands and elbows as if an electric current flowed between bodies. A slow clockwise movement began as they moved, the better to hear or see the guide, who could not stay in place and walked inside the circle; the crowd tightened ranks, and when the guide recounted how the tsarevich's coffin was opened, the circle froze, a charged emptiness in its center.

Despite the coolness of the day, it was hot, it smelled as though something were being heated up, the smell of the crumbs that collect in the bottom of pockets, of poorly washed stains, of the dirt under fingernails, and the metallic bitterness of buttons. There, in the center of the circle, in the emptiness, someone had to appear, different, pure, untouched by our foul lives.

A cry rang out, a boy in the front row must have sensed a threat in the movement of the adults and tried to hide, but his mother held his hand so tightly that he bit her palm.

We shuddered and moved apart—there was no longer a compact crowd, just a group of adults shivering in the breeze and a boy being scolded by his mother, as she wrapped her bitten hand with a used hankie.

No one was looking at the guide, as she lightly adjusted her heavy bracelets, silver fetters, amber and malachite bridles; her hair was snaking in the wind again, and the passion cooled in her eyes.

The return trip on the boat was like a half-dream; I remember only the excursion in the shoe factory in Kimry. They were fulfilling an order for the military, and I saw thousands of wool boots; they were piled up, but in one place one of the workers jokingly set up a line of pairs of boots, as if they belonged to a unit of soldiers. There was something upsetting in the emptiness of the boots, as if somewhere there were people for whom the boots were intended but who were still living their individual lives, not knowing that their lives were predetermined.

The banks, not yet covered in green, were empty; the emptiness of water surrounded the boat. Mother was still sick, and I spent all day on deck.

I sensed significant images and faces leaving their usual places inside me, my inner arrangement changing, like a map of the heavens in the hands of an astronomer ready to add a newly discovered constellation.

I ended the school year poorly, my final May grades spoiling the quarter and the annual assessment; I could not do exercises or solve problems, and my parents decided to send me to the dacha as soon as possible, thinking I was exhausted by the end of the school year and that summer life would heal me faster than lectures and admonitions, than concern and care.

I was clearing space for future emotions, feelings, and events; they were prearranged, and I was the only draftee who knew that the factory was already making his boots.

PART THREE

THE SUMMER OF MISTER

The summer began with a household catastrophe—the old stove, built by Grandfather Trofim, collapsed; he had not been a professional bricklayer, but he learned to build, to create out of nothing, and his stove had served for three decades, until it buckled under its own weight.

It was cold and damp in the house, Grandmother Mara tried lighting the stove a few times, but the rooms immediately filled with smoke coming through the cracks in the plaster; the village stove builder refused to repair it, he said it had to be taken down and a new one built.

Grandmother Mara was not prepared to do that; I think she secretly felt that the collapse of the stove was retribution for infidelity to his memory, since she was marrying the retired captain; the old submariner was told not to come to the dacha for now, and he obeyed without complaint; Grandmother ordered Father to find a temporary stove.

Rather shady characters, of an inscrutable age and who knew their way around money, gathered at the village market-place, ready to procure what was not available and would simply not be found in the stores. Father bought a *burzhuika* cast-iron stove from them, paying an arm and a leg and overcoming his disdain for swindlers and cheats. He brought the stove home in a wheelbarrow, seeking approval for obtaining the hard-to-find item and his willingness to overlook his principles for the good of the family.

But Grandmother Mara burst into tears: she wanted the stove carted off, Father to go away, everybody to leave her alone.

Outrage, confusion, Father's explanations—we understood

that Grandmother Mara had spent her whole life trying to escape from the freestanding stoves that gobbled firewood and fit into the smallest barracks room—and now, completing an enormous historical circle, the *burzhuika* was back.

Grandmother Mara was so enervated by the sight of the stove wrapped in wax paper that without raising her voice, in a monotone, she started telling me what she discovered when she returned from wartime evacuation in the winter of 1943: her former room in Moscow was occupied by new people registered to live there; of the things she had left with relatives to hold, only the *Great Soviet Encyclopedia* survived. They had traded the rest for food for the winters of 1941 and 1942, but kept the encyclopedia, maybe because it garnered a paltry exchange rate.

That cold winter in a tiny cell right by the barracks door, which opened and closed five hundred times a day, letting out the warmth and letting in the crisp frosty air, in that tiny room where she lived without official permission, Grandmother Mara waited for nighttime, so that no one would see, to feed the cracked and corroded stove with volumes of the *Great Soviet Encyclopedia*, two volumes a night.

Things improved quickly, a package came from Grandfather Trofim, and she began receiving food parcels at work. But even decades later, she could not forgive her apostasy. She chose the volumes that did not have Lenin, Stalin, the Communist Party, the USSR, the RSFSR, Communism, or Bolsheviks—but even so, she said, she probably burned a volume that should not have been destroyed, on which everything depended. All our misfortunes come from that, Grandmother repeated, all our troubles! And there is worse to come!

Grandmother Mara told us how she and Grandfather Trofim traded alcohol for the GSE with some small town council, where the books had been sent for the local library, and where the set stood unopened. She and Grandfather didn't need an encyclopedia but they were thinking about their future children, they wanted the GSE for them. And now the stove appeared before Grandmother as a testament to her ancient crime, an accusation of an unforgivable sin.

So that's why there were missing volumes, I realized. My parents tried to console Grandmother Mara, saying, There are no troubles, no misfortunes, everything is fine—but I could tell they didn't believe their own words and sensed changes on the horizon that were unlikely to be for the better.

The dacha areas were being rebuilt very quickly in those years to accommodate new arrivals; the empty lands and former fields gave rise to new lots, with six hundred square meters instead of the previous thousand. Forest borders were chopped down, roads and paths laid through the woods to the train station; the new residents settled in, and suddenly there were too many people, the forest ravines started filling with garbage, the excess of their existence. Previously, everyone knew everyone, the villagers and the dacha residents knew one another, the mushroom collectors knew the mushroomers, the fishermen the fishermen; and then in just a year or two the summer population doubled or tripled; and the appearance of a "stranger," which used to elicit wariness and talk—Who's that wandering around here?—became routine, but it transformed the atmosphere.

Feeling this change or perhaps alerted to the new times and the disintegration of the former order by nomadic and unsettled instincts, tramps began appearing.

From behind stoves, from seemingly abandoned cabins on the edge of villages, from a neighbor woman's shed, from storage buildings, came the men hiding there, as if awakened from sleep.

For many long years they stayed put—living wherever they had washed up—under someone else's roof, some did petty thieving, others drank, but all found a food source, leaned on something. Suddenly they seemed to have found willpower, intention, strength; they used to be ashamed of themselves, knowing their pathetic position in the strict village world, but now they were forming groups that quickly turned into gangs. They went out into the woods and found an abandoned forester's hut or a child's tent, which they furnished into a scary parody of living space: they dragged in cast-off couches and refrigerators, trashed television sets, and set up this trash around a bonfire covered by an awning or in a pit; they probably stared at the broken screen of the Rubin or Yunost TV, put leftover and stolen garden vegetables into the refrigerators, and tossed piles of clothing snatched from the line while the housewife wasn't watching into listing cupboards.

A method of earning money appeared in the forest strongholds—stealing metal and robbing dachas; the tramps climbed over the barbed wire of the military airfield to unscrew things from planes and established an exchange with the guards. In the winter they found shelter or moved south or died of the cold, but the gangs reappeared in the spring, with new members, and the forest world grew stronger. The tramps looked down on the dacha owners, uselessly puttering in their gardens, the way in times of pestilence, starvation, and plague they must have looked at the people guarding their houses and fields.

Former convicts became tramp leaders, stupid girls were sent out to beg on their behalf, strange rumpled women walked around the villages and dachas casing the places for their friends. Of course, there weren't many tramps, they couldn't ruin the entire forest, and they weren't seen in every yard, but they set something off, and rumors started in the villages, touching the dachas, too; rumors as musty as a bread box moldy from the inside, rumors that must have spent half a century under a bushel, crept into roach holes and spider corners and old women's trunks with their burial underwear; mad, inarticulate, and portending disorder and trouble.

About army deserters hiding in the woods who killed two people last week in Pyatikhatka and burned down the house to hide their traces; about the Chernov daughter who took a short-cut to Stary Gorodok and saw two men harassing a dacha owner; about the coming revaluation of the currency, after which everyone would be impoverished; about how planes land every night at the airfield with coffins from Afghanistan and they burn the bodies in the furnace so that no one will know the real losses there—they really did switch the furnace from coal to oil, and the smoke it produced was different.

Grandmother Mara's village women friends took grim pleasure in retelling what they heard, and in doing so took on the appearance of limping birds of prey. Their conversations revolved around coal, firewood, manure, salt, and sugar, and were interrupted by the next in a line of rumors, as if they could sense the approach, the return of something terrible and for-gotten, and were happy that life was just, and that the present prosperity, albeit a relative one, was only temporary, and no one could escape their comeuppance.

The deserter theme was most frequent, the old women savored that city word in a special way, as if it were a lump of sugar to suck on while drinking tea, syllable by syllable; deserters, deserters, they repeated, and I think they meant every escapee, every tramp who went off into marginality, having abandoned their usual world order.

Or maybe they were remembering the war years, men hid-den out of fear of arrest, memories of brothers or husbands who fled the front, secretly or with faked papers; cellars and distant farms, foxholes where deserters hid in the chaos of the retreat in 1941. There was a devil-may-care tone, as if they knew some-thing no one else did, hidden in the crevasses of their wooden houses; echoes of ancient artillery thunder and astounding events were bursting inside them, demanding to be told.

Whenever an unknown man dressed in an old army jacket walked past the most distant village yards, looking at hanging laundry or a fowl that came out to drink from the big puddle, and maybe thinking about stealing something to sell for a drink, the old women knew by evening that a deserter had been seen by the Nefelyev place. Her friends brought their stories to Grandmother Mara for certification of authenticity, as if she were a notary, for her to say whether the man who looked greedily at the goose was a deserter or just some fellow; Grandmother Mara generously confirmed it—a deserter!—as if she understood the women's need to live not ordinary lives but to be in final, terrible times, and she shared it completely.

Simultaneously with the deserter theme, another old story came up, and the children told it, but it originated with the grown-ups. The story was about a mother who had a daughter who banged her finger and her nail stayed blue from bruising for life. One day the daughter vanished—the circumstances were given variously—and the mother sought her in villages, train stations, and marketplaces; six months later at a faraway station she bought a meat pie from a platform vendor's army-issue thermos and found her daughter's blue fingernail in the filling.

The old women, who all seemed to be childless (either there were no children or they had moved far away), gabbed about the inconsolable mother, the vanished daughter, and the blue fingernail, as if it had happened yesterday, as if they had known both; it also seemed that they knew it was all lies, and they were sorry and wanted it to turn into truth.

The third theme, which came up on its own and roamed in and out of conversations, was rats; in fact, no one had encountered any rats, there were no rat infestations or stores of grain gobbled up. Once in a while people glimpsed one visiting the garbage pit. Yet there was the feeling that they were expecting rats. If you already had deserters and an inconsolable mother

looking for her missing blue-nail girl, then rats were sure to follow; instead of harmless mice, sturdy rat teeth would soon be
chewing away at the wooden supports of our houses. And that
meant you had to look in the sheds for long-forgotten rat poison, set rat traps, and fill in holes in the floor with clay mixed
with ground glass.

Grandmother Mara liked to recount how she killed a red rat
with a shovel when it jumped at her from under the floor, and
with each telling the rat grew bigger until it was the size of a dog.
With the rapture of exaggeration, Grandmother Mara told them
how smart rats were, how hard it is to poison them, how cats fear
them, how the rat dismembered by the shovel lived on for a few
seconds and stared at her with hatred. I got the feeling that they
weren't talking about animals, however smart, predatory, and
dangerous in number and stubbornness, but about monsters
that came from the beyond. I was amazed that Grandmother
Mara and her friends had once seen these monsters, it wasn't
their imagination at work but knowledge. I couldn't understand
it, the source of this intense fear, but understood when I heard
Grandmother Mara with her friend Grandmother Vera.

During the war, Vera worked as a switchman at the Leningrad Station in Moscow. In February or March 1941 a train
arrived from Leningrad with evacuees, and rats poured out of
the cars.

A train with flour stood on nearby tracks, and the rats
streamed across the rails; the train was guarded, but some of the
men with guns panicked. Vera grabbed a crowbar to chase the
rats away from the grain, but then realized that these rats had
eaten corpses on the streets of Leningrad—evacuees had told her
about it—had survived by eating human flesh and had escaped
the city in the trains with surviving humans.

Her enthusiasm vanished and she ran—from the rats and
from the people with them in the train, in the same cars; one

didn't know who had the real power there: the weakened people or the strong rats. One of the guards had the sense to run to the engine. Still coupled, the driver moved the train with flour, the rats jumped and fell under the wheels trying to get at the flour, and then scattered, making for the platforms and the ware-houses. Vera shuddered for years afterward at the sight of a rat in Moscow or in her village—Was it an ordinary one or a Len-ingrad man-eating rat?

I think the old women were expecting the progeny of those rats, or rather, they were willing them to come, predicting, luring them, as if they feared the looming disasters would not be bad enough. The old women put on their mended flowered dresses and shawls, met at the well or the mailboxes on the village street, and talked about exploding gas canisters, drowned fishermen, overturned buses. Their talk made the dacha area fascinatingly hostile, mysterious, open to the drafts of history, the winds from the past, its restless shadows. There will be famine, the old women said, you can't even buy ordinary grain any more—and I recalled the submarine captain's white locust flowers; we had one growing by our fence.

And finally, the old women got what they wanted: horrible news rolled through the dachas and surrounding villages; chil-dren were forbidden to play far from home or go alone into the woods, and soldiers patrolled the roads. They claimed to be catching deserters, but everyone knew that a maniac child killer had appeared in the region.

The maniac had a nickname—Mister; no one knew why it was the English word, but everyone said he called himself that. The bodies were found in places where you think the killer could not be unnoticed, and that increased the fear; it seemed that Mister was absolutely unrecognizable and therefore elusive; no one would suspect him of being a maniac, inhuman, the devil's spawn.

My friends and I felt no fear at first; in a few days of playing and running around the idea came up, just for empty chatter and boasting: Why don't we catch Mister?

Naturally, no one believed in it; but it was so exciting to imagine ourselves as brave and clever hunters, capable of doing what the police and soldiers could not. We talked ceaselessly about capturing Mister. We knew the area better than the adults, all the secret places, the dangerous corners; gradually, without a plan, we began acting like detectives, scrutinizing people, armed at all times with a penknife, nails, or metal electrodes sharpened on a brick.

None of this turned into a real search, and nobody actually wanted that; everyone wanted to amaze his friends with a story about how he found a mysterious boot print on the path by the fence and sat in ambush, we invented suspicious drifters allegedly seen in the field or by the pond; we all knew that these were just made-up stories, but we enjoyed competing in heroic lies with the knowledge that by unspoken consensus no one would be exposed.

But these fantasies did promote the idea that we could really try to catch Mister; each succeeding lie made the idea a bit more real.

The idea fermented like yeast, fed by the boredom of the longest, hottest summer days, the old women's stories, the whispers of the adults, the rules, the faded raincoats of the patrols, young soldiers fatigued by the pointless length of their tours who sneaked off to bathe in the pond, closer to the still-white bodies of girls lounging on towels. Something was going to happen, we were all expecting it, and inside me the feeling grew slowly, slowly that I was distancing myself from my gang and that part of me was already taking the idea of finding Mister seriously.

I did not realize it yet, but the maniac murderer, elusive in the dacha area, had become a fact and phenomenon in my inner life. The rumors, the boys' braggadocio, the details related by the villagers, were one layer—everything that is scary but does not affect you elicits interest; but there was another layer.

The dacha area changed with the appearance of Mister. I was drawn to the contrast between light and dark at the edge of a thick fir forest, the dry crackle of wires, the fragrance of peas in the field where you can open a pod and find tiny green pearls, sense their infancy, their softness that will turn to hardness. But I knew, whatever you did, whatever engrossed you, you were always either getting closer to Mister or moving away from him, and you never knew what was there, at the end of the forest path.

The world became a terrifying fairy tale realm, where nothing is random, where every object means something, says something, increases the danger that threatens the hero or mitigates it. My age kept me from feeling compassion for the ones who died in torment, and I accepted the appearance of Mister as what had been missing from my life.

THE APPEARANCE OF IVAN

Lazily discussing the latest "news" about Mister—who found which clues or traces—we played "knifesies" at the fire pit at the dacha dumping ground; what a strangely attractive game it is, you can play it a thousand times day after day and never tire of it. On the hard, ash-covered ground, you draw a circle with the knife blade and then divide it in half; two get into it and throw a knife onto the territory of the opponent; if it sticks, another line is drawn, and now you own three-fourths of the circle, and he has one-fourth; if it sticks again, your territory grows and his diminishes, but he still has room to stand. If your knife doesn't stick, then the opponent throws, scuffing away the recent borders with his foot, scratching in new ones, and now it's you and not him who balances on one foot.

Sometimes we'd play knifesies all day—there comes a time when frictions and unspoken injuries accumulate in a group of children; they were removed, channeled on the days we played many times against various opponents. The number of wins, the pressure and excitement of the game reset the relationships of seniority, first place going to the luckiest player.

I don't know how other children played in other places, but for me knifesies was inseparable from the bonfire ground. The soil smelled of ashes and was cleansed by fire—as if something had been burned, destroyed completely; we smoothed the surface so that it could be cut by a knife like bread, still warm, transformed in the fire, having lost its memory of all previous borders, divisions, markings. Soil and metal, soil and knife were like paper and pen; "pen" was criminal slang for knife, and we played with a homemade knife that had a broad and thick blade, which stuck into the ground less reliably than a penknife. Konstantin Alexandrovich, my mother's cousin, gave it to me secretly, telling me that a famous criminal had owned it and used it in self-defense when he was arrested; but I guessed that the knife had once belonged to the general, who grew up in workers' barracks, and in giving it to me, he was remembering the boy from the lawless, thieving outskirts who'd had a greater chance of becoming a bandit than a policeman.

In my mind, knifesies belonged with books and films about the Civil War; with the Red Cavalry, machine gun carts, "in the distance by the river, bayonets flashed," the psychological attacks by White officers, stars carved into backs, death in locomotive boilers. Not the invasion of the Germans, foreigners attacking from outside the circle, but the struggle of two implacable foes inside the disintegrating and simultaneously existing, "flickering" whole; knifesies was a Russian national game, somehow internalized and intimate.

So, we were throwing knives at the dumping ground beyond

the dacha fence; I won, having pushed my opponent out of the circle, removed the line of his last holdings with the sole of my shoe, and was enjoying the ideal emptiness of the circle that belonged to me alone. At that moment, we heard a voice from the edge of the circle. "May I play?"

The day was coming to an end, swifts swooped low near the ground, scooping up mosquitoes; something was cooking in the sky's kettle, towers of cumulous clouds rose higher and higher, deep blue on the bottom, colliding and devouring one another, the setting sun's rays burst through the gaps in the clouds, the light was harsh, thick, and dangerous, as if a battle was looming on high. It was the time before evening when the shadow is so much longer than the object that it seems it will overbalance it; space consists of those shadows, everything is elongated, distorted, stretched on a rack; it was out of the intertwined shadows, the stifling pre-storm air, and the agitated darting of the swifts that Ivan appeared.

We had seen him before, from a distance, but we knew who he was and his name. He was about ten years older than we were and he visited the dacha area sometimes, for his grandfather had a house here, but he never made friends—he was always on his own.

I looked at Ivan and understood that we had a long, one-sided connection, originating from me. I had met him thirty or forty times, briefly, the meetings scattered, lost as insignificant among what seemed more meaningful and memorable encounters, impressions, discoveries. But they had accumulated in secret even from me, and suddenly, in a moment, they were all there, open; words spoken about Ivan by the grown-ups, our childish conversations—it all came together and filled the emptiness that appeared while I was on the boat cruise.

This must be the way a man who runs into a woman who lives nearby might automatically or with the whim of a voluptuary casually toss into a drawer of memory the rustle of her winter wool skirt clinging to her legs, the barely noticeable limp revealed by the wear on her right heel, the slight discomfort that arose when they met by the elevator with a mild hint of flirtation, and then he let her pass, thinking lazily, why bother? And then one day, opening that additional little drawer made for ornament rather than utility, he sees her, all of a sudden, revealed to him radiantly and tenderly, sees her and feels her as if he held her in his arms.

For three, no, four years I had noticed Ivan at the dachas, playing badminton or hide-and-seek as I went to the well; he went to the well, too, I had often seen the bench damp from the water that had slipped from his pails, and once I left the well bucket full, and Ivan, who came after me, carried that water home, and drank it, swallowed tea and soup made with it— water that I had collected, water that I raised from the icy depths by turning the handle, while the liquid reflected my phantasmagorically distorted face.

Our connection was forged long ago; and now all its component parts, all the links in the chain, all the moments isolated from the rest of time in which we were connected by the delayed and hidden work of my heart, were electrified, under tension; we recognized, we saw each other, and blazed with the triumphant and ruthless light of understanding—it's him!

His figure was awkward; every adolescent goes through a time when his body behaves like a traitor, when everything you try to hide is callously revealed, the body's stupidity, actually, its stupefaction; shyness, constraint, fear—everything is exposed, comes to light; the body is afraid to grow and change; the act of becoming a man is confounded.

The awkwardness of Ivan's adolescent figure was different; there was something about him of a colt of magnificent breed, born to run, and the awkwardness was because his body grew faster than he could comfortably inhabit it, but would live in it tomorrow, and with great power.

He was tall, thin, blond; he stood out among our crew-cut boys with his long hair parted in the middle; he changed his hair later, but the first time I saw him I remembered him this way.

When I first saw this person, it seemed he hadn't been there a second ago, had stepped through an invisible opening from another space, from a time of eternal summer; it was all in his hair, as if the locks of a beautiful woman at the peak of her youth had been transplanted onto a teenage boy. The wavy locks glowed like the sun, with golden sparks, threads, quick zigzag snakes; the youth's gentle, slightly frightened beauty—Acteon looked like this when he saw his crazed borzoi hounds—was combined with an avalanche of hair, sensual, arousing the flesh.

We saw Ivan rarely, when he came to the dacha in his grandfather's cream-colored Volga—his face behind the window, his profile against the backseat. Every boy's dream was to ride in front, next to the driver, but Ivan rode in a car like an important person; a boss, a writer, in the back, by himself, alone with his thoughts, indolently looking out the window.

Ivan's whole family lived differently from the neighbors, with aristocratic casualness they returned the intended function to things that had been warped by our lifestyle. No one had ever seen sacks of potatoes hauled in the cream-colored Volga, nor was the car ever crammed with passengers, as if Ivan's family was not subject to the powers of life's necessities, forcing people to clump together, huddle, fit into a prescribed space. Laundry never hung on a line in Ivan's yard—inner secrets revealed—and the property was planted with twining plants that formed a living screen; only sometimes, walking past, could you see, through a gap in the foliage, Ivan reading a book in the garden.

You couldn't say that the dacha kids liked or disliked Ivan. If he had been one of the gang, his behavior would have been considered a challenge, they would say he was being snotty and would take revenge—they would break the dacha windows or jump him and beat him up; but for the dacha youth Ivan did not exist, as if no one knew which language, which words to use to think about him.

Over the dacha summers, everyone observed him, everyone probably understood that Ivan was a kid like any other, then an adolescent, then a young man; not burdened by excessive physical strength, unlikely to stand up for himself in a fierce fight— we had learned about fighting from the local village lads who were not averse to brawling with bike chains and pieces of metal pipe. It seemed that a boy three or four years younger, who was used to scrapes, roughhousing, and clumsy cursing, could scare and beat up Ivan; but Ivan never landed in that kind of story.

Yes, there was something feminine about Ivan, but there is a necessary correction here: if boys sense something girly about a boy, they will inevitably make him miserable. But the femininity in Ivan was—and this was clearly felt—not a weakness or flaw, but just another side, inaccessible to others, of his strength, a plastic, flowing strength, the strength of a much greater emotional range than an ordinary person.

Ivan entered the circle; I bent down to draw a line dividing the circle in half with my knife and it looked as if I were bowing to him; he looked at me without surprise or mockery. But I felt an aching anger: I want to stab Ivan, kill him in this circle, on this slightly salty, ashy, velvety soil scorched by fire; this was no game at all. My friends watched with interest, they did not consider Ivan a serious competitor, and they were happy to watch someone their own age beat him.

We did rock-paper-scissors; I showed a fist and Ivan covered it with his hand; Ivan got to go first. I usually threw the knife to immediately cut the opponent's side in half; then divide the remaining fourth; Ivan acted the same way. The knife we used had a secret—the handle was weighted, filled with lead; it had to fall absolutely vertically to stick into the ground, and that required practice. I hoped that Ivan would fail on his first throw; however, he threw it, very carelessly, without looking, as if he'd merely dropped it; the knife plunged into the dried soil and divided my part of the circle exactly in half.

Ivan erased the line just as unhurriedly and carelessly, increasing his space to three-quarters and reducing mine to one-fourth; he threw again, and each time I thought the knife wouldn't stick. But no—it entered the earth smoothly and firmly. I experienced a strange excitement; I had never lost this easily and indisputably, but it wasn't just the loss; as Ivan's share swallowed up mine, my desire to run away or attack Ivan vanished. I wanted the game never to end, for the division of my piece of ground to continue to infinity, so that I would diminish before Ivan and that there would be another chance to grow smaller, give up yet another part.

The burning ground inside the circle was my life now, and Ivan was reshaping it, taking everything for himself; he was whole and I was becoming part of that whole. I seemed to know that Ivan, in humiliating me and herding me into a reduced sector of the circle, would later make up for it.

Ivan threw the knife the last time; there was no place for me to stand, and I left the circle, acknowledging his victory.

"Come over some time," Ivan said. "Gate's not locked. Or I'll come over and pick you up. Well, so long."

He turned and left as if he hadn't just been playing; before me was the circle, still full of him, belonging to him; the knife stuck in the ground, casting a long evening shadow, like the marker on a sundial.

Ivan won me—from my own self. My pals could tell that I had not simply lost the game, I was happy to have lost, I wanted to be friends with Ivan.

They dubbed me Ivan's girlfriend; I couldn't go past our fence, they were waiting for me, hiding in the bushes, armed with rock-hard sour apples. I would creep up to the bushes and hear their conversations, which I'd but recently been a part of, and I bitterly missed the idiotic friskiness of speech, the hurrying, the gasping, the rush to talk, the constant exaggeration, the lies, the stupid boasting. The group was talking about Mister again, telling the same old stories, overgrown with outright falsehoods, while in my solitude I sensed that so many things had been rolled together into one clump: Ivan, Mister, my desire to show Ivan I wasn't like my pathetic comrades, to show my comrades I was braver than them, that they could only make up stories and pick on someone ten against one; the desire to do something exceptional, to block a black car's path, to prove to myself that I'd been right to turn away from Grandmother Tanya and the brown book; yes, yes, I thought, I'm like the son of the regiment, I will draw fire away from others; one dream hurried and pushed the next, and with the relief of a soldier weary of waiting for an attack, I sensed that soon I would take a step.

THE GENERAL'S VISIT

It was June, close to the solstice; the summer was dry, hot, and scorchingly sunny; it made the heavy fir forest beyond the dacha fence seem even blacker. Late evening and nighttime, when children are usually afraid, did not seem scary that summer; scary and horrible were the afternoons, when the streets were empty, hot haze shimmering above the asphalt, distorting and hiding perspective and the horizon; in the boiling jelly of that haze, the figures of passersby could suddenly appear very close, shimmering, inaccurate, flowing, and worrying; blessed was the cool of the evening, clearing the air and chasing away the ghosts of the day.

Those were the days when Konstantin Alexandrovich always visited the dacha. No use in hiding it—I was proud when his black Volga stopped at our gate, the numbers and letters on the license plate not random gibberish but a brief readable code, a sign of power and strength.

The general arrived at the moment the first cucumbers were ripening on the vine; Grandmother Mara brought them out on a plate, freshly washed, fragrant with the energizing, cooling scent of early morning and dew, which seemed to bring out the bumps on them. Konstantin Alexandrovich ate these first vegetables of the summer when they were still babies, thin-skinned, covered with a transparent and tender silvery fuzz. I honestly couldn't understand what made the general so happy, why this ritual was repeated year after year.

Then the table was set in the garden, the gramophone was brought out, a square box with a windup handle and an orchid-like trumpet. Manufactured in 1900, the gramophone was older than everyone around it; you could study its history in its scratches, lumps of lacquer, and dents in the trumpet. They used records, heavy ones, one song on each, and the gramophone rasped out "La Cucaracha," "La Cumparcita," and melodies from Alexandrov's comedies. No one remembered how the gramophone came into the family; I even thought that the family appeared because the gramophone was first; it was one of those long-lived objects that are unthinkable without a certain lifestyle, and if a gramophone shows up in someone's life, it will unite a man and a woman, marry them, give them children and grandchildren, a dining table, and curtains.

The record spinning, the slowing of the viscous sound when the springs wound down—the gramophone was a machine for producing familial happiness, and I was happy to turn the handle that dozens of hands had touched before me.

This time the general arrived toward evening, when everyone had thought there was no point in expecting him that day—that often happened, when urgent business held up Konstantin Alexandrovich or canceled his visit.

Watching Konstantin Alexandrovich's pleasure in washing up with well water, wiping his face with a linen towel that Grandmother Mara handed him, how he hung up his uniform jacket in the closet and came out in ordinary clothing, handily setting up the chairs, adjusting the tablecloth, carrying out the narrow faceted shot glasses between his fingers, and constantly looking around at the apple trees, the vegetable plots, the old house with flaking paint—I understood that the dacha was the closest thing to the lost world in which he was born. He was relaxed here, stopped being a general, returned to his postwar childhood, to the villages where soldiers settled; one lieutenant or captain joined the police as a patrolman, another became a bandit, and the boy grew up seeing both.

Later, just as the party was warming up, I was sent to bed. Usually, because of my attachment to Konstantin Alexandrovich, I was allowed to stay up to the end, but here, I noticed, the general glanced over at me to show it was time for me to go to sleep.

Mister!—the general knew something that he wanted to tell my parents.

I had the idea that if I could tell my friends what Konstantin Alexandrovich said, casually dropping his name, lying that he had told me personally, I would be able to get back in their favor, end their campaign against me, and become top dog: the reflection of Mister's horrible fame would make everyone listen and obey.

I said good night. I was to sleep in the attic, because Konstantin Alexandrovich was here, and after waiting a few minutes, I opened the dormer window, the hinges of which I had oiled because I liked climbing out on the roof at night. I crawled on my belly to the drainpipe and sat above the garden party. While

I crawled, I decided that I wouldn't tell my pals about the general—let them sit in the bushes with apple cores—I would go to Ivan. Now I would have something to intrigue him and keep him. For some reason, I had no doubt that Ivan was interested in Mister.

"They're not talking about this now," the major general spoke softly. "Trying not to talk. We have just one witness, a boy, a friend of the first victim. The artist's renderings are made from his description. They were together at Pioneer camp and sneaked out during quiet hour. Some people think the witness is a phony. He did see something, but much less than what he's telling us. He gave a description of the man who led his friend into the woods, very detailed, without any discrepancies, he said the killer scared him, warned him not to tell the police anything or he'd come back for him. We're hunting for the man described by the boy—height, hair color, a navy tattoo on his hand, something complex, and so on. And that nickname, Mister, allegedly he called himself that.

"It all seems true, but I've talked to that boy ... I think he got scared and ran off before the killer even noticed there were two of them. Our witness saw nothing but a shadow, a silhouette. But he invented this Mister, told the camp counselors about him. He wanted the attention. Then the police and the prosecutors kept at him, and now the boy can't admit that he lied. He knows he'll be punished. He's heard about giving false testimony. However, a lot of the investigators believe the boy. It's easier to hunt for this Mister. Lots of distinguishing marks."

"This doesn't sound right," Father interrupted. "Doesn't he understand that he is putting other people in danger?"

The general did not respond. I had conflicting feelings. On one hand, I was embarrassed by my father's question; didn't he understand what power there was in that lie? And on the other hand, I was scared, because I could easily picture myself in the boy's place and I knew I could have done the same thing, invented Mister.

"He must have a car," said Konstantin Alexandrovich. "And a place where he does it all before tossing the remains in the woods. A garage or a cellar. Probably a cellar. And here's one more thing," he added. "He is attracted to boys of a very certain type. Aged ten or eleven, not shy, not spic-and-span with no physical flaws. Not mama's boys, but boys who like to wander around on their own. The faces of all six boys are similar." The general stopped. "Bold, clear. Even at that age, no one would say, 'What a nice boy,' rather 'What a great guy.' Something was going through my mind," the general said and struck a match, tobacco smoke rose to my rooftop, "they reminded me of something. I finally remembered. It seems strange, but I keep thinking it. When I was a kid and we played war, you'd go into the woods, find an old hazel with thick, far-flung branches. You'd climb into the center and that's where the thin new canes are, completely straight, as if they came from a different root than the clumsy branches. You cut down a switch like that, you can make a bow or an arrow, anything at all—it's flexible, sturdy, springy, as if it has absorbed all the power from the ground. I look at photographs of those boys, and I think of the hazel tree. Maybe I'm just making it up, but I think he senses that quality in them. He sees it from afar. And he chooses them."

I froze. Konstantin Alexandrovich was saying something he could not know. It was my secret: I cut hazel switches like that and hid them in the nettles outside the fence, they were my weapon against the confusing deep forest, filled with spider webs. With a cane like that, turned into a sword, I could enter deep into a grove with borrowed courage, knowing that it did not have power over me.

Konstantin Alexandrovich told them about increased checkpoints at all the suburban stations along our line; about military

helicopters flying over the region; about soldiers combing the
woods; about checking old files and solving dozens of crimes
along the way; about undercover police pretending to be mushroom hunters, bathers, fishermen; about a group of immediate
responders, ready to come instantly; about the fact that both
the MCID—Moscow Criminal Investigations Department—
brought in to help the local police, and the Minister of Internal
Security himself were in charge of the case; and that the killer
would be caught any minute, the ring was narrowing, he would
definitely make a mistake and reveal himself.

My parents didn't consider taking me back to the city to
wait until the maniac was caught. No one even brought it up.
Instead, they sat there, depressed, helpless, Mother wrung her
hands, bringing them up into the air as if pleading to a cruel
power for mercy.

I remembered where I had seen that movement before,
those maternal pleas; I remembered the album of pictures from
the Dresden gallery that my father brought back from the GDR
and I leafed through secretly; a painting by Breughel the Elder,
with snow, redbrick houses, dark sky, hounds, trees—and men
in red on horseback, scattering throughout a village, dragging
women by the hands, killing infants.

The mother and father in the painting also clasped their
hands, fell on their knees by the stirrups, stared lifelessly in the
direction of yellow patches of thawed snow, wept by the walls of
houses. No one interfered, picked up pitchforks or scythes, the
villagers showed not just docility but a primal readiness to accept
the deepest suffering.

I might have wanted to leave the dacha, but my parents
couldn't break the usual rhythm of life, to act differently than
they ever had, sharply and roughly—you couldn't even consider
that. The adults were worried by the threat to their child, but
they looked at the neighbors, who also lived in dachas with chil-

dren, and told themselves not to panic—as if submitting to the habit of bearing things and obeying the power of circumstances, awaiting their fate like the men and women in Breughel's painting. The power was Mister, Mister-Coming-From-the-Woods, Mister-Taking-Away-Your-Children. Not a single resident of the dacha complex left, took away their children, they all lived as if hypnotized by a boa constrictor.

The more confidently Konstantin Alexandrovich talked about posts, helicopters, and special groups, the clearer it was that he was simply calming my parents. Despite the ban, I went into the woods, wandered around the area, not knowing why, just absorbing impressions that would later prompt me to act.

For example, when I picked strawberries on the sunny side of the railroad tracks, where freight cars were parked far from the station awaiting formation into new trains, I could sometimes sense the evil sticky smell of oil on the gravel, and how strangely predatory the berries looked, red and spattered with tiny hairs, how dark the water was in the pond, and how the forest reflected in it was also reflected in my gaze, not allowing me to see inside, as if all of nature was on the side of Mister.

Garage … Car … Cellar … Human remains … You couldn't say that I didn't believe the major general, but it seemed to me that there was something he was leaving out or didn't understand. Mister had become an otherworldly creature for me, Konstantin Alexandrovich's logical, clear statements about a flesh-and-blood man contradicted my ideas; I thought I could see farther and deeper than the old detective.

"The soldier patrols must have come across him," Konstantin Alexandrovich said. "More than once. But he's a simple good Soviet man. Can't recognize him."

"You mean he looks normal?" Father asked, stressing the word "normal."

"Soviet, he looks Soviet," the major general replied. "I have a theory. He must have something that makes people like him. And that shows he's a responsible person, not in authority, but nearly so. An armband of the national volunteer force, a badge of the Green Patrol, an ID as a fisheries inspector, something like that. A socially involved person."

A Soviet man, I thought. I didn't even listen to the rest. A Soviet man. Mister. I couldn't understand why I didn't believe in a killer finding pleasure in torture. Of course, it didn't fit my picture of the world, but there was something else, some backstory.

A Soviet man. Mister. Mister Soviet man.

Enlightenment came.

There were so many of them in children's books—various "misters," unremarkable fishermen, hunters, campers, soil scientists, nature photographers, herb collectors! Even the experienced eye of the border guard did not recognize them as violators of the border, spies, saboteurs, devils incarnate who crossed the no-man's land in shoes that leave hoof prints, in order to kill, poison wells, set explosives, to sow evil that was as cruel as it was ultimately pointless, evil for evil's sake, or to learn military secrets.

In the twilight hour, the time without shadows, he appeared, the werewolf, the perfect changeling, more Soviet than any Soviet man. Invulnerable, like a mirror, he strode across our country, absolutely "not one of us," an invader from the world beyond who preached the destruction of the Soviet Union, living only for hatred of the USSR. He left death and destruction in his wake, fooled sentries, tricked peasants and city folk, everyone. The only thing he feared, as the books all taught me, was the gaze of a child. Only a child, an unsophisticated child, could recognize him.

That was why Mister killed children—they were a danger to him! With the military airfield nearby, everyone in the village knew the secret information that the regiment posted there was the first to be equipped with the latest MiG-29 fighters.

"The regiment has achieved combat readiness," my friends and I repeated variations on the words someone overheard at the station, repeating them like a spell. "The regiment has achieved combat readiness!" That's why Mister was here, circling the airfield. And just like in the books, no one believes he's a spy, they think he's just a killer!

Could I tell the grown-ups my discovery? Why bother, the narrative *required* them not to believe me, not to pay heed to my warning.

I think this was the first time, with sadness and regret, that I realized the limited nature of Konstantin Alexandrovich's power, which had once seemed boundless to me.

Konstantin Alexandrovich was a detective, he was in the MCID, but I sensed that he was helpless here. He was a policeman, he caught thieves, bandits, and killers—humans; what could he do about the elusive, otherworldly Mister? The police don't chase spies, and if they do, they don't catch them.

I was the grandson of Grandfather Mikhail, the secret agent, the grandson of Grandfather Trofim, the tank soldier; at last I could prove I was worthy of them. I joyfully sensed that I was on the right side, on solid ground.

I began thinking what weapon I would use against Mister.

Father kept a double-barreled shotgun in the attic; two or three times a year he would spread an oilcloth on the floor and take the gun apart and clean it. I was allowed to hold the oil, take out the dirty rag, and once, only once, to look into the barrels, separated from the butt; the two ideally round openings looked like the entrances into infinity.

Probably, I could have swiped the shotgun, but I sensed that it wouldn't help in the hunt for Mister. Rather, if I took the gun, there would be no hunt—it would be like a flotation device, a life preserver, that would keep me from going deeper into the space where Mister was found.

In his desk drawer, Father had a German bayonet knife; Father found it when he was a boy in piles of military metal— smashed tanks, weapons, machines, platforms of armored trains, which were brought to the Hammer and Sickle Factory in Lefortovo to be melted down. Sometimes when Father was away, I secretly took it out, a patina covered darkened blade; but no other hand could be the master of this weapon, it would probably slip out of my grasp to be gripped by Mister's fingers.

There was the Finnish knife, the one we used to play knifesies, a gift from Konstantin Alexandrovich my parents didn't know about. But it couldn't help me in my search for Mister or against Mister—like the German bayonet knife, it would take the side of the saboteur, the man with a thousand faces, who could pretend to be a soldier or a thief.

I was missing something, things weren't coming together. Only a child could recognize Mister. He feared a child's gaze.

I understood: I had to come out unarmed and recognize Mister—my death, its circumstances—someone was bound to remember where I went, someone would see me minutes before I met Mister, notice his car—would give the detectives a sign that would lead them to Mister, make me his last victim, which would destroy him, snatch him from the other world.

I quickly convinced myself that there was no other way; I was delighted by the correspondence of my plan with the Soviet faith in which I was brought up, which considered sacrifice the highest and noblest act.

Still mulling over my plan, I recalled how last year they were filming a movie near the tank trial field of an army camp in a neighboring village. They set up a scaffold made of old boards on the village square; the script called for the hanging of a partisan messenger.

The soldiers from the camp were used as extras, and dressed in German uniforms they surrounded the square; local residents were asked to wear old clothes—the ones without any were issued jackets, sheepskin coats, trousers, boots, and bast shoes. My friends and I went to watch them making a movie, but there was no film magic to be seen; however, we noticed something else: the soldiers and sergeants had very quickly gotten comfortable in German uniforms. I thought it was almost criminal to even put one on, I thought they would want to tear off the foreign uniforms before they dirtied their souls. But on the contrary, there seemed to be an evil temptation to try on "the enemy's skin," to be a fascist for a while.

They readily formed a perfect encirclement, they pushed people with the butts of their guns so naturally into the square, that it couldn't be explained just by the desire to have some fun after the boredom of the barracks, by the taste of short-lived power. I imagined what it was like—to see things from inside a German—and suddenly understood the intoxicating freedom that came with the role. All the rules, all the symbols, everything that was specifically Soviet from clothing to words was supposed to elicit hatred, or a degree lower, scorn. Here was the opportunity to legally wipe their boots on the red flag—there was a scene like that, but they used a red rag rather than a flag—and that enflamed them: "protected" by the German uniform, the image of a Nazi who holds nothing dear, the soldiers probably would have burned down the village if the director told them to and forced people into the burning houses.

The locals, herded by the soldiers, also were transformed; suddenly, without the director, but by memory and instinct, the men started taking off their hats, revealing the heartbreaking nakedness of heads, the loneliness of each head before the noose. The bodies were pushed close together, and the heads seemed to be in the stratosphere, in rarified space, where the cold winds have a shade of a razor's raven blueness; the gesture—taking off your hat, recognizing the unity of death, the unity of destiny—

cut into my heart.

What happened next was no longer perceived as a film shoot, as something unreal, so I will not speak of acting and the suspension of disbelief.

The executioner's henchmen, two *Polizei*, Nazi collaborators, dragged out the partisan messenger. He struggled, kicked, perhaps sensing that things had gotten out of hand, that what was unfolding was much older than an episode from the Great Patriotic War, something as powerful as rebellion, as a whirlpool—it was elemental.

The messenger was a boy, just a little older than I was—maybe thirteen or fourteen. An impulse passed through the crowd—not horror, not fear, not compassion, but the first wave of enchantment.

The director had made a good and bad choice in the actor. Fair-haired, with perfect features, they boy was too remarkable to be a messenger. There was no confusion, fear, or shyness about him, he was proud and bold and the first sentry he passed would notice him. But in another sense, it was a good choice: holding his hands behind his back, the Polizei tried to get the noose around the boy's head, a boy born and brought up with reserves of goodness and belief in life.

The boy was sturdy, he would have grown into a tall, strong man—but his future was canceled by the execution. When they pulled his hair to get him to stretch his neck and stop resisting, suddenly, like a flood, like something observed secretly, his throat glowed with the tender light of vulnerability.

I don't know if the others standing there saw what I did. I think that if they didn't see it in such details of imagination, they sensed it for sure.

Thanks to that flash, that vision of the throat that would be lashed by the noose, the crowd and the victim joined in a familiar closeness, brothers and sisters, parents and children. That boy on the scaffold was so dear to each one that—with an inversion of feeling—he had to be, must be given up to the executioner.

The point of the no-longer just cinematic action, but of exIstence in general, was that the best had to die, the strongest and purest shoot had to be pruned, so that his death would enter each of the others as their own death, in which everything petty, egoistic, coming from nature, personality, and education will die so that you can be reborn.

The death of one hero gives birth to many his equal, greater than he was, that is the universal law, the only path for the creation of heroes. But the first one must die, and if he does not, the rest will die remaining just as they were without partaking of the seed of inspiring death.

This memory of the boy actor on the scaffold is what convinced me that my conception was correct. I didn't wonder why the other children did not expose Mister with their deaths, I had a ready answer: not every child can reveal a spy or saboteur; he has to be, for example, the grandson of a watchman, a retired Red Army soldier, or the son of the head of an outpost; heir to their skills and then surpassing his elders. And who, if not I, the grandson of combatant grandfathers, was better for the role? Who had figured out who Mister was?

Of course, I hoped sometimes in my daydreaming that I would stay alive, that Mister would only wound me heavily—there were stories like that in my book, too. Or maybe not even heavily, just in the arm or leg, so I could talk and show where the spy had gone; but then I reproached myself for cowardice and enjoyed the anticipation of fame.

Then fear would come over me, animal fear at the thought that I was wrong about myself, that despite knowing the true nature of Mister, I was just like all the other children, and he would simply kill me the way he had his previous victims.

I needed an advisor, an arbitrator, who would relieve my

doubts; Ivan, Ivan, he was the only one capable of understanding that Mister was not a sadistic killer but something more frightening; but if Ivan said that I was wrong and making things up, well then, I'd give up my idea, for after all I didn't want to die. But if Ivan confirmed my supposition, then the very fact of his support and involvement would save me, give me a chance not to die, for Ivan also was not like everyone else, and maybe he knew something about Mister that I did not. Oh, this secret would make us closer than brothers, closer than friends, despite our ages!

Ivan, Ivan, Ivan!

A BATTLE WITH THE GENERALISSIMO

The next day, as I wondered how to find out if Ivan was home, I walked down the dacha street toward his place. My friends had ceased their siege while the general's car was in our yard and were in no hurry to resume; I ran into one along the way, and he said "Hi!" as if there was nothing wrong; tireless Grandmother Mara had already told all the neighbors that an MCID general was visiting us, as she did every summer. My friends, naturally, wanted the details.

I had no hostility toward them; I told them everything I had heard from the general, but in a way that would give them no clue about the real nature of Mister.

Ivan's property was empty.

Back home, I started a casual conversation with Grandmother Mara about Ivan's family. But my grandmother, who seemingly knew everyone, and everything about them, merely shrugged, almost angry with Ivan's people for being so secretive. Ivan's parents worked abroad, as economists or diplomats, they hadn't been seen at the dachas for many years. His grandfather used to be a big shot in the KGB, but then fell into disgrace, demoted and pensioned off.

Grandmother told me this with a grimace, conveying that she disliked Ivan, disliked his family, disliked my new friendship; she tried to make sure I saw it. But I was thrilled: his grandfather in the KGB, his parents abroad—of course they weren't economists, they were spies! And that meant I was right about Ivan: like me, he was an heir to intrigue, he would know many things; I was so sorry I had not asked Grandmother earlier, for now I understood Ivan's aloofness, his reluctance to hang out with the dacha crowd; what a great surprise for him when he would learn that among the ordinary kids there was someone like him, his junior fellow traveler, his student!

Late in the evening I climbed out the window, down the apple tree, crept past the fences and the sleeping lazy dogs toward Ivan's property and climbed up onto the fence.

A lamp was on on his veranda; it was big, spacious, glassed in on all sides, and Ivan sat in his armchair as if in an aquarium of dim yellow light. It was dark all around, midges flew at the light and bumped into the glass, and I climbed over the fence and stood in the middle of the darkness, unnoticeable by Ivan, even if he were to look in my direction.

Ivan was alone at the dacha; he was drinking fortified wine in a thick green glass, setting it down on a tablecloth of the same green; this was my first look at the interior, I had climbed onto the wood pile by now. It was strange for me, accustomed to our dacha and the fact that a dacha is built out of whatever is at hand, furnished with whatever God sends your way, to see the heavy antique furniture, the big mirror in an ornate frame, and paintings on the walls; we all made do with paper reproductions, while these were real canvases.

No longer aware of what I was doing, unable to resist, I came out of the darkness, walked along the paved path, trying not to step on a crack, stepped up to the porch and knocked, hiding behind the door, the only nontransparent part of the glass veranda.

"Hello," Ivan said, opening the door. "At last you've decided. You were out there, behind that birch, right? I've gotten tired of waiting. Come in, come in. Have you ever tried fortified wine? Will you have some? You sneaked out, right? They wouldn't let you out this late, your parents, yes, I understand. Come in."

I was suddenly embarrassed by my old, patched trousers, torn T-shirt, and sweater frayed at the elbow, but I also knew that Ivan didn't care about such things, he was totally indifferent. A sip of the wine, which I had never tried, left a sweet tingle on my tongue, tempting me to confide in him.

Afraid that I wouldn't have the nerve, I started talking right away—about Mister, the general's story, how I guessed who Mister really was and the child's gaze he feared; about my intention to sacrifice my life for the sake of catching Mister, about Ivan who must be thinking about the killer, too.

Ivan listened in silence, sipping the wine.

Then he replied, as if weighing something. "I have to think about it. I was expecting something else. Go home now. I'll see you tomorrow."

He placed his hand on my shoulder in farewell. I walked down the dead street, where someone had marked out a hop-scotch ground, in confusion: What had I just told Ivan? Would he get in the way of my efforts? But the dark night told me: no, he won't, you'll be too scared alone, it will remain just a dream and someone else will catch Mister. Ivan will help, Ivan won't let you be scared. Without him you are weak, he is your strength, your desire, your courage!

The next morning a car honked at the gate; Ivan waved from a beige Volga, as though there had been no conversation the night before.

"Let's go for a swim?" he said invitingly.

"A swim?" I repeated; it had never occurred to me that Ivan could go swimming. No one had ever seen him at the dacha pond where every adult and child spent time splashing in the water, sunbathed on old towels in the trampled grass, played cards, baked potatoes and caught fish and crayfish. I thought that his skinny body—he never wore shorts, T-shirts, or shirts with short sleeves—was too aristocratic to bear openness, his nature could not stand the democracy and casualness of water that turned everyone into similar amphibians, bringing them closer, while air separated them; bathers are amazingly similar, they form a subspecies of humanity, and the only way I could picture Ivan at the pond was in the role of a natural scientist studying that subspecies.

"Swimming," Ivan replied. "Let's go."

"What if we get stopped?" I asked, embarrassed, even frightened by this swift new closeness with Ivan that had required nothing from me.

"I actually have a license," Ivan said, opening the glove compartment, with his wallet inside. "Get in."

We drove off; we drove past the pond, the nearby woods, the village, and the pea fields. Ivan drove smoothly, enjoying this unrushed "grown-up" style of driving, as if he were an old hand at it. The Volga passed a tractor, with kolkhoz women sitting in the hay in the trailer, returning from the field. Ivan slowed in the empty oncoming lane, and on my right a multiarmed, multifaced, tanned female creature floated by; the wind ruffled the dresses and kerchiefs, the fabrics were sweaty with labor; a young woman, using a burdock leaf as a visor against the sun, waved it like a hat, while another cupped her heavy breasts with a significant gesture. I was embarrassed, but as he drove in front of the tractor, Ivan gave a quick wink, as if to say all sorts of things can happen when you're with me, he winked without salaciousness, enjoying the burdock leaf, the smile, and the lovely breasts.

We were driving to the Moskva River; the car dove into an old fir forest, the road led down into the valley, I knew this road, sometimes I came here with my parents by bicycle. But Ivan turned in a different direction, honked at the barrier, said something to the guard, and we drove inside the brick wall, where the same forest grew, but here it seemed darker and quieter, as if it were warning visitors. Another few hundred meters, two turns, and we came upon a brick castle in the English style, red and white with ornamental towers; people in bathrobes strolled along the paths, paying no attention to the Volga. I had never known this castle was in our neighborhood, it was my first time on the property closed to outsiders, and this was yet another miracle that occurred when you were with Ivan.

"The castle of Prince Kerbatov," Ivan said, as if he were a personal friend of the prince and was about to introduce me. "If not for the walking corpses, this would be a perfect place."

The place was beautiful; the fir grove gave way to a pine grove, hazel bushes ran down toward the river, and I could see patches of white sand through the grass, and it seemed that just stepping on the warm ground sprinkled with fragrant needles would release an invigorating sensation that mounted from your heels to your lower back. This was the slope of the valley, with hidden layers rising to the surface, natural springs, and the vegetation was thicker from the proximity to the river and its fertile fogs.

I recognized that the strollers were high-placed old men, perhaps generals, officials, men of power. Before, when I met them in the courtyard of the building on Sokol, I was afraid they would notice me, think it wrong that I was wandering on their sidewalks. I was used to the importance of their uniforms, their gray overcoats and hats, their right to barricade themselves behind barriers and fences, to live in special buildings, stroll in bathrobes down paths of an unknown castle, while their heavy uniforms and suits, ironed by servants, hung in the closets here.

But Ivan's remark showed me a different picture: the old men were turned into ridiculous figures who did not suspect that their time was coming to an end. I was sure he had the right to talk that way—without adolescent irony, just as a person who knows.

Leaving the car, we went down to an empty wooden dock, where there were several rowboats without oars. Children and teenagers from local villages were swimming on the other bank, flickers of tanned bodies, shimmering splashes, and a fast current carried the swimmers down around the river bend. Here it was quiet, the nettles had a bitter and delicious tanginess, and the orange fins of tiny roach fish flickered amid the long shaggy water grasses.

Ivan had a white body; in the sunlight, against the rampant bright green grass, in the inflorescence of the clover, it seemed almost like marble. The sun, the rushing water, the splintered boards of the dock, the shouts and merriment on the far bank—all that was nobly alien to Ivan, and he squirmed in the sunlight, as if it burned.

Then he turned, and I saw the birthmark on his left shoulder blade. It was a delicate coffee and cream color; not a disfigurement of his skin, but a parchment seal, the form of which could have been an oak leaf, or a bat, or the paw print of an imaginary beast; it was noticeable, the size of half a hand.

Ivan's mark spoke of his inner scale, the sign was beautiful, it attested somehow to Ivan's already obvious specialness and superiority, a manifestation of higher powers.

Uncomfortable, I decided it was better to swim than to reveal my interest in his birthmark. I dove, swam to the middle of the river, and came back struggling against the current, while Ivan watched me from the dock, perhaps enjoying the simplicity of my joys—river, light, the bleak fish leaping near the surface in the translucent layer of sun spots.

I climbed out onto the dock; Ivan stretched, and then slipped into the water without a splash, as if he had been waiting for me to finish my swim and leave the river to him alone.

Downstream from the dock and closer to the middle of the river, a glacier boulder lay on the bottom. Above the surface there was a small gray roundness, like an elephant's forehead, that looked harmless. But if you looked closer, you would see that the clear river water darkened behind the boulder—there was a powerful whirlpool there, pulling in the river streams, you could feel its hidden power from the shore.

Ivan swam toward that funnel. He did the crawl, then the butterfly, he was a fish then a bird taking off, and the current was carrying him to the boulder. Standing on the dock, I pictured the river to the very bottom, saw its depths, shallows, and snags, sand banks, and flinty rapids. I perceived the entire boulder—huge, the size of a railroad car, separating the river in two; the whirlpool had dug an enormous hole behind it, and the icy springs could burn muscles into spasm; no fish entered there.

The boulder was waiting in the river—for a weakened swimmer, a child risking to cross to the other bank, and I had time to wonder if it had once lain on the neighboring sandy cliff, if people made human sacrifices upon it.

I shouted to Ivan not to swim toward the boulder, but he did not hear me, his head appeared only for a second at a time, he must have been swimming with his eyes open, looking at the fish and grasses.

He swam headlong, fast, on a straight path. But now he crossed the outer circle of the whirlpool, his arms caught in a deadly chop, and his agile body started moving against his will, sucked into the deep.

Ivan dove, then surfaced, and started stroking harder, but the whirlpool slowly spun him around, and the strong swimmer became a trapped, floundering creature. Why had he swum in that direction? I thought, while I looked around for an oar; if there were boats tied up, there had to be oars, and I doubted they were far away. I found them under the dock, I pushed out a light plastic shell and rowed to Ivan. He was trying to reach the boulder, to climb on and catch his breath, but the rock pushed him back with a wave, filling his eyes and mouth with foam; Ivan stopped swimming, hoping the current would carry him out, but the whirlpool dragged him down.

The boat scraped against the stone, the vortex turned it around. Ivan, crazed by the struggle, waterlogged, still saw the shadow that blocked the sun and grabbed hold of the line I threw him. A few moments later, soaked, he was in the boat; his eyes held fear, anger, and joy. "You saved me," he said with unexpected pleasure. "You saved me."

I knew that I would never have dared to fight the whirlpool and regarded him as a hero who took on the water spirit in his den; who was Ivan, where did he come from, what did his spot mean, what was he doing among ordinary people?

Then we sat on the shore, and when he was rested, Ivan told me that he sometimes came here to fight the whirlpool and that he always survived. They must have released water from the dam upstream and the river had not calmed yet, supposed Ivan, and that's why the whirlpool was more dangerous than usual; I examined him quietly, saw how his muscles were strained, the veins swollen, and I was in awe, as if I had created this body, pulled it out of nonexistence in a single motion.

I never did understand what happened that day. Was Ivan acting from beginning to end, pretending that the whirlpool was sucking him in and he could not swim out? Had he started off pretending only to have the water unexpectedly get the better of him? Or was he not pretending at all and had he actually underestimated the vortex?

"You know what the old generals call this rock?" Ivan asked unexpectedly. "Generalissimo. Some call it Iosif Vissarionovich. But mostly, Generalissimo. They've been coming here for decades, they know all each other's war wounds here. The head of the sanatorium is also an old frontline soldier, this is their favorite place, their own little private club. No one remembers now who first called the stone Generalissimo. They bring the new ones over to meet it. Here's the fresh spring, here's the dock, here's the pine allée, and here's the Generalissimo. I saw them bring one over, an aviation major general, gray-haired, scarred ..."

Ivan paused, finding the right words, and I thought back to the building on Sokol, the generals coming down the steps, the gray-haired pilot who pretended to be a plane for his grandson—could he be the one?

"A very serious old man, the locals are mostly flabby now, but this one seemed to be hewn from metal," Ivan continued. "I thought he would laugh and say the geezers had gone gaga, too much rich food at the sanatorium has gone to their heads, the mineral water bubbles affected the brain and soon they would be naming the trees. But the pilot, and you could tell he had been shot down, his face cut by pieces of the windshield, stood there and then saluted. The old men nodded and swayed: he's one of us, he is, and they led him to the main building and looked at one another as if their impotent little crowd might have drowned him, if he had not acknowledged the stone as the Generalissimo."

Ivan stared at the rock that almost took his life, while I processed the meaning of his words, remembering the two boys who ran across the street in front of Stalin's black car. Who was he, who was Ivan, if he could throw out this challenge to the Generalissimo and fight him? I had no doubt that the ancient boulder, deified by the old generals who gave it the name of the Supreme Commander, was in some sense today's Stalin.

If I had been more attentive, I would have realized that Ivan had made up something in this story; after all, I did the same thing.

At school, where my teacher knew that my parents had traveled extensively around the country, I began making up journeys for myself: saying I had seen Mount Communism in the Pamir Range and had even gone up into its foothills, had been in the Ural River in the place where Chapayev had drowned, had visited Shushenskoe and gone inside the house where Lenin and Krupskaya had lived in exile.

I made up the first story because I was bored, and I based it on a few facts—they really had considered taking me to Pamir. But I realized that our strict teacher, who never allowed us to stray, was treating me as if I had made a pilgrimage to holy lands; I, a child, had become more significant and authoritative than the adult. I couldn't resist continuing the fantasies that protected me from disciplinary zealousness and moved further and further from reality.

But I couldn't ever imagine that Ivan was fibbing or lying. Why lie to me? Knowing my tendency to mislead, I felt it had been forced upon me: I didn't completely believe my grandmothers and parents, I could feel that they were leaving a lot of things out, hiding things, and I had become wearily accustomed to my own lies of omission. But Ivan? Ivan had come to me as a messenger of truth, an outsider who certainly had no need for me not to know something or to believe in some allegedly redeeming deception.

Could I have guessed that Ivan used falsehood as a tool? The one who lies has power over whoever believes him; Ivan was not interested in deceit per se, as are fantasizers and fabulists like me. Deceit was a form of power, it *created* the power; out of false assumptions he cultivated real feelings, real attachments, and I think that was what thrilled him.

But this kind of reasoning was beyond my abilities.

"Last night I thought about what you told me," Ivan suddenly said. "You're right. Mister is really a spy or saboteur or they would have caught him a long time ago."

After the battle with the Generalissimo, I was prepared for Ivan to give me clear marching orders on how to catch Mister; he continued slowly, still exhausted, "It's your mission. Only yours. I can't help you. I'll only scare him off. Or he'll kill me." Ivan shut his eyes for a second, as if examining his exhausted body, and I lost my breath from the sincerity of his words, his confession of weakness.

"I would risk it anyway," said Ivan, "but you'll be better at it. And I'll help however I can."

Maybe I would have come to my senses, pretending that nothing had happened—even at the cost of breaking apart from Ivan—if not for a single detail, a circumstance that decided everything.

While talking to me, Ivan grew agitated, blood infused his usually pale face, and a thick crimson bead of blood slowly dripped from his left nostril. Ivan sensed my look before he tasted the salty viscous warmth over his lip, took out a handkerchief from the shirt lying on the dock, patted the blood, leaving a pink print on his skin, and as if forced to apologize for something improper, said, "Weak vessel."

That phrase—weak vessel—decided it. While the blood dripped—a second, two seconds, an eternity—along his pale skin, I experienced physical lust for Ivan's blood, saturated, overfilled with red. I was in love with a man whose body literally bled when he was agitated, I understood the flawed superiority of my body and my mission—to protect Ivan so that nothing would upset this higher being who elicited dizzying delight and anxious pity.

"Weak vessel." Ivan's body was a weak vessel, and I—as life had decided—became guardian of the vessel, that was the reason

I was born into this world. I would catch Mister so that Ivan would be unharmed, so that he would not go on a hopeless hunt that would result in his death.

FISHING WITH LIVE BAIT

Day after day I stubbornly wandered around the empty areas near the dacha, trying not to be seen by anyone I knew and to be noticed by the terrible unknown Mister. The occasional people I came across showed me that everyone, almost everyone, had a secret life that can be discovered in the keyhole of a random moment, if you know how and want to see.

It started with a bicyclist, the village mailman, I recognized him eventually, but at first I just saw a man on a bike. He was riding through the wheat field, going uphill, he was bent over the handlebars and for a second I thought the pedals were being pushed by a headless body in dark trousers and a patched jacket. The headless corpse flickered, and once again there was a man riding toward me, but I felt a jolt of fear. The bicyclist came closer, and I grew even more frightened, not of him, but of his bicycle.

The bicycle looked like a ferocious torture machine—the spokes were spinning and they could tear off your finger if you stuck it in the wheel, the sharp teeth of the gears worked the chain that could break bones.

The scariest part for some reason were the nickel-plated handlebars, with a shiny bell with a metal "ear" attached to them like a well-fed snail. I thought that if the rider were to ring the bell at me, it would be the last loud sound I would hear in my life. The bicycle, its quiet tires making an unobtrusive trail ... no one would consider tying the murder to a bicycle track, there were many trails on the road, plus it sounded silly—the killer got away on a bike. We were alone in the field, visible to all and to no one, because no one was watching, this was a convenient moment for villainy, the evil hour. The cyclist drove past, nodding at me, and only then did I realize it was the familiar mailman.

There were others. Early in the morning a man was carrying a large unframed mirror along the side of the highway. He was passing a dangerous curve where there were frequent accidents. Alders, impregnated with the roadside dust, grew in the ditch, and faded, worn wreaths hung on them; a monster that devoured people and cars must live in the messy den of the forest.

The mirror was too big to carry under his arm, and the man held it in front of him, with a newspaper folded in four to cushion his hands. This made the sharp edge of the broken mirror come sharply—literally—into focus. I was walking toward him, and toward myself, reflected in the mirror. On my side were the rotting alders, the ditch, never cleared of the debris of car accidents, and it was filled with broken headlights, crumbled windows, pieces of upholstery, rubber snakes of belts, clots of oil, spark plugs, leaking batteries. I walked and waited for my face to be changed through the opaque amalgam into one with warts, tight red nodules, like on aspen leaves, the face of a satyr, a forest spirit, as if from inside the reflection. I would become frozen, understanding everything, and turn off into the woods, while only the mirror would remain on the road, leaning against a clumsy alder and reflecting the dark undergrowth on the other side of the highway.

There was a mushroom hunter, an old man who wore a black raincoat in all weather, with a big, frayed basket and long kitchen knife, thinned by sharpening, turned into a thin steel probe, that could deftly slip through fear-stiffened muscles, squeezing under the ribs; its thin point, as narrow as a bird's tongue, would find the most sacred and alive part in the darkness of your body and end life with a single touch. The old man wandered in the distant aspen forests, rummaging through the leaves with a stick, even though it was too early for the mushrooms that grow under aspens, and it seemed that he was seeking a meeting, a knot in the confused clump of small forest paths.

There was the store night watchman, who picked raspberries during the day and sold them at the train station before his work began. In the hot stifling air of the prickly berry patches, where you can only hear and see the mosquitoes and horseflies thickening the heat, the watchman moved noiselessly, pulling and shaking the raspberries from their branches into the can tied to his waist. Dressed in dark heavy clothing, so as not to feel the bites and thorns, he would appear unexpectedly from the breaks in the berry patch in his white hat, and the hat that hid his eyes, unnaturally, a sterile white, contrasted sharply with his big, spade-shaped hands covered in ichor berry stains.

The juice of the berries, which ripened in just two or three days in the humid heat, had eaten deep into his skin. Soiled hands dangling, the watchman stood resting in the empty intersection of forest passages by the red orienting pillar. The matte underside of leaves glowed on the smashed raspberry plants, and it seemed that just a minute earlier there had been a fight, an attempt to escape, breaking the bushes. The watchman stood, smoking and wiping his brow, but I could see that he wasn't picking berries, that there was a body hidden under the branches farther back.

One day I went really deep into the woods, where my parents and I went only rarely, when the mushrooms appeared in fall on stumps and fallen trees; firs grew there, tall, heavy, far apart. They shaded the ground, not letting underbrush grow, moss spread beneath them, and in the space between the ground and their lower dry branches an invisible daytime twilight collected, fed by the endless decay of fallen needles.

The air was filled with the sour dampness of decay, with wood sorrel ranging among the fir roots. Yellow mushrooms, as wrinkled as brains, poked out of a rotten log; pale toadstools, a light greenish tinge around the cap, formed witches' circles all around. I walked and I thought that my presence was awakening the witches' circles, and they were expanding, like drops on water, and the old fir forest was expanding, opening a corridor for me, a path to the deepest part of the grove.

I saw something through the trees: a tramp's hovel of boards and bitumen set up in an old tank bunker. I sensed that someone or something was inside; not necessarily a human or an animal, but perhaps an ax, knife, nail, or hammer pretending to be stolen, when in fact it had been used to smash someone's skull.

But a thought came to me, like redemption, that the tramp's hovel was made in a bunker where maybe a T-34 had stood, and that meant the place, even if defiled, could not be fully *evil*. Picturing the tank, camouflaged by branches after it had squashed the supple forest mud with its treads, I stepped inside.

From inside, the hovel was like the belly of a gigantic animal; thin tree roots, like blood vessels or feelers, hung from the ceiling; the walls reeked of rot and the dampness of the earth's womb. Once my eyes adjusted to the dim light, I saw plank beds by the wall, human nests of filthy rags, and the floor, ankle-deep in food scraps, bottles, tin cans, cigarette butts, and rotten cabbage leaves—the people who lived here must have stolen them from the store near the station. A tall thick block of wood held dozens of candle stubs with dead, tormented looking wicks, and burned matchsticks were scattered everywhere.

Was this where Mister was hiding? I suddenly got so scared that I ran home, imagining dying there, wounded, amid the putrefaction and mud; that disgusting death seemed so real that I dropped my intention of catching Mister. I thought that even Ivan, who had listened raptly to my stories of the headless mailman and the watchman with bloody hands and told me I was getting closer to my goal, that I had a good eye—he was now getting weary of the hunt, as if he thought he'd been mistaken in me, I was not the one to recognize Mister. It took a great effort to keep from going to Ivan and giving up the hunt, one more day, I told myself, just one more day, one more attempt, and then it's over.

And so the next day, I walked along the highway; it was that hot afternoon hour when yards and roads are empty, and sleep, as viscous as the drool from an idiot's mouth, a sleep without dreams or feelings, submerges the area into a warm, starchy pudding. People, dogs, birds, cats—everyone hid, moved into the shade, and only flies wandered like somnambulists along the plains of lunch tables, clambering up the porcelain or cut-glass temple of the sugar bowl, the porous boulders of bread crumbs, and avoiding the lakes of tubs with soaking dishes to be washed later, when the heat let up.

The smell of chewed chicken bones, soap, and burned butter fills kitchens and verandas, seeps into the rooms, and the flies, while people nap, slowly move their tiny feet over the bodies of the sleepers, approaching the eyelids, as if trying to peek behind their cover.

No one drove along the highway. There was a pause; for kilometers in both directions, from the station and from the village, there were no cars on the road, no sand trucks from the military quarry, no sedans or buses. The few who had intended to go somewhere, maybe to meet the first commuter train after the break, delayed, or chose another road, or decided to kill some time, stopping to chat with someone near the store closed for break time, and have a smoke.

That created a window of absence, ten or fifteen minutes lost from shared existence. The well-used highway was guaranteed to be unoccupied, as if it were the deepest corner of the forest.

I froze: so this was the time when Mister was active, he knew, he could sense these intervals like a ballet dancer, he "landed" only in them. He was like a locater that calculated the holes outside the field of vision of people busy with their own affairs, inaccessible to their hearing, and he dove from hole to hole, appearing *between* people, in the quiet intervals from one passerby to another. Only a random boy could come across him, a pathetic little fool who'd wandered into the wrong place at the wrong time, which is why his victims were found in places that seemed impossible to leave without being noticed. But no one ever saw Mister.

Then, as if through the veil of a landscape, the windshield of a parked car flashed from the bushes near the road.

A child's eye is always focused on hiding places. An adult sees an unremarkable landscape, while a child will find a loop in the path, where the bushes could hide a standing person, a dark space between two low pines where you could lie down; that ability is the basis of hide-and-seek, the competition of who's best at vanishing. I understood that the car owner had not picked this place accidentally, this descent from the highway was a hideaway that pedestrians and drivers would miss. I should have walked past, looking the other way, pretending not to have noticed the car. But I turned, I turned off the road, telling myself it was only curiosity about the Lada, which I could touch, look to see what was inside, imagine myself in the driver's seat.

The banged-up gray Lada 9 with rusty fenders was dusty from the rural roads; a crumpled oilcloth jacket was tossed on the backseat. There was nothing else that gave a clue about the owner; but there was nothing scary, it was just a car.

Crooked lines were etched in the mud of the doors—it often drove into the woods and had been scratched by branches; it had rained last night, but there were no drips in the dust—it had been in a garage overnight; almost bald tires, sagging suspension—it was used frequently; the license plates were illegible, covered in front and in back with clay and grass, as if the car had been stuck and had to go back and forth, to work its way out, hitting dirt with both bumpers. An ordinary rural car, there were dozens of them by the station, changing owners frequently, worked on in garages or the kolkhoz tractor station.

But there was something else that I couldn't catch, and I circled the car, peeking inside, under the car, sniffing. I realized what it was—the crushed grass where the car had driven was still trying to spring back into place, which meant it had driven here recently and the owner was nearby—hiding?

He came out of the woods, slipping sideways through the thick growth of rowan bushes at the edge. He was around twenty-five or thirty, dark-haired, thin, small-boned, not a man, despite his age; his face was narrow and elongated, rather anemic, as if it did not know strong passions. He probably wanted to look cool, fashionable, but he had a bad barber, the jeans, denim jacket, and sneakers were bought at the village outdoor market, where they sold fakes. These details—unfortunate haircut, clumsy clothing, an early stoop, a slight drag of one leg—formed a recognizable type. If I had met him at the station, I wouldn't have given him a second look: this driver was simply, tastelessly unattractive, and I would have lost interest in him before remembering his features.

Walking to the car, he smiled uncertainly and waved at me, I pretended to be embarrassed but continued observing him attentively through half-closed eyes. As I looked closer, he reminded me of someone.

His softness and not complete adultness made me think he was a coach or gym teacher, people who are always around children. They like to touch, caress, hug, tickle with a blade of grass, they like to fake wrestle, they like sports, camping trips, making up competitions and games to keep up the constant running and scrambling of bare arms and legs. They are not attracted to children but to the strength that accompanies growth, which makes scratches heal by morning and quickly forgives yesterday's hurt.

The guy who came out of the rowan grove could never be Mister. I knew a spy could wear any guise, and I would have believed any but this one. I had a counselor like this in Pioneer camp, who adored boys' elbows and knees, skinny, sharp, and always scraped. He softened and applied plantain leaves to scratches, smeared them with green iodine, and before taking you to the doctor he examined swollen lymph nodes or glands himself—he was tempted by these illnesses of growth, their ugly manifestations, as if he sought the ugly duckling in each child, who was rejected, needing protection and patronage. The counselor had the same pathetic haircut, avoided the loud fat cook and her jokes about him, and often walked alone in the woods.

Mister a mailman, Mister a shepherd, Mister a forest ranger, Mister a rail watcher, Mister an electrician, Mister a tractor driver, Mister a hunter, Mister a mower, a hundred variants, a hundred faces, only not this harmless fellow who probably worked at the village school or the big Pioneer camp on the other side of the woods.

But why was I so anxious?

"What's the matter, boy?" he asked, coming right up to me. "Are you all right?"

He probably did think that I had sunstroke or was sick from the heat.

I looked around in confusion; it was about a kilometer to the edge of the dacha settlement, no one would hear me scream even though it was quiet. We were surrounded by piles of garbage overgrown with nettles, this unattractive turnoff from the highway had become a garbage dump, and mushroom hunters and people out for a walk avoided this place; the only ones who came here were tramps and feral dogs, I saw a mutt with a low hanging belly gnawing at a plastic bag of scraps.

"You must be really scared and think I'm Mister." The guy smiled, gave a short, good, kindly laugh, his eyes narrowed slightly, his cheeks lifted and filled with merriment, and light wrinkles ran to the corners of his eyes. "I'm not Mister, I breed horses, you know the farm across the lake? One of our horses, Diana, is sick. She loves berries, she can eat a bucket of raspberries." He pushed his lips forward and stuck out his tongue, showing how a horse eats berries. "I don't know the berry places around here. Maybe you do? I've been wandering around for an hour, the nettles are killing me. Do you know a berry place? Just point the way, if you're afraid. If you're not afraid, help me out, and then I'll show you the horses on the farm, take you for a ride."

He's not Mister, not Mister, not an evil otherworldly saboteur. But why was he lying about looking for a berry patch for the last hour, when just a few minutes ago I'd seen the recently bent grass straightening under the car?

He shook cobwebs from his plaid shirt, pulled out a pack of Opals, and offered me a cigarette.

"Smoke? I started at your age, too. Go on, don't be shy, I know you don't have your own yet." He held out the cigarette. "You all smoke, I know."

He was taking me for someone else. I had never smoked and didn't want to, and who was "you all?"

I stepped back, my back up against the car.

"You were trying to get into the car, yeah? Wanted to steal something?" He spoke sympathetically, persuasively, not threateningly, not raising his voice, as if he would be happy to be proven wrong.

"Thank God it's not Mister, not a killer, just a weirdo," I thought, looking at his hand, pale, with small red ridges—from tight rubber gloves? Small black hairs, like animal fur, grew on the back of his hand and fingers, but his face was clear, he barely needed to shave.

"Wanted to go for a ride, yeah?" He leaned his arm on the car roof, as if he wanted to embrace me. "Wanted to go for a ride, but you can't drive. Want me to teach you?"

Learn to drive, even just sit in the driver's seat, that was my dream. Besides the drive with Ivan, which didn't even seem real to me, I'd only ridden from the dacha four times with neighbors who agreed to drop off our heavy baskets of apples in their old Zhiguli, and twice with my parents in a taxi coming home late from a party.

The smell of the car, the blinking arrows, wheel, pedals, gear shift, mysteriously connected, that brief moment of delightful supremacy over pedestrians!

Once again, as I had felt at the wharf in Uglich, I realized that neither at school nor at home was there attention paid to my insignificant wishes; we all lived that way—some look to borrow a smoke, others dream secretly of a rare stamp or toy car, still others wander around in search of drink. And it's not the cigarette, car, or bottle of beer that matters, but a small friendly sign from fate, the satisfaction of your expectation of kindness.

A random stranger says, "Would you like me to …" without even knowing how much you want it, to be shown how to drive, to be talked to as an equal for a few minutes, and then you can live, trusting the near future. He was a messenger with good news, this stranger from another life, where there are no limitations of childhood, sent to build confidence in growing children.

I was about to admit that I dreamed of driving, but the man interpreted my prolonged silence in his own way.

"Fine, if you don't want to," he said regretfully. Then he brought his face close to mine and looked into my eyes. "I left a tape recorder in the car, an expensive one, what have you done with it? I wanted to be nice about it, give you chance to confess. But you're being stubborn. That's not good. We'll have to go to the police." He took my arm. "They'll figure it out. Get in the car." He opened the back door. "Get in right now!"

I resisted, not letting him push me into the car, while my thoughts raced: Maybe it would be better to go to the precinct? They knew me, the local cop often came by when Konstantin Alexandrovich was visiting, it would be safe there.

"He must have a car," I remembered the general's words. "And a place where he does it all. A garage or cellar. Probably a cellar."

He pushed me into the car, my face ground into his crumpled jacket on the seat, and I saw the badge pinned on the lapel: "Public Environmental Inspector," dark green, shaped like a shield, with a golden hammer and sickle on the bottom.

"An armband of the national volunteer force, a badge of the Green Patrol, something like that. A socially involved person." Once again I heard the general's voice.

I finally understood. The evil was real, my fantasies about a saboteur were not.

The guy was leaning on me, pushing me against the seat, and I was kept from struggling and screaming by a profound regret: how could I have deceived myself, how could I have believed Ivan, who probably listened to my stories about searching for Mister with the relish of a person who had played an incredible, dangerous hoax!

It suddenly started to rain—a brief summer shower that forms in a few seconds, falling out of nothing, from weak clouds, as if an invisible cup had overflowed in the sky. Its gigantic drops spread in flight into a rainbow of vertical strokes, unfolding a radiant curtain, so thick that at twenty paces you can make out only silhouettes, and then the rain increases for two or three minutes, making noise, hiding all other sounds, and even the silhouettes will vanish beyond the veil of water. It weakens quickly, falls into silvery threads, and then vanishes completely, leaving the steaming ground—but the silhouettes will vanish with the rain, as if they had been created by the rain, as if no one had stood on the forest path.

"We won't go to the police," the "horse breeder" said. "I'll punish you here myself, your little thief. Get out. You deserve to be whipped with a belt, don't you?"

I got out without a word.

There was nothing but the flying drops, the rain that swallowed up space. I realized that behind that rain, inside that rain, he would kill me; sensitive to nature, he had been waiting for something like this—and he found the minutes of cover.

The world fell apart, I felt its tiniest particles, the raindrops, but I did not feel the whole; the rain glowed, the rain blazed, deepening the victim's dreadfully triumphant joy, which would in seconds be replaced by horror, but for a second filled me entirely as if it were the most important thing in my life—I was brought to the altar of just retribution.

"Turn around," came his voice from behind me, not angry but agitated, hoarse with his breathing that sounded like a dog's. "I'll tie you up. Behave. I have to get something from the trunk."

He opened the trunk and reached below, to the well where the spare tire is kept. I might have tried to run, but I couldn't even move a finger. I sensed that the pause in time the killer was using was coming to an end; far away a car appeared on a rise and in ten minutes it would drive past on the highway, its wipers removing the decreasing raindrops. The commuter train from Moscow was three stops away from ours, crammed with passengers, the store would be opening soon after the lunch break, everything would come back to life, move, fill with people. Perhaps the killer had never taken such a risk, but the quieting rain brought us together intimately, like lovers under a raincoat.

He came up from behind, put his hand on my shoulder and tickled my ribs with a knife; he turned me to face him, and put the tip of the thin, nickel-plated scalpel on my nose; my eyes focused on the shiny blade, it was blinding me.

"Fucking lousy weather!" Behind the "horse breeder," so very close, unheard because of the rain, several men were cursing without anger, clambering over the garbage.

Mister cursed, too, as if he had never done so in public, pretending to be the well brought up examplar, and maybe he couldn't even curse alone, because it came out feeble and pathetic.

He weakened instantly, becoming a child, the loud, brazen voices reminded him of something, and he lowered his hands. Four tramps came out of the garbage mound, young, hard-drinking, I think they were deserters from the army. He sobbed and exclaimed strangely, as if his liver or kidneys were moaning with pain.

The spell was broken, I shouldered him aside and ran through the nettles to the tramps, slipped, slashed my hand on a tin can, but jumped up and ran. The car door slammed, the engine started, and the car drove off through the brush ...

I woke up on the plank beds of the hideout I had entered, thinking this was where Mister lived.

"Who are you, young fellow?" one of them asked. "Where do you live? What was that all about?"

"That was Mister," I replied, barely able to get the words out.

"We just went out to find some tarp, we were getting soaked in here," someone else muttered in the dark.

"You have to call the cops, boy," the first said. "Let's go, we'll walk with you. But not a word about us, all right? Tell them you escaped on your own."

They walked me to the fence of the dacha area, wrapped my hand in a dirty rag; the rain was long gone, the sun was shining, and the water from the bushes had washed their hands and faces; the deserters were even younger than they had seemed in the dugout, around eighteen, their first year in the army.

"Listen, bring us something to eat, huh?" the smallest one asked. "There's nothing in the gardens yet. Please?"

I crept into the cellar behind the house, pulled out a half-full sack of potatoes, and dragged it back to the forest. The four of them grabbed the sack, said, "Be sure to call," and ran off, sensing that the police would be combing through the woods soon.

Grandmother Mara was still napping in her room.

I went up to the attic, sat at the window, and gathered my wits to wake her up and confess everything.

Ivan. I thought about him. My thoughts were short and clear.

Only the deserters and I knew who the killer was. But the forest tramps would not go to the police. They would hide as far away as possible or maybe leave the area.

The "horse breeder" would also lie low, he had to understand that every policeman would know his description within an hour. He would run away, hide, stop killing. He would never imagine that I wouldn't tell. The elusive Mister would continue to exist for everyone.

If Mister killed Ivan, caught him on a forest path, no one would be surprised.

I finished this thought and sensed a black liquid, a poison, slurping in my chest. Black, sticky, smelly, it came from my old offense against Grandmother Tanya, it had been inside me a long time. It all came spewing out, until the last spasm made me pass out.

DELIRIUM AND AFTER

I dreamed that Grandmother came and pulled me by the tongue, which unrolled endlessly like a telegraph's perforated tape. She held me by the tip of my tongue, while I ran off, jumping over fences and railroad tracks, swimming across lakes, leaping over cities, trying to cut it off by putting it in the path of a slamming door or a hurtling express train, but the tongue wouldn't tear, and Grandmother tugged, and I was thrown in the opposite direction through high grasses and forest branches, until I was back in the room and it all started again.

"Did you see the deserters?" Grandmother Mara asked.

"Yes," I replied and only then realized that this was no dream but a sunny morning with Grandmother at the head of my bed.

"I knew it," she said, shaking her head. "They stole our potatoes. And scared you to death, you were unconscious all day. Well, stay in bed, here's some hot milk for you. We won't tell your parents, or they'll fuss at us."

From the doorway, she said, "Your Ivan came by. If he comes again, shall I let him in?"

"Yes," I replied.

I hadn't readjusted to the world yet, the only thing I felt was my lightness, as if I had no body. The drapes, floor, ceiling, furniture, everything was scuffed, scraped, and dusty, but it all seemed new and amazingly clean. Had yesterday happened?

Hurried steps sounded outside the door. It was my pals, who burst in together, chattering and paying no attention to Grandmother Mara.

"They caught Mister!"

"The highway cop waved his baton at him, but he didn't stop!"

"The cops chased him, stopped him, asked him why he kept going."

"He said, I didn't notice you wanted me to stop!"

"They started writing a ticket—"

"And the MCID cop with them said—"

"Search the car—"

"They found a scalpel under the seat—"

"And all kinds of things in his garage—"

"Mister was arrested!"

They couldn't understand why I only lay back weakly in the pillows. The approaching hum of a car came through the window, and I raised myself up on my elbow—Ivan's Volga was driving toward Moscow, he was at the wheel; as he passed our house, he didn't even turn his head, and a sixth sense told me that he was leaving *forever*.

I had but a remnant of summer left, even though there were still six weeks before school. Ivan had vanished, Mister's dangerous shadow was gone from the area, nothing flickered threateningly at the dark end of forest paths. I wandered aimlessly, retreading the routes I had taken in my search for Mister, but I felt nothing, just clocked up the kilometers, breathing dust and heat, watching indifferently as wheat, apples, and corn burgeoned.

Only one place suited my mood. Far from the dachas lay large swampy ponds surrounded by reeds. Huge catfish lived there, and to catch them, people used special hooks made by blacksmiths and smelly dead crows as bait. They shot the crows right there, on the edge of the field where a garbage heap had formed, as it often does, from a large hole where someone had dumped a truckload of construction rubbish. Over a few years the trash spread outward from the pit filled with eviscerated sofas and broken barrels.

I wanted to be at those ponds, walking along their swampy shores, risking falling into duckweed-covered ooze, trying to feel the edge, the edge of something in my life and destiny. The water hid big fish, blunt-headed killers I had seen swallow up ducks from the surface of the water.

July passed and two-thirds of August, the falling stars had finished their cascades, and the long rains and packing for the return to the city began; Grandmother Mara was picking which gladioli still in bud would go in my back-to-school bouquet for the teacher.

It was a particularly glum day, the rain pouring drearily, the puddles bubbling, and beyond the fog the express trains to Brest blared their horns. I went out on the porch and the first gust of wind from the north, scattering the clouds and clearing the sky, cooled my face. It was an autumn wind, the air was clearing, the fog heading into the distant woods, the puddles covered with tiny wavelets. I could see the heights of the heavens, marked by cirrus clouds frozen on the border of the stratosphere, and something cleared up inside me, too, and as if I had just noticed that my key was gone and there was a hole in my pocket, I recalled that the light had not been on in the second-floor window of the house opposite.

Before Ivan there was one person I had wanted to call my friend. He was a slightly younger boy who lived across the street. I could have, but did not call him a friend; we both sensed that we should not be friends; individually, each of us was accepted in the dacha groups, but if we had shown a mutual connection, we would have been ostracized.

Other children grew energetically and boldly, with no fear of the future, like greedy and agile shoots of a strong plant. We existed with uncertainty, feeling our way as if in constant pain and unable to heal, unable to feel the mind-numbing and unsubtle energy of a perfectly healthy person.

We knew, even though we never discussed it, that were we to go off and do what we wanted, drop soccer and tag and instead read books and share impressions, look for belemnite fossils among the railroad gravel, wander in silence around the dacha streets without looking for a branch of ripe plums hanging over a fence, or plant an oak or rowan tree in the far corner of the garden in honor of friendship and watch it grow—if we were to reveal our real wishes, we would be punished, our lives would be turned into a living hell over that silly tree, even if the horde of rude pals knew nothing about it, only sensed that we were sharing a secret, delicate and lofty.

So we spent many summer seasons side by side without becoming closer, and it was only in the twilight, when the streets were empty, I could see the light come on in my friend's window—home after playing outside and a late dinner, he went up to his room. I watched sometimes, waiting to see if his curtains would move—that would mean that he was looking at my house, my window, illuminated by the night light, and pining over the impossibility of friendship.

They had a gazebo, covered in vines and tiny flowers, the only one in a neighborhood where people borrowed the village habit of setting tables out in the garden or on the open veranda, of which there were not many, either. They drank tea from thin porcelain cups in the gazebo, and after lunch, his grandfather sat there with a book; he was a doctor who always came when children were sick, gently refusing payment as soon as he came in, and gave the disease its Latin name, as if that would scare off the illness; Grandmother Mara disliked him because he used Latin, torn between the need to cure me and her hatred of foreign speech in her house, which underlined her illiteracy.

How promising the gazebo would have been had we become friends! How delightful to have to sit there, hidden by the vines!

I was inside the gazebo three or four times when his grandfather invited us to play there; we were embarrassed and hastily refused. He listened to my excuses suspiciously while I tried to retain a snapshot of the old lettuce-green paint, bristling with splinters, the smell of the vines, so that I could re-create it later in my mind: the gazebo in the middle of the garden, no kids, no adults—just the two of us and our conversations that never happened.

Once I grew close to Ivan and began my search for Mister, I practically forgot my pal from the house opposite; sometimes I promised myself to think about him tomorrow or the next day, to miss him the way I used to—but Ivan reigned inside me.

We met a few times playing games, and he looked at me meekly, as if to ask, Could I be third, could you introduce me to Ivan? But I was submerged in the dark spaces Mister inhabited and regarded my abandoned friend with the harsh determination to bid farewell to the past. And then he stopped falling into my field of vision, as if our time had ended.

There was no light in the window! With belated regret I rushed to their gate. I remembered the interior, the German sewing machine turned into a workbench, the small photographs, like openings in a birdhouse, in wide wooden frames on the walls, with microscopic people reduced by time; how could I not have noticed them, how could I not have understood that he was my brother, my fellow traveler, my twin!

His grandfather opened the gate and politely told me that his grandson had left for the city two days ago. The old man said his good-byes for a very long time, telling me how much he liked me, thanked me for my friendship with his grandson— and all the time I was dying of shame, because I thought he had guessed my treachery and was trying to console me. The old doctor would not let me go, he would stop for a second, watch the north wind tear wet leaves from the apple trees, and then repeat his words of farewell, as if he were parting with his past and his life and not with me.

In the morning their house was empty and boarded up. We all did that, leaving the dacha for the autumn and winter, but that day the boards crisscrossing the windows seemed to be shutting me out of the big room of summer, where I had left Ivan, Mister, Konstantin Alexandrovich, the mailman, the watchman picking raspberries, the mushroom collector, the passerby with the mirror … The north wind brought the cold, and Grand-mother Mara, no longer blaming the *burzhuika* stove for its huge appetite, fed it happily and started packing bags and baskets with jams and pickles, while I thought that inside the packages was my memory, divided up into pieces and taken away.

I did not want to lose this, I wanted to stay in that terrible summer that meant as much as all my previous life; in my boots and raincoat and with a bag of food I headed for the dugout, where I hoped the deserters who had saved me would return; the patrols on the roads were long gone and the wanted posters for Mister had been turned to papier-mâché by the rains. How are they going to winter over here, I wondered. I'll spend the winter with them, I'll bring them grain in glass jars to protect it from mice, I'll steal my father's jacket …

The weight of the water had torn through their roof of slab and polyethylene, and the dugout was filled with a puddle in which a soaked mass of stolen clothing floated.

The summer was over, having stolen years of my life ahead, making them empty and almost unnecessary.

PART FOUR

SPRING NEIGHBORS

Autumn and winter slipped by as if they never happened. I was awakened only by anniversaries of last year's events: a year ago I had been at the Kremlin, a year ago the comet passed, a year ago Father went to Chernobyl, a year ago Grandmother Tanya showed me the "eternal bullet," and then we had an argument. I lived with this refrain, existed on last year's calendar, as if I still had to sail to Uglich, meet Ivan, fall into the hands of Mister.

It was only in the spring, when we arrived at the dacha and I saw the neighbors' boarded-up house, that I began to wait for my friend to arrive with his grandfather and parents; I wanted to replay last year and set it on another path. They should have come out on a weekend, aired out the house, put the bedding, blankets, and pillows in the sun, chased away the stale mouse smell. But they didn't come, the garden was not dug, the fir branches that covered the flower beds were still there.

Summer came, the grass grew and swallowed the paths, the occasional perennials drowning in the greedy weeds; we weeded regularly, but the weeds seemed to have run away from us to hide behind the neighbors' fence. I secretly crept into the yard once, moving aside one of the pickets, a trick I learned from a friend. The floor of the gazebo was covered in autumn leaves and a couple of birch twigs brought in by the wind. A floorboard had rotted over the winter, tilting the table; a glass fruit cup forgotten on the table was covered with fine rings of dirt from the numerous times water collected and then evaporated in it.

None of the adults talked about where our neighbors were, where the whole family was. I finally asked and I was told, "They moved to Israel," in a tone suggesting they'd left on a risky adventure, and while they didn't condemn it, they didn't approve of it, either.

I thought I was partly to blame for their move; I couldn't believe it could be a good thing if they had left their house and gazebo, which would be quickly ruined by the weather—for things left unattended and uncared for develop special signs that are clear to rain and snow—pour here, fall here, drift here.

Like the adults, I suspected that the neighbors had left on the eve of something; coming events were in the shadows, creeping up quietly, but invading the horizon. The departure, like a wartime siren, shook off their invisibility.

Then I noticed there was someone there; I was sure the family had returned, that they'd never gone to Israel or had returned for the sake of the old house and the old gazebo. I decided to drop in right away and tell my friend I'd missed him.

But there was a pile of unfamiliar things on the porch, a teenager five or six years older than me was walking on the overgrown paths, a nail puller whined at the back of the house, and the nails came out of the boards with a screech.

The layout of the yard had been created by people who loved neatness and coziness, with a sentimental attitude toward flowers and birds, a touch boring and sweet in their love of trees that they grew not for the apples but for their look, shade, and rustle.

The teenager wandered around, irritated by the layout, picking out what to criticize, what to try to break off, "accidentally" spill, knock over, kick, or smash; he struck the weather vane with his shoulder and then stepped on the meaty leaves of the faded tulips in the grass.

"Just don't let him go to the gazebo," I thought. And he went inside the gazebo, started moving the glass jar around the table top, deciding whether or not to push it into the hole in the floor; he was bored, he didn't like the dacha, he didn't know why he was there, but just in case, he looked and sniffed around.

What amazed me about him were his movements; he resembled a rat, mole, or shrew who knows how to find the narrowest crack, gnaw itself into it, and squeeze through where any other creature would be stuck.

One summer a skunk began visiting a neighbor's henhouse. The first time, the dog scared it off, but the skunk started coming every night, looking for a way in. The chickens squawked, the neighbor lost sleep, so he put sheet metal all over the henhouse and got a second dog. He depended on his laying hens, he sold their eggs every morning at the train station. But the skunk would not retreat; the neighbor sat up all night with a rifle, shot at a moving shadow in the dark and killed two cats; one was a pet, beloved by its family, and he and the owners got into a feud; then he wrapped electrified barbed wire around the henhouse. It drove him crazy that he, a former sapper sergeant, builder, and decent hunter couldn't handle a lousy little creature. The skunk seemed to sense the sergeant's fury and would vanish for a while, then return again, until one night the neighbor got drunk and forgot to lock the henhouse.

In the morning, hungover, sobbing, he brought out hen after hen and spread the white bloodstained chickens on the grass; they lay there, just piles of feathers, and he moved them around and called them by name. The dark forest beyond the fence was filled with the malicious glee of the skunk that had killed all the hens and had waited three months—ages for a small creature—for the owner to make a mistake.

Nimble, quick, and as sensitive as an animal, the teenager turned around, feeling my gaze. I recognized him: it was the teenager pretending to be the ideal Pioneer who met Mother and me at the Palace of Congresses, enjoying his role as usher and his part in the party at the Kremlin. It was his face; but my imagination could not put the Pioneer uniform on him, as if he had outgrown it, like a snake shedding its skin. It had happened a little over a year ago, and I sensed that I was falling behind, unable to let go of last summer, while everything around me was changing rapidly and irrevocably.

I watched the new neighbors for several days as they surveyed and circled their property, chopping it up with their eyes, and I understood that my worry over the gazebo was pointless: they would tear down the gazebo and the house, redo the entire lot and would not stop within its borders.

The dacha association had 150 members who could vote at meetings, they'd been there a long time, and they discussed the poor manners of the new neighbors who had not come to introduce themselves, did not make a polite visit to the association chairman, and who had already filled up the communal dump—an annual fee of a ruble per household—with stuff that belonged to the previous owners. People were angry, and the angriest were ready to go over and explain how things were done and that the old ways had to be respected.

I saw workers carting things away. I watched the first trip out of boredom, the next with growing interest, and then I couldn't tear myself away.

I wasn't attracted by the private life that now belonged to no one and was being discarded, but by its absence. In the first cart I had noticed an old radio, just like the one we used to have, a lampshade that I'd seen at the dacha of Father's friends, and a few other things that were familiar in color and shape. So I decided to wait for the next cart—I was curious.

There were familiar things in the second, third, and fourth cartloads. When they formed the interior of someone else's house, standing together, shoulder to shoulder, they were hard to recognize as "doubles." But separated, loaded like corpses on the cart, deprived of mutual support and protection, they lost the domestic charm that gave them individuality and color. All day long, without haste, taking smoke breaks and drinking a pint of vodka over lunch, the workers brought things out—and I knew that if you were to open and gut any of the other dachas, the workers would bring out the same light fixtures, cabinets, refrigerators, and armchairs; that similarity held a vulnerability that the old dacha residents did not recognize.

The time had come for all those things to be worthless, old-fashioned, ridiculous, unneeded, laughable. That would happen tomorrow, or the day after, or in six months, all of a sudden, like a stock market collapse, and the people who bought lot No. 104 were harbingers of that change.

"These are new people here," the association chairman said to the women gathered at the well with their buckets. "New people, understand? They'll get used to it, they'll become like everyone else."

"New people," I said, testing the words. "New people …"

STALIN'S INCANTATION

When Father arrived for the weekend, Grandmother Mara demanded he immediately rebuild the fence that faced the street. She wanted solid planks so that when she was on her own property—the dacha was hers—she would never see the new neighbors.

Grandmother Mara was in mourning—the submarine captain had recently died, having been her husband for just a little over a year; but through her grief you could sense her gratitude to him that he had died well, in his sleep, as if he had lived through something very important with her, something he had previously lacked, and then left. Grandmother dressed in mourning, but she was cheerful and worked in the garden, as if she had paid a debt and that gave her strength.

Father was stunned by her harsh demand and launched into explanations, but Grandmother Mara stood her ground: if he didn't build a tall, solid fence she threatened to sell the dacha the very next day—she shoved a packet of documents under his nose—and she would sell it to people like the new neighbors, show-offs and scoundrels, who had no regard for elderly and respectable people.

Grandmother's fury had a simple explanation; the day before she'd been out planting strawberries and she had a few runners left of some precious and prolific variety. She went over to offer them to the newcomers, and at the same time learn what kind of people they were. They explained indifferently that they didn't need the runners, they could buy strawberries at the market, and they had no intention of "mucking around in the soil." Just before that, Grandmother Mara had shown the new neighbors an example of hard work, digging up long potato rows by the fence in the hot afternoon.

She visited all her friends that evening to tell them the shocking news—the new dacha people weren't going to plant anything at all! Forgetting that the Latin names the old doctor used had upset her, forgetting their move to Israel, which she used to mock—the hyenas ran off—she now hit all the chords in her changed tune about the wonderful old owners; she promised to write and tell them who had moved into their old place, even though, of course, she didn't know their address.

She had a very hard time dealing with the strangers' lack of connection with the soil. That night as I was falling asleep, she was still upset, heavily pacing the room, using a cane, which she never had before. Like a sleepwalker, she kept repeating the same words in a low, mindless voice—What if there's a war? A war! No, it's too soon to give up on the potatoes! Only potatoes will keep us fed! Potatoes! They've never seen how people plant just the eyes, no they haven't! Time will tell, if Stalin were still alive, he'd grab them by the ear and toss them over the wall for that kind of behavior!

It seemed that Stalin was just like her, an embittered old gardener or a lame spirit thrown out along with the furniture of the previous owners, circulating under the foundation, creaking the floorboards to make the newcomers feel uneasy. Grimly, as if he himself had grown out of an ugly potato plant, he demanded that they plant potatoes. "Don't fool with the soil," as Grandmother Mara repeated.

"Stalin, Stalin, Stalin"—she was roaring like an airplane now, realizing the uselessness of all other words. Just that terrible hooting, owl-like, "Stalin, Stalin, Stalin," merging with the nocturnal wind, with the scrape of a branch on the waterspout.

Her voice started to change, there were modulations now; it was the voice of a little girl in the dark woods calling for her father, who was cruelly hiding behind a tree, the voice of a nun suffering from the destruction of a sacred place, the voice of a widow many years after her husband's death whispering his name, forgotten by her lips. Then the various voices disappeared, leaving only one, moaning and groaning, like the blade of a scythe on a sharpening stone.

"Stalin, Stalin, Stalin"—and then everything stopped, no more creaking floorboards and thumping of her stick. A few minutes later I peeked into her room—she was sleeping at the table, her head on her arms, and her head was reflected in the mirror illuminated by the moon, as if she had been trying to tell her fortune, looking into the mirror's depths, seeking a glimpse of a beloved's face, a shadow of her intended.

Father did what he always did in these situations: he got a book on do-it-yourself building for dacha owners, took drafting paper marked in millimeter squares, and started sketching various fences, calculating the spacing of the posts, counting the number of posts and boards, cleaning away excess pencil marks

SERGEI LEBEDEV

with a razor blade, and grumbling that he didn't have a good ruler, and without one the fence might not be right.

Grandmother's heart, which had required instant action—hurrying to buy boards, hammering, drilling, banging in the posts—settled down. She couldn't stand Father's measured drawing, and she made a face and told him to forget it—I'll do it myself later, later—as if he had been moving the pencil point on the part of her herself she could not protect.

Knowing her personality, I assumed that she would start sniping at the neighbors, writing to the district attorney to demand they check where the money to buy the dacha came from, and that she'd soon drive them away with the secret help of her village friends, who could send kids to break windows or saw through the seat in the outhouse toilet.

But Grandmother Mara retreated instantly, as if she sensed her death in those new people. The fence was never built, but it existed in her imagination. For the rest of her life she never looked in the direction of the neighbors' house or spoke of lot No. 104. Everyone thought she was expressing scorn, but I knew she was suffering. One day we were supposed to go to the store for flower seeds, but when the bus pulled up she scowled and said we'd walk—the bus was on route 104.

For some reason I was sure that the young Okunenko boy (Grandmother had learned their last name) would definitely try to befriend Ivan once he started running into him at the dachas.

But it happened faster than that. Okunenko, who had no idea Ivan existed, who never exchanged a word with any of the dacha people, nevertheless met Ivan on the first day of his arrival, when Ivan was getting out of his car to open the gate. He had predisposed Okunenko to himself, as if he were billiard ball rolling along a hustler's table, always in the direction of the needed hole.

Ivan did not drop in to see me that day or the next; however I often saw him at the gate of the neighbor's house and even

216

more frequently saw Okunenko heading toward Ivan's; sometimes they walked down the road together—a strange couple, resembling a nucleus and an electron.

I was still troubled by occasional ghosts of last summer, I still retained traces of my former adoration, my former attachment to Ivan, but I now preferred the role of aloof and independent observer. Now I could see what an invisible effect he had on me since I last met with Ivan; he had poisoned me, in the unique way to which I was susceptible by my age, with extracts of feelings and emotions that could have killed me but, once the danger was past, also accelerate maturity.

I did not seek a renewal of our friendship; I watched Okunenko hang around Ivan, giving him American cigarettes—Ivan had taken up smoking; watched them drive off in the Volga to Moscow and return happy and excited, as if they had pulled off a successful deal—and perhaps that was the case.

Coming back from the store one day, I saw Ivan heading toward our neighbors' house. I was going to slow down and avoid him but realizing that I wasn't expecting anything from Ivan, I kept up my original pace.

It was the first time in a year that I'd seen Ivan up close; he was a completely different person now, as if last year's hunt for Mister, when like a hypnotist he moved me between life and death, feeding on my delight, fear, and hope, had aged him by three or four years. I alone would not have been enough for Ivan. Or maybe he wouldn't have been able to deceive me so easily and naturally now, for he had acquired a seriousness that interfered with pretense and deceit.

"Hi," he said, as if we had parted just yesterday. "How's life?"

"Good," I replied. I felt the difference in our ages, which had not seemed apparent last year.

Ivan stood still for a few seconds as if pondering which toy in his pocket to give me; then he seemed to realize something and said, "I'll drop by one of these days. We'll go for a walk."

And one of those days, Ivan kept his promise. A storm was coming from the west, from Borodino and Smolensk, and whirling columns of clouds with imprisoned lightning bolts within them moved toward us. The trees shivered, sagging power lines began to whine, ripples covered the darkened ponds and moved into the reeds. We strode past the railroad station and the freight trains in the sidings. Platforms, cisterns, bunkers with grain, containers—everything seemed filled with anxiety, as if on the eve of war. With the first drops of rain we reached the old House of Culture—patches of plaster falling from the bas-reliefs, cracked columns, worn steps. Opposite, in the scrawny park, stood a propeller on a foundation—a monument to pilots killed in the war; carnations rotted in a jar with green water beneath the propeller.

"Look." Ivan pointed to the building's pediment.

I didn't see anything except for the faded spackling. Something had been written there many years ago, but now there were only vague shadows and runny letters left.

"Just look," Ivan repeated.

Rain bucketed down on the settlement, bending trees. The drops flew horizontally, harshly, the streets were boiling with water, lightning struck the rod on the boiler plant chimney, and the nearby thunder rattled windows. The rain lashed the pediment, the violet flashes of electricity outlined the shadows of the columns. The shadows fell to the left, then to the right, as if the old building were tottering on its foundation.

Suddenly I saw the inscription appearing from inside the soaked spackling, and in an oval above it, a portrait.

LONG LIVE COMRADE STALIN—the erased letters were clearly visible in the storm's strange light; so was the profile, hair brushed back and large, predatory nose.

A profile—Stalin was not looking at you, but he could see you, he saw everyone everywhere, his gaze was not a line but a bell jar that covered the universe in all 360 degrees.

LONG LIVE COMRADE STALIN—the storm raged, tossing old crow's nests from the trees, breaking branches of apple trees, the foamy sap meant for the apples spraying into the air. I thought that long-dead corpses would start rising at the village cemetery from beneath the pyramids with red stars, the metal and wooden crosses, the slabs of granite and labradorite, the forgotten blurred earthen mounds, and the new coffins lowered on top of the old rotten ones.

I thought of Grandmother Mara's fervent pleas—"Stalin, Stalin, Stalin!"—and understood that after her death she would join the army of these corpses, that the lifetime connection would become an inseverable umbilical cord.

The leader had stamped his name on them—and they responded to that branding, they were enslaved in the afterlife. They were people of *his* era; I saw that I had lazily united them all by the name Stalin, repeating their own loyalty to him when he was alive, the way serfs were called by their master's name.

Ivan stood entranced by the rain, which was penetrating deep into the soil, to the roots of the cemetery trees, hammering on the sheet metal, tearing away weather vanes and downspouts, seeping into the dried-out attics. He was a priest of a new, victorious faith, come into the temple of the old gods in order to sense his own power; he did not sense the awakening of the dead, he heard and saw something else: the spectral letters, the irony of oblivion that allowed the generalissimo to feel how completely he was forgotten—there was nothing but the inscription on the gable that appeared in storms with a westerly wind.

The rain was letting up; I was soaked, shivering, and my face was covered with cold drops.

Ivan was next to me, tired, drained; I understood that he had showed me the most personal and intimate thing he could show another person; he had come across that inscription and held on to it as if it were a jewel, showing it to no one, so as not to turn it into a local attraction.

I wanted to tell Ivan how Grandmother Mara cried out Stalin's name, but I didn't think he would understand, he would just laugh at an old woman's stupidity. He had brought me along because he needed an audience and because he did not want to be remembered only as a deceiver; he could have not bothered about me at all—who cared what the little kid thought of him?—but he liked the opportunity to turn a difficult situation in his favor without having to admit guilt, easily resolving the unsolvable.

He was giving me a gift, allowing me to join in the glory of his power, in the feeling that the future was his, that his time had come, which meant that he'd been right about everything.

We were back at the dachas, soaked in the muddy streams carrying rubbish and leaves, and we stopped at my gate, opposite the Okunenko house.

"He's a zero who dreams of standing next to a one, to make ten, and to be able to call that ten 'us,'" he said, having guessed my secret and most burning question. He was generous, the way people are generous before a final farewell. "But I will need zeros like that. Many of them. He's the first. You have to respect precedence."

I thought Ivan was wrong; he haughtily thought Okunenko sought his society and was nothing on his own, he amused himself playing with what he considered an empty man. But I had seen Okunenko at the Palace of Congresses, and I was stunned by his ability to change, I sensed that Okunenko was not a zero. Grandmother Tanya, who liked to play solitaire, explained the meaning of the cards to me, and I thought that Okunenko was the joker, the card that can become any other; the fool who in certain circumstances can acquire the highest power and disrupt the balance in an instant.

"So," Ivan said. "Go. Go dry off."

He turned and strode off to his place. I wondered—should I run after him, tell him what I knew about Okunenko? And I stopped. I was interested in seeing what would happen with the two of them. The situation was reversed: now I had Ivan in my power because I knew what he did not. Without feelings of revenge or jealousy, I said: let things be.

I went home, knowing that Grandmother Mara would scold me for running off and for my wet clothes, but I had no fear of her now, as if I had suddenly become the older one.

A LETTER INTO THE FUTURE

Ivan never came back to the dacha, Okunenko didn't visit much, either, and I was there less and less—my grandmothers were sick, they had trouble walking, and Mother and I took care of them. No sooner would one illness pass, than another would appear, and we spent years following a schedule of pill taking, both apartments turned into hospital wards; school, homework, friends—everything was left at the door, everything took a backseat to the endlessness of illness, its power that inexorably forced me to pay attention to other people's pulses and breathing.

Father was traveling more frequently to places where ships sank, gas exploded, planes crashed, and buildings collapsed. He rushed from one catastrophe to another, no longer knowing what to do with them, how to explain it all; he drafted new tables, clicked his calculator keys, and brought home an aluminum cap, a part from a plane or rocket that he kept erasers in, but sometimes in the morning the cap stank of bad cognac and Mother tried to get me out the door for school faster.

The southern borderlands, the Caucasus mountains already echoed with future gunfire; with the coming of somber times, Moscow and other cities were plunged into darkness—some crazy force had declared war on lightbulbs, and the lines were getting longer and there were fewer things to buy; I grew taller, my physique changed, and Mother resewed and refaced old clothing for the third time.

My body demanded food, pleasure, and fun, but money, without a day's rest in my parents' wallet, turned into boxes of medicines with foreign names, into yellow and pink granules, green tablets, white pills, pale blue plastic capsules filled with liquid; syringes and oilcloth, bandages, ointments, and powders.

Father came and went, weary, bowed down, argued with Grandmother Tanya, who got up when we were out and tried to help with the housework; the two grandmothers could not be kept in the same apartment, so Mother lived between two houses; Father understood that he should be helping her, but she understood that he was waging war against the elements gone mad, facing defeat after defeat. Malignant lightning flared over the distant mountains, over the borderlands.

Father broke down in late December, in the black hole of winter, home from an earthquake that killed tens of thousands of people. He was a stranger to Mother and me, exhausted, permeated with the smell of dead houses and generator fuel.

Late that night, refusing food, he told us what he had seen with a disconnected urgency; it was not a story but a mash of words, the ruins of narrative.

Darkness, lit only by bonfires and headlights, mounds of coffins at intersections, tanks and roadblocks, looters; the special hour when all work stops and they take acoustical soundings of the ruins in case someone is still alive under the concrete, stone, and brick.

"We couldn't stop the machinery at the same time," Father said. "They brought rescue workers from all over the country, and their watches were not synchronized, everything was plus-minus fifteen minutes."

"One block survived," Father said, with no connection to his previous sentence. "The usual five-story houses. The neighboring ones collapsed. We drew profiles of seismic waves in order to understand how that happened. An engineer found the documents. That particular block was built by workers from Czechoslovakia, on an exchange. They hadn't stolen cement during its construction. The orders came to blow up that block." Father drummed his fingers on the table. "Blow it up."

Mother suggested gently that he go to bed, she seemed even more tired than he was from the story of the destroyed city.

"I can't sleep, I haven't slept in three days," he replied softly, without expression. "There was a factory there, built by Komsomol workers. The factory was destroyed. Some Komsomol official came and said that there was a time capsule in the foundation, a message to future citizens. It was put there in 1972. He asked us to find it. We sent him packing, but he called somewhere, and the bulldozer was ordered to dig. He had brought a blueprint at least, he knew where to dig. He said a museum would take the capsule. We found it—a silver tube, dusty and dented. The engraving was beautiful: "With a Komsomol greeting to the builders of the future! To be opened in 1992." The tube was dented, so it opened. And inside there was nothing but cigarette butts. And a note written on a pack of Prima cigarettes: "The Battalion Does Not Surrender."

"To be opened in 1992," Father repeated. I think he felt like a woodsman who cut down a beloved tree and discovered its rotting core.

"There it is, the future," Father said. "Cigarette butts."

THE LAST PARADE

Father went back to the earthquake zone. Despite the horror, he seemed happier there; indisputable and obvious, the ruins cut off any thoughts of the future. He had ceased being rational, he thought that the massacre in Sumgait, the Spitak earthquake, and other small and big disasters were related somehow, that nature and humans had become one. "It will start soon," he would say, and I could see why he did not perceive everything that had happened thus far to be the beginning; the more threatening the shots and underground tremors and the longer the lines at stores, the clearer it became that these were the events that could set off an avalanche, but were not the avalanche itself; Father knew this field, he dealt with snow issues, and he used a dynamic mathematical model of avalanche for his theoretical model of catastrophe.

And just a few months later—Father was still on the trip—I came home in the evening; Grandmother Tanya was watching television with a very strange picture on the screen—an enormous line of tanks, kilometers long. And the line was moving fast.

They moved across a huge bridge with angular trusses, they moved in an endless flow across the Amu-Darya River back from Afghanistan, the tanks and armored carriers wreathed in blue-gray smoke with their gun barrels raised, headlights burning, and red flags waving; soldiers with their hands at their temples stood knee-deep or chest-deep in the tank hatches. It was like the movement of ice, like ice cracking in the upper reaches of a river; a chain of events had begun, events that, like people, *stood in line to happen*. There was such power, such impatience in that movement home that it seemed the tanks would never be able to stop anywhere, they would drive and drive, like windup cars that never run down.

And it was true—that fall I saw the parade on the anniversary of the October Revolution. Our family and my parents' friends had a tradition: we would meet near the U.S. Embassy on the Garden Ring Road, to see the columns of war vehicles headed toward the Kremlin through the eyes of American diplomats. The children grew up, others were born, but the tradition was unchanged. We all climbed up on a parapet, while the tanks and missiles rolled by, followed by the trucks, and marines threw their collars, navy blue trimmed with a triple line of white, with handwritten signs—DMB-84, 85, 86, 87. That moment—the flying collars with fluttering ribbons, the hands reaching for them—was repeated annually, making the parade a city holiday, not a military one, turning the military machines into something theatrical, not quite real, the setting for a film shoot.

But that autumn the collars didn't fly into the crowd—maybe there had been an order not to waste state property—and the tanks were grim and menacing, as if they were the same ones that could not stop, the ones that crossed the bridge over the Amu-Darya.

Soldiers in the cab of a tented truck—I think they were border guards—waved meekly to the crowd, and then one who must have seen family in the crowd along the sidewalk shouted at the top of his lungs:

"We'll be back, wait!"

The tanks, armored vehicles, trucks with marines, missile haulers, and self-propelled artillery turned onto the New Arbat, toward the Kremlin, moving out of sight, going, going, going; the huge canvases of military banners carried in open cars seemed vulnerable.

"We'll be back!" the solider yelled again, and now it sounded like a threat; the troops stayed in formation, but it seemed that they could also move helter-skelter, for the flags of the military controllers no longer had the same power and there might be a shell hidden in the equipment; the moving vehicles made windowpanes rattle in a high mosquito-like whine.

I don't remember any more parades; they may have still taken place, or maybe the marshals also sensed the *new mood of the tanks*; we stopped going to the Garden Ring Road, my parents' group of friends fell apart. My father quit his job and became eccentric, inventing crazy alarm systems, rescue methods for a fire, and was a regular at the patent bureau, which was a gathering place for scientists like him and stubborn autodidacts, as well.

I grew closer to him and my mother, the grandmothers' health kept deteriorating, and we had trouble remembering our previous life, when everyone was healthy. Illness lived in our apartment, not us, we were merely its servants and messengers, illness consumed time, took away the right to make plans, and made tomorrow both predetermined and yet uncertain; we almost never watched television and rarely opened the papers and magazines that were bloated with news and had huge print runs. To make money, they found work for me as a laborer on archeological and geographic expeditions, and in the winter I studied and indifferently passed from one grade to another.

Two years passed this way.

THE FAREWELL TRAIN

The grandmothers were brought back to life by the March referendum on preserving the USSR. It's not that they were cured, more as if they had asked the illness to give them a reprieve from infirmity, a last surge of strength. When 77 percent of the people voted "yes," Grandmother Mara remembered the planting, the dacha where she had not been for a few years, and began reproaching us—probably we had not whitewashed the apple tree trunks for the winter or dug up the beds in the autumn for spring planting; and Grandmother Tanya asked us to buy her new glasses and resubscribe to newspapers.

They both demanded to be with me, once again they competed in signs of attention, giving me trifles from their pensions, and they were happy that we could go to the nearest park, that I had grown, and they could brag about me to the neighbors; having lived through feebleness and knowing it would be back, and for good, they hastened to give me everything, they opened accounts in my name at the bank without consulting each other; and my parents, seeing how the former family was being reborn, asked me not to go away for the summer, not to apply for jobs, but to stay with the grandmothers.

I was uncomfortable and embarrassed, I noticed signs of their frailty that should not be noticed, I was clumsy, self-conscious, pathetic, and unable to respond to their love. Grandmother Mara kept talking about my future, my wonderful wife, and my good apartment—she meant hers, and this kindly rejection of her own future grated on me. Grandmother Tanya was much quieter, but she started holding my hand much more frequently, as if trying to slip something into it or seeking support.

That summer I was attracted to bridges, ancient houses, factory chimneys, and monuments. I avoided rallies, loudspeaker voices, screaming posters, and took side alleys; old stones and bricks and cast-iron bridge trusses had a better sense of the future than any orator; monuments knew more than those agitating around them. I wandered around the city, looking for advice—who should I be, how to live; I went through the places, names and events imprinted on the city's memory.

One Sunday I found myself at the Paveletsky Station, where the steam engine that brought Lenin's body from Gorki in 1924 was placed on a pedestal.

In school, we were taken to see the steam engine and a nearby monument marking the spot where Fanya Kaplan shot at Lenin during a rally at the Mikhelson factory. Back then I was unpleasantly surprised by the nearness of those two points: the shot with a poisoned bullet, as we were told, seemed to pin Lenin to the place of the assassination attempt, and six years later they brought his body back here.

The steam engine seemed to be complicit, its wheels, connecting rods, pistons, furnace, and boiler made history; but now the steam engine looked aged, knowing it had been rendered useless and scorned by the electric commuter trains.

To my right, thousands of dacha dwellers were emptying out of trains onto the station platforms. Into the humid and dirty city smells rolled in from the Garden Ring Road and from the Moskva River covered in mucky seaweed, the aromas of thousands of baskets with the first apples, with fragrant *grushovka* tomatoes, and endless bouquets of dacha flowers and jasmine came like fresh streams of scents and perfumes.

Jasmine had bloomed during the week; everyone coming home from the weekend cut some of the flowers and saw that everyone else on the train was carrying sweet, cloying jasmine as well and the suburban platforms were covered with the tiny cups of its flowers, which resembled the tea sets of fairies.

A storm was gathering over Moscow, the wind was rising, the dry wind that comes before a shower, not yet very strong but capable of wrinkling the heavy fabric of men's jackets and trousers and lifting and fluttering women's light dresses, skirts, blouses, and scarves. In the wind, the men seemed to be moving calmly and unemotionally, while the women—buds of fabric—slightly intoxicated by the jasmine, pupils dilated by heart palpitations and difficult breathing in the crowded train, were vibrating, expecting the approaching rain, listening to the car horns that had become too jarring.

Another dozen such evenings and something was bound to happen in the city, compounded out of the electric atmosphere, dilated pupils, and excitement taken for nervousness. A woman tripped on the metal-trimmed steps, and dozens of teaspoons fell from her purse and spilled out across the stairs, ringing merrily, dazzling with their polished dimples, but everyone turned around as if there had been a shot.

Drawn by a morbid interest, I went where Lenin had been wounded; on a Sunday evening the streets around the station were empty except near the hospital that gave rabies shots around the clock where several men with bandages were waiting—obviously attacked by a dog—and smoking silently, listening to their bodies: Was the sickness, the madness, the frothing at the mouth, coming, were the shots too late?

The square where Kaplan had taken the shot was empty except for a bronze Lenin. Only once in a while, cars drove by on neighboring streets, the dusty and unwashed windows of the former factory looked down, recognizing nothing, and the silence seemed padded, as if the entire area had been covered with poplar fluff. The place that was once open and tragic was now surrounded by the wild growth of new houses and courtyards.

I spent the evening wandering the streets, coming out by the Donskoi Cemetery and then the Shukhov Tower; force lines— the shining trolley tracks—led me, not letting my movement become a relaxed and unimportant stroll, pushing me forward; through them the city communicated its magnetized, edgy state before the storm.

When the rain began, I went home, almost falling asleep on my train, where it traveled aboveground and the raw air, filled with creosote from the ties, poured into the windows.

In the metro I had a vision, half-asleep, of an empty compartment, the long corridors of the cars, the curtained windows, the tedious jangle of a spoon stirring sugar in a glass with a metal holder, so prolonged that you couldn't imagine that tea could absorb that much sugar; voices in the distance, muffled by the vestibules at the end of cars, flashes of light—the crossing lights—and once again the rattling spoon.

The quickest way home from the metro was along the railroad; the signal lights shone over the empty crossing and a large pack of homeless dogs ran along the embankment.

I was exhausted when I got home; my parents and grandmother were sleeping, and I went to bed without even washing up—a heavy sleepiness that portended a bad dream was knocking me off my feet; I fell asleep just after hearing the piercing blare of the freight train's horn, forcing late-night idlers to recoil from the platform edge.

I dreamed I was walking in the cool morning through a field along a railroad track; in the distance, by the switchman's hut, enveloped in fog, a train had stopped.

It was the train that had carried Lenin's body. The engine huffed steam, a sentry stood by the stairs to the cabin, wearing an old Red Army uniform. Coming closer, I recognized him— his photograph was probably the smallest one on Grandmother's wall of photographs, hung on the periphery, like a distant planet or Sputnik; he was Grandmother Tanya's great-uncle, the first in the family to sign up for the Red Army and the first to die at the age of nineteen in an armored train hit by artillery and captured by General Shkuro's "Wolf Division."

He stood on watch, swaying clumsily, for he consisted of two parts, separated by a saber slash from right collarbone to left leg. But he did not fall apart, some force held the dead body together, dressed in an undershirt marked by two hoof prints.

Seeing me, the sentry nodded toward the cabin—go in—and blinked, probably to indicate that he had recognized me, too.

There was no one in the cabin; the tender was empty, it didn't smell of coal near the furnace, but fire roared inside it, and the steam engine was slowly restoring the connection among pistons, wheels, and axles, becoming a machine again.

A shout came from the boiler, but the dead sentry was unfazed. A shout, then another shout, and someone struggled in the boiler, being burned alive, trying to break the door, get through the iron walls. The train started, the screams blended into the powerful roar of the machine, as if the burning man had turned into thrust, flames, and the energy of the furnace.

I walked through the cars; in the first was the coffin with Lenin's body, heaped with winter fir wreaths. The fir fragrance was strong, and frost covered the windows; the black mourning crepe, stretched into tight folds, resembled the wings of bats, and the coffin seemed to be embraced by a gigantic bat.

The stink of stale river silt filled the hallway, and a shiny black centipede crawled out from a compartment door and climbed up the wall; near the ceiling, several others waited for it. Someone was vomiting in the compartment, murky water poured into the hallway with small fry and seaweed floating in it.

Chapayev was inside, vomiting sand and filthy water, centipedes climbing out of his ears, and his eyes were white, like a boiled fish.

In the restaurant car, twenty-six men were celebrating, black-haired, so tanned that even death's pallor could not touch them; they drank wine from clay jugs and the wine poured out through the bullet holes in their chests.

Also in the restaurant car, sailors in striped shirts and round caps were gathered around a basin of macaroni, and watched entranced as the noodles turned into white maggots that gobbled up the meat.

There were other cars, other people, men, women, missing legs, arms, and eyes, marked by torture, in uniforms of various eras or half-naked with red stars carved into their backs.

Alongside the train, a hundred cavalrymen raced over meadows and ravines, passing through trees and strata of earth, creating fox fire in the decaying swamp wood. The horsemen passed the train, then fell behind, swooping out on the right, then the left, galloped in the air over the roofs of the cars, nimbly, like swallows or swifts. Semitranslucent, with silvery moon faces, the riders pointed the way with their sabers, and their horses—clots of forest shadows, flowing and slipping—picked up speed effortlessly, leaping over rivers that could not catch their reflection.

The train exited the forest and hurtled down a long valley; in the distance, by the horizon, more banks of fog appeared. The riders sped through hay ricks without disturbing a single straw, occasionally startling a bird; I was thrown from the car, the train vanished in the fog, and the horsemen galloped in farewell, dissolving into swarms of lightning bugs and sparks from steppe campfires.

. In the morning, I did not remember the dream right away but I awoke with a sense of loss—I did not yet understand what or whom I had lost.

Noon found me near the metro station at Revolution Square.

The famous sculptures—the army scout with a dog, the sailor signalman, the revolutionary laborer, the young woman who was a Voroshilov sharpshooter, the Stakhanovite worker with a raised hammer—had turned from ordinary monuments into monuments to a lost era, as if overnight the historical clocks had been reset.

PEOPLE AND ANIMALS

In mid-August I dropped by to see my mother at the Ministry of Geology on Krasnaya Presnya Street. Her windows opened onto the zoo, and in the summer heat you could smell the animals, a scent unthinkable in a city, foreign to asphalt and glass.

The hippos, elephants, and crocodiles wallowed in the pools in their enclosures, ate, excreted, mated, and the zoo stank of putrid water, rotting cane, and tainted meat.

A vulture's revolting call from behind bars was answered by a jackal or hyena. Once in a while, a random pedestrian, aroused by the scents of hay beds, nests, and dens, wet puppies and naked fledglings, the odors of predators and herbivores, mutually repellant, would discover the prehistoric creature within and with a quick look around send up a pithecanthropic hunting cry, responding to the animals with a ferocious animal sound.

The ministry hallways, carpeted in long runners, were filled with the clacking of electric typewriters; there were oases of quiet near the doors to the bosses' offices, where people slowed down and lowered their voices as they passed.

The ministry countered the wild scents of the zoo with the smell of paper—it seemed that opening any door would reveal papers piled to the ceiling; even in the cafeteria on the first floor, the paper smell mixed into the flavor of soup, schnitzel, and fruit compote.

That day something had changed in the ministry corridors. The machines would start typing and then stop. There were fewer people. But most important, there was a new kind of air current, as if previously the draft had moved along the corridors in accordance with a general plan, decorously and strictly, and now the currents were all mixed up, new ones appeared that did not know how to behave in a ministry; they tore papers out of people's hands and slammed doors and windows shut.

The ministry bureaucrats, extremely sensitive to such things, waited it out, staying put at their desks; the document flow stopped until it was clear what was going on, and the huge ministerial machine spun its wheels. There was still a long line at the security desk, maps, reports, and rolls of millimeter-marked paper were still carried from office to office, but the tension of power, the electricity that generated decisions, had slackened suddenly, and the four floors of the ministry building resembled a hive where the queen bee had died.

I went into my mother's office; it was empty, she had gone to lunch with her colleagues. The insolent draft had pushed open the poorly fastened window and the office was filled with flying papers stamped "For Internal Use Only" and "Secret" that had been left on desks in violation of the rules. The zoo smells were no longer just swamp decay and rancid feed, but unrest, anxiety, as if the animals' blood, warmed by the heat, was taking in a constant drip of hormones, and every gland was awakened, swollen and pulsating, responding to the stirrings in the air. The animals sensed this more deeply than the humans.

The animals were not lying down, they wandered, pushing against the cages, whipping themselves with their tails; suddenly an elephant trumpeted, lions, bears, and tigers roared, rhinoceroses and oxen screamed, as did every creature whose jaws were big enough for their voices to be heard. The noises clashed, tumbled, whirled until they blended into one sound that was no longer the cry of wild animals. It seemed it was not flesh and blood but a *thing* screaming, as if suddenly there was an onset of metal fatigue at some gigantic construction site, seams bursting, I-beams and channel bars collapsing, a wave of deformation traveling across all its elements, and the tower—I imagined it was a tower—began falling sideways, twisting into a corkscrew and emitting that scream of a disintegrating whole.

THE FRACTURE OF AUGUST

The next day was Saturday and my parents went to the dacha, leaving me in charge of the grandmothers. They were taking a long weekend, planning to return in a few days, but we did not meet until a week later.

Over the weekend it felt like there was a human flow across the city, the start of a vortex; the seemingly relaxed passersby were going about their business, but one had the impression they were carried along, led by an invisible force. I wandered the streets; I thought that everything had a secret meaning, and the policeman who didn't pay attention to the Zhiguli that crossed a solid line knew something and was lost in thought, and the man with a suitcase hurrying to the train station had reason to rush; something had happened, people and things had changed, you could push your finger through a brick, fall into the metro through the thickness of the sidewalk, meet a talking dog, win five thousand rubles on a trolley ticket, and walk by unnoticed through the security at the Spassky Tower entrance to the Kremlin. It was only the general habit of belief that bricks were hard, the ground solid, and sentries vigilant, that kept the city in its former state.

Monday morning, the human flow in the city increased when the radio announcer, seemingly sedated, read: "In the aim of preventing chaos and anarchy ... The collapse of society ... Forming the State Committee on the State of Emergency in the Union of Soviet Socialist Republics"; the voice wanted to calm people and called them to order, but it was so recognizable, so laughable, that when it used the simple-folk pronunciation of Vice President Yanaev's patronymic, calling him "Ivanych" instead of "Ivanovich," more and more people left their radios with every word and went out into the street, albeit not yet knowing what to do or where to go.

That evening I found myself by the White House. The period had begun in which the concepts of "day" and "date" had lost meaning—it was a gap in eras when time itself becomes an event. Rumors moved among the thousands of people like rustling waves: "The Dzerzhinsky Division is headed this way," "There's a column of tanks on Komsomolsky," "The 'shoot to kill' order has been given." Barricades appeared and grew out of nothing.

Benches, newspaper kiosks, boards, pipes, cars, buses, streetlamps, grates—they remained in their places, they had a precise function. Suddenly, as if someone had looked at the city with a different view, the view of a revolutionary, a fighter, things began to move on their own, forming obstructions, lying down and dovetailing beneath memorial plaques commemorating the first revolution, the battles of 1905.

The White House, as the House of Soviets of the Russian Soviet Federative Socialist Republic was known, hearkening back to the history of the Soviet regime, was built in a "dormant" historical zone, with the Barricades movie theater, the Barrikadnaya metro station. Like an enormous paperweight, it held down the crumbling ground of Krasnaya Presnya, which was already squashed by a high-rise, the house on Uprising Square.

The power of names turned out to be longer-lived than the power of stone, and the memory of the uprising, encoded in monuments and street names, responded as soon as it was hailed. Druzhinnikovskaya Street, named in honor of worker combatants, Shmitovsky Alley, named for the revolutionary factory owner, the Trekhgornaya Mills, where Lenin was elected as a deputy; the sculptures by the 1905 Street metro station—a woman catching the bridle of a Cossack's horse—the sculpture by the White House—a worker in an apron picking up a dropped rifle; symbols of uprising, protected and multiplied, were gathered here.

Volunteers were gathering at Presnya River again, 1905 was being repeated, but on a larger scale; barricades grew around the White House, and this was an inversion of history—the House of Soviets was turning into a bastion of resistance to the Soviet regime.

But just a few hundred meters from the White House people sat in cafés, strolled, shopped; men's shoes were delivered to the store on 1905 Street, and the line for them looked more tight-knit than the ranks of defenders of the barricades. From inside the defense rings, the White House looked like the epicenter of events, but if you moved just a bit to the side, it began to seem that the White House and everything around it was suspended in midair and taking place with no grounding whatsoever; part of the capital had plunged into a different dimension.

I found its border as I walked down the street, the ground beneath my feet was oscillating slightly, as if predicting a coming storm. In the next block there was only the trembling caused by the metro trains traveling near the surface. You could choose one or the other register of perception, but there was no smooth transition between them; an invisible line divided the city.

That night by the White House people sang songs around bonfires, and dozens like me sought something among the heaps and smoke, among the arriving crowds; men in civilian cloth-ing with guns appeared, attentively surveying the scene—who were they, who sent them? The more people, the harder it was to understand who was one of us and who wasn't, and whether there was an "us" and "them" or whether it was all a masquerade, a phantasmagoria, that there weren't any foes or any clear antag-onists but only the blood-raising attraction of major events.

Okunenko was in charge of building a barricade at the entrance to the White House; he was giving orders to three dozen people, most of whom were older than he was, but he was more energetic, more precise, he gave smart and accurate direc-tions on where to put what, where to place the concrete plate, the dozen benches, the tracks; it seemed he had a special mind that could easily combine mutually exclusive objects—plates, benches, tracks, concrete flower boxes, and furniture—into a sturdy construction that would be hard to break and move.

Okunenko, matured, electrified by the events, stood on the top of his barricades, indicating "left, left, more to the left" to men dragging a lamppost knocked down by a bulldozer.

The barricade was finished; I expected Okunenko to tell his comrades to move on to the next one. But he got down, lit a cigarette, spoke with his subordinates and stepped away, and it was no longer clear whether he had commanded anyone or it just happened that the men building the barricade took him for a manager of elemental construction.

He walked among the bonfires and barricades, no longer the clever and efficient builder—he had turned into a concerned simpleton, for whom everything was new and interesting. He looked inside camping kettles, respectfully studied the armature prepared for hand-to-hand combat, stopped near people arguing, smiled to a pair of policemen with automatic guns, struck a match for a soldier's cigarette, and gave disorganized civilians a pitying look.

Okunenko had gestures and objects for every situation, like an improvising magician; he did unnoticed work, helping, joining, supporting, advising, approving, sharing cigarettes—whatever it took to make the crowd more focused and thicker. He made several circles around the White House and later that night moved toward the Arbat; I followed him, and I saw a common thread in the patchwork of events.

Parked in the courtyards near the Arbat, which looked empty from the sidewalk, were cars with men in suits, doing nothing, and heavyset men were smoking in dark doorways; no one looked into the faces of passersby, no one stopped anyone, everyone pretended to be there by accident.

I almost lost Okunenko a few times, but his way of moving made him easy to spot. Both the military and the police—they were the ones smoking in doorways—were tense, and many must have understood that the symbols on their uniforms would soon be meaningless; they stood listening to their radios, awaiting belated orders, but Okunenko delighted in this night, he was practically dancing, sensing that there would be no orders given.

He sat inside a Moskvich car for a few minutes, then jumped out and ran back to the White House, to the intersection of Novy Arbat and the Garden Ring Road; in the quiet, well-lit courtyards where sounds seemed to fall from the sky, the distant rumble of military machines grew stronger.

The infantry vehicles came down the Garden Ring Road from the side of the zoo, along the old parade route.

The mechanical reptiles crawled along, warping the asphalt with their caterpillar tracks. They represented the ancient threat of nature, which had created shells, spines, claws, and teeth; the teeth were for opening up the shells, the spines to protect the neck from the teeth, claws to get to the soft belly, and armor plates to protect the belly; behind all that power was the narrow brain of the predator, its tiny eyes peering out from deep inside the skull.

The city rose in buildings, spread in lanes, glittered with lit shop windows, signs, kiosks, and street signs, and the armored vehicles were moving in, waiting for the order to destroy everything, to find and destroy the sources of the rebellion. The exit from the Novy Arbat tunnel was blocked by trolleybuses, as if the civilian urban technology had come out to stop its crazed relatives; the boxy blue trolleys with their snaillike antennae huddled together, blocking the tunnel's throat; it was clear that everything would be decided here, at this intersection.

The armored vehicles drove into the tunnel and crawled out, pushing aside the trolleybuses, which the crowd had moved toward the army machines. Above on the overpass, a long-haired man was trying to light a Molotov cocktail, but the matches

kept burning out; Okunenko grabbed his hand—I thought he
was going to hit him, but no, he struck a match while protecting it from the wind with a graceful gesture, and the bottle flew
in a basketball arc, flames shot up on the armored car into the
sky and seeped into the ventilation holes. The truck swerved,
another bottle was thrown from the overpass, two more armored
vehicles broke through the trolleybuses; there was a mash up
of men and metal and then everything stopped—someone had
been crushed to death.

I lost him there by the tunnel; I went back to the spot where
Okunenko came either to report or to get instructions, but the
cars were gone, the courtyard empty, and there was nothing but
butts in the doorways. I spent the next two days rushing around
Moscow, trying to understand where the main events were taking place.

Thursday night I was on Lubyanka Square; the pedestrian
flow brought me there at the moment when the mountain
climber had reached the neck of the secret police boss Dzerzhinsky's statue and was slipping a noose attached to a crane around
it; I was tired and dizzy, and I thought it was all a dream—how
can you hang a monument?

Next to me by the wall of the Polytechnical Museum several
men, dressed identically in civilian clothes, obviously KGB officers, were smoking; they stood and watched calmly as their chief
was dragged off his pedestal.

Observing them, I noticed their colleagues, leaving by a side
entrance and mixing with the crowd. On the sidewalk you could
still tell they were KGB, but then they became faces, sleeves, hats,
shoulders, and heads in the general crowd, vanishing without a
trace, without adding a single person but raising the density of
the living mass. Probably later you could find them in photographs, chanting about freedom, raising their arms, embracing
neighbors, waving their fists at "Iron Felix Dzerzhinsky."

Beneath the windows of the KGB, Lubyanka agents were enjoying the overthrow of the Lubyanka god; they had developed the art of mimicry to such a degree that it was stronger than their dutiful respect. I had thought that some general had given orders to the surveillance service, but orders no longer had their former power, and the surveillance agents had changed into civilian garb and left, beginning their private lives from that moment on.

The moment was joyful and partially comical—albeit with a note of danger; the spies were gone and the moment when they could have been identified and counted was gone, too.

The statue of Dzerzhinsky fell across the square, the soft and heavy thud of metal on asphalt blocking the roar of the crowd; and at that very moment Ivan came out of the museum.

I was still trying to figure out who was coming toward me so headlong, as if he wanted to arrest me, when he was just three steps away; he was practically running, like an actor performing in two plays on the same day, buttoning his jacket on the go; he did not recognize me as he went past to open the door of an empty car, parked right there; the car came alive, flashed its headlights, the driver, who had been hiding or sleeping, appeared; the rear lights drew red looping lines in the twilight and disappeared into a lane.

I went into the museum, up the empty stairs to the roof; there were no workers or guards, just a toy robot's blinking lights on one floor; the door to the roof was wide open.

From above, the dark heads of the crowd looked like black caviar, a viscous mass that had filled the square, a strange dish for gourmets of this sort of spectacle. I stood on the roof in front of a barrel of caviar, an accidental guest at someone else's banquet, and I expected cutlery to appear from the sky for the real diners prepared for the feast, for gluttony, to devour as much as possible without even tasting it.

Moscow had spent the previous years in lines; there were fewer individual pedestrians on the streets than people standing queuing up, looking at the back of another's head. At any one moment, sometimes even at night, a family member was in line, sometimes people passed along their number to somebody else, writing it down on somebody's hand, and my school pals and I tried not to wash them off—number 87, number 113—showing off what long lines we had been in.

The ability to form a chain was a skill, a form of existence; there were lines for lines: you had to stand in one for the right to sign up for another.

And this was just such a line spread out over Lubyanka Square, taking up its entire area and splashing out into the lanes, where human currents were pouring into the big sea of people standing in line for the future. If I had been in the street, I would have wholeheartedly rejoiced, kissing and hugging strangers; but from the roof I could see the waves of emotions and unstable feelings traveling over the square; I was happy to see them born and grieved over their quick death.

The year before I had worked as a laborer on an expedition in Kazakhstan. We traveled across a steppe where half-wild horses lived; the magnificent, free creatures galloped across an ideal plane, animals that had never seen a tree, house, fence, or corral, born for an unbounded plain. To me they weren't animals, not flesh and blood, but spirits of motion.

A month later our expedition came back the same way—there were thousands of dead horses in the steppe; there had been a pestilence.

I was astonished by the speed with which a heavy mass of beauty became a mass of dead meat; the stench was unbearable, and it was impossible to believe it came from bodies that I had seen so recently not as bodies but as spiritual symbols.

I could not believe that beauty could die this way, it should have had a different death, pure and incorporeal. But the sun had turned the steppe into a rupturing abscess, and small predators scurried around the horse carcasses, foxes intoxicated by the abundance of meat were not afraid of cars and got run over, the horse plague had overwhelmed everything, and vultures circled in the sky, hypnotized by the sight, not knowing where to land, which carcass, for there were thousands of carcasses. This chewing, burping, grunting, and flying horde, consisting of teeth, beaks, and bellies, made a sound like the quiet buzz of a circular saw.

On the roof, where the emotional wave did not reach, spreading horizontally and sending throbbing sounds upward which resembled the tide, I realized that this communality was held together by short-lived emotions. Disintegration awaited it, the decay of feelings that, like the meat of victims of a cataclysm, will clutter the space, and in that environment ideas with the air of deterioration would form and carrion-eating creatures would be born. The physical sensation of feelings doomed to an early death moved me away from the edge of the roof.

It was time to go down.

THE BOOK WITH THE BROWN COVER

I got home late; Grandmother Tanya went to sleep without waiting up for me; the high moon filled her room with a weak emulation of the blue glow of the lamp she used to radiate herself with long ago. I went to my room; the light was on—I thought she had gone in and forgotten to turn off the lamp.

On the table, in the lamplight, among last year's textbooks I had forgotten to turn in, lay a large book, the size of a barnyard ledger, in a brown binding, with neat stiches of waxed thread. Next to it was Grandmother's porcelain statuette, the three frogs

"See nothing, hear nothing, say nothing"; it seemed to me that they were no longer covering their mouth, eyes, and ears.

Frightened, I went to check on Grandmother Tanya: after writing *that*, even though I didn't know what *that* was, she could die, maybe she had lingered on in order to complete this work.

Barricades and bonfires still filled the city's squares; shells and bullets were still loaded in weapons; and the book—had Grandmother really been writing it for five years, hiding it from everyone?—seemed like a kind of a weapon, too.

Grandmother Tanya was breathing, breathing more evenly than usual, more calmly, as if her illness had left her. I envied her, she seemed so at peace, complete and finished; I wished that someday I would lie as calmly, and I lightly touched her gray hair, thinning with every year; the planet of another person's mind, weightless in sleep, rested on the pillow.

Carefully, I turned the heavy cover and leafed through the pages, not reading the words, recognizing the colors of the ink—I had seen these pens on Grandmother Tanya's desk—recognizing the various forms of her penmanship, the various stages of illness, when pain directed her fingers and the letters grew bigger, childishly disobedient, and then diminished in size when the pain weakened.

Here were the first lines, the first sentences. But what was it—had she decided to write a novel instead of a memoir, a novel stylized as a family chronicle, invented from the first letter to the last, kindly and edifying? Why fiction, why artistic invention, when I had thirsted for truth, even if it were meager, but still truth?

"The history of our family goes back to the XIV century," Grandmother wrote. "Our family had military men, heads of the nobility, priests and metropolitans, generals and naval men, revolutionaries and philosophers, officers tried in the Decembrist plot and terrorists in the Socialist Revolutionary organization. Your great-grandfather, about whom you know nothing, was a nobleman and military doctor. And you, my grandson, are the seventeenth generation in our line."

"You, my grandson." It was only on the third reading that I understood this was not a stylistic turn and that Grandmother truly was addressing me. I was the seventeenth generation of the line.

A swarm of dead men, previously invisible, appeared and turned into the rustle of August foliage, into moonlight, as if they had seeped one by one through a crack in time, into the joint of eras, awakened by the soldiers' boots stomping on cobblestones, the fall of monuments, the rumble of tanks, and the din of the crowd.

The wind picked up and trees trembled in the dark, and I thought, honestly sensing my own smallness, that it would be better to destroy Grandmother's manuscript and throw myself from the balcony; no one would understand, but living with this was more than I could bear. I had been counting on a personal truth, a small, manageable piece of it, and I had been given too much.

Mechanically, I reached out in a farewell gesture and touched an apple; we brought them from the dacha and kept them in boxes on the balcony. Sharp, angry, boiling with an excess of flavor, the juice burned my mouth; I discovered that I was like an animal, chewing and choking on that apple, enormous, juicy— the harvest had been a good one that August, the tree branches cracked under the weight of the fruit, even though we propped them up—and the desire to live seethed and raged within me.

I was to be born anew.

IF VENICE DIES BY SALVATORE SETTIS

INTERNATIONALLY RENOWNED ART HISTORIAN Salvatore Settis ignites a new debate about the Pearl of the Adriatic and cultural patrimony at large. In this fiery blend of history and cultural analysis, Settis argues that "hit-and-run" visitors are turning Venice and other landmark urban settings into shopping malls and theme parks. This is a passionate plea to secure the soul of Venice, written with consummate authority, wide-ranging erudition and élan.

A VERY RUSSIAN CHRISTMAS

THIS IS RUSSIAN CHRISTMAS CELEBRATED IN supreme pleasure and pain by the greatest of writers, from Dostoevsky and Tolstoy to Chekhov and Teffi. The dozen stories in this collection will satisfy every reader, and with their wit, humor, and tenderness, packed full of sentimental songs, footmen, whirling winds, solitary nights, snow drifts, and hopeful children, the collection proves that Nobody Does Christmas Like the Russians.

THE MADONNA OF NOTRE DAME BY ALEXIS RAGOUGNEAU

FIFTY THOUSAND PEOPLE JAM INTO NOTRE DAME Cathedral to celebrate the Feast of the Assumption. The next morning, a beautiful young woman clothed in white kneels at prayer in a cathedral side chapel. But when someone accidentally bumps against her, her body collapses. She has been murdered. This thrilling novel illuminates shadowy corners of the world's most famous cathedral, shedding light on good and evil with suspense, compassion and wry humor.

MOVING THE PALACE
BY CHARIF MAJDALANI

A YOUNG LEBANESE ADVENTURER EXPLORES THE wilds of Africa, encountering an eccentric English colonel in Sudan and enlisting in his service. In this lush chronicle of far-flung adventure, the military recruit crosses paths with a compatriot who has dismantled a sumptuous palace and is transporting it across the continent on a camel caravan. This is a captivating modern-day Odyssey in the tradition of Bruce Chatwin and Paul Theroux.

ADUA BY IGIABA SCEGO

ADUA, AN IMMIGRANT FROM SOMALIA TO ITALY, has lived in Rome for nearly forty years. She came seeking freedom from a strict father and an oppressive regime, but her dreams of film stardom ended in shame. Now that the civil war in Somalia is over, her homeland calls her. She must decide whether to return and reclaim her inheritance, but also how to take charge of her own story and build a future.

THE 6:41 TO PARIS
BY JEAN-PHILIPPE BLONDEL

CÉCILE, A STYLISH 47-YEAR-OLD, HAS SPENT the weekend visiting her parents outside Paris. By Monday morning, she's exhausted. These trips back home are stressful and she settles into a train compartment with an empty seat beside her. But it's soon occupied by a man she recognizes as Philippe Leduc, with whom she had a passionate affair that ended in her brutal humiliation 30 years ago. In the fraught hour and a half that ensues, Cécile and Philippe hurtle towards the French capital in a psychological thriller about the pain and promise of past romance.

ON THE RUN WITH MARY
BY JONATHAN BARROW

SHINING MOMENTS OF TENDER BEAUTY PUNC-
tuate this story of a youth on the run after
escaping from an elite English boarding school.
At London's Euston Station, the narrator meets
a talking dachshund named Mary and together
they're off on escapades through posh Mayfair
streets and jaunts in a Rolls-Royce. But the
youth soon realizes that the seemingly sweet dog
is a handful; an alcoholic, nymphomaniac, drug-addicted mess who can't
stay out of pubs or off the dance floor. *On the Run with Mary* mirrors the
horrors and the joys of the terrible 20th century.

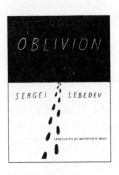

OBLIVION BY SERGEI LEBEDEV

IN ONE OF THE FIRST 21ST CENTURY RUSSIAN
novels to probe the legacy of the Soviet prison
camp system, a young man travels to the vast
wastelands of the Far North to uncover the
truth about a shadowy neighbor who saved his
life, and whom he knows only as Grandfather
II. Emerging from today's Russia, where the
ills of the past are being forcefully erased from
public memory, this masterful novel represents
an epic literary attempt to rescue history from the brink of oblivion.

THE LAST WEYNFELDT BY MARTIN
SUTER

ADRIAN WEYNFELDT IS AN ART EXPERT IN AN
international auction house, a bachelor in his
mid-fifties living in a grand Zurich apartment
filled with costly paintings and antiques. Always
correct and well-mannered, he's given up on
love until one night—entirely out of character for him—Weynfeldt decides to take home
a ravishing but unaccountable young woman
and gets embroiled in an art forgery scheme that threatens his buttoned
up existence. This refined page-turner moves behind elegant bourgeois
facades into darker recesses of the heart.

THE LAST SUPPER BY KLAUS WIVEL

ALARMED BY THE OPPRESSION OF 7.5 MILLION Christians in the Middle East, Journalist Klaus Wivel traveled to Iraq, Lebanon, Egypt, and the Palestinian territories to learn about their fate. He found a minority under threat of death and humiliation, desperate in the face of rising Islamic extremism and without hope their situation will improve. An unsettling account of a severely beleaguered religious group living, so it seems, on borrowed time. Wivel asks, Why have we not done more to protect these people?

GUYS LIKE ME BY DOMINIQUE FABRE

DOMINIQUE FABRE, BORN IN PARIS AND A life-long resident of the city, exposes the shadowy, anonymous lives of many who inhabit the French capital. In this quiet, subdued tale, a middle-aged office worker, divorced and alienated from his only son, meets up with two childhood friends who are similarly adrift. He's looking for a second act to his mournful life, seeking the harbor of love and a true connection with his son. Set in palpably real Paris streets that feel miles away from the City of Light, a stirring novel of regret and absence, yet not without a glimmer of hope.

ANIMAL INTERNET BY ALEXANDER PSCHERA

SOME 50,000 CREATURES AROUND THE GLOBE— including whales, leopards, flamingoes, bats and snails—are being equipped with digital tracking devices. The data gathered and studied by major scientific institutes about their behavior will warn us about tsunamis, earthquakes and volcanic eruptions, but also radically transform our relationship to the natural world. Contrary to pessimistic fears, author Alexander Pschera sees the Internet as creating a historic opportunity for a new dialogue between man and nature.

KILLING AUNTIE BY ANDRZEJ BURSA

A YOUNG UNIVERSITY STUDENT NAMED JUREK, with no particular ambitions or talents, finds himself with nothing to do. After his doting aunt asks the young man to perform a small chore, he decides to kill her for no good reason other than, perhaps, boredom. This short comedic masterpiece combines elements of Dostoevsky, Sartre, Kafka, and Heller, coming together to produce an unforgettable tale of murder and—just maybe—redemption.

I CALLED HIM NECKTIE BY MILENA MICHIKO FLAŠAR

TWENTY-YEAR-OLD TAGUCHI HIRO HAS SPENT the last two years of his life living as a hiki-komori—a shut-in who never leaves his room and has no human interaction—in his parents' home in Tokyo. As Hiro tentatively decides to reenter the world, he spends his days observing life from a park bench. Gradually he makes friends with Ohara Tetsu, a salaryman who has lost his job. The two discover in their sadness a common bond. This beautiful novel is moving, unforgettable, and full of surprises.

WHO IS MARTHA? BY MARJANA GAPONENKO

IN THIS ROLLICKING NOVEL, 96-YEAR-OLD ornithologist Luka Levadski foregoes treatment for lung cancer and moves from Ukraine to Vienna to make a grand exit in a luxury suite at the Hotel Imperial. He reflects on his past while indulging in Viennese cakes and savoring music in a gilded concert hall. Levadski was born in 1914, the same year that Martha—the last of the now-extinct passenger pigeons—died. Levadski himself has an acute sense of being the last of a species. This gloriously written tale mixes piquant wit with lofty musings about life, friendship, aging and death.

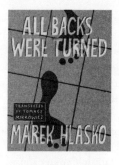

ALL BACKS WERE TURNED BY MAREK HLASKO

TWO DESPERATE FRIENDS—ON THE EDGE OF the law—travel to the southern Israeli city of Eilat to find work. There, Dov Ben Dov, the handsome native Israeli with a reputation for causing trouble, and Israel, his sidekick, stay with Ben Dov's younger brother, Little Dov, who has enough trouble of his own. Local toughs are encroaching on Little Dov's business, and he enlists his older brother to drive them away. It doesn't help that a beautiful German widow is rooming next door. A story of passion, deception, violence, and betrayal, conveyed in hard-boiled prose reminiscent of Hammett and Chandler.

ALEXANDRIAN SUMMER
BY YITZHAK GORMEZANO GOREN

THIS IS THE STORY OF TWO JEWISH FAMILIES living their frenzied last days in the doomed cosmopolitan social whirl of Alexandria just before fleeing Egypt for Israel in 1951. The conventions of the Egyptian upper-middle class are laid bare in this dazzling novel, which exposes sexual hypocrisies and portrays a vanished polyglot world of horse racing, seaside promenades and nightclubs.

COCAINE BY PITIGRILLI

PARIS IN THE 1920S—DIZZY AND DECADENT. Where a young man can make a fortune with his wits … unless he is led into temptation. Cocaine's dandified hero Tito Arnaudi invents lurid scandals and gruesome deaths, and sells these stories to the newspapers. But his own life becomes even more outrageous when he acquires three demanding mistresses. Elegant, witty and wicked, Pitigrilli's classic novel was first published in Italian in 1921 and retains its venom even today.

KILLING THE SECOND DOG
BY MAREK HLASKO

TWO DOWN-AND-OUT POLISH CON MEN LIVING in Israel in the 1950s scam an American widow visiting the country. Robert, who masterminds the scheme, and Jacob, who acts it out, are tough, desperate men, exiled from their native land and adrift in the hot, nasty underworld of Tel Aviv. Robert arranges for Jacob to run into the widow who has enough trouble with her young son to keep her occupied all day. What follows is a story of romance, deception, cruelty and shame. Hlasko's writing combines brutal realism with smoky, hard-boiled dialogue, in a bleak world where violence is the norm and love is often only an act.

FANNY VON ARNSTEIN: DAUGHTER OF
THE ENLIGHTENMENT BY HILDE SPIEL

IN 1776 FANNY VON ARNSTEIN, THE DAUGHTER of the Jewish master of the royal mint in Berlin, came to Vienna as an 18-year-old bride. She married a financier to the Austro-Hungarian imperial court, and hosted an ever more splendid salon which attracted luminaries of the day. Spiel's elegantly written and carefully researched biography provides a vivid portrait of a passionate woman who advocated for the rights of Jews, and illuminates a central era in European cultural and social history.

SOME DAY BY SHEMI ZARHIN

ON THE SHORES OF ISRAEL'S SEA OF GALILEE lies the city of Tiberias, a place bursting with sexuality and longing for love. The air is saturated with smells of cooking and passion. *Some Day* is a gripping family saga, a sensual and emotional feast that plays out over decades. This is an enchanting tale about tragic fates that disrupt families and break our hearts. Zarhin's hypnotic writing renders a painfully delicious vision of individual lives behind Israel's larger national story.

THE MISSING YEAR OF JUAN SALVATIERRA
BY PEDRO MAIRAL

AT THE AGE OF NINE, JUAN SALVATIERRA became mute following a horse riding accident. At twenty, he began secretly painting a series of canvases on which he detailed six decades of life in his village on Argentina's frontier with Uruguay. After his death, his sons return to deal with their inheritance: a shed packed with rolls over two miles long. But an essential roll is missing. A search ensues that illuminates links between art and life, with past family secrets casting their shadows on the present.

THE GOOD LIFE ELSEWHERE
BY VLADIMIR LORCHENKOV

THE VERY FUNNY—AND VERY SAD—STORY OF A group of villagers and their tragicomic efforts to emigrate from Europe's most impoverished nation to Italy for work. An Orthodox priest is deserted by his wife for an art-dealing atheist; a mechanic redesigns his tractor for travel by air and sea; and thousands of villagers take to the road on a modern-day religious crusade to make it to the Italian Promised Land. A country where 25 percent of its population works abroad, remittances make up nearly 40 percent of GDP, and alcohol consumption per capita is the world's highest – Moldova surely has its problems. But, as Lorchenkov vividly shows, it's also a country whose residents don't give up easily.

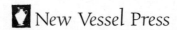

New Vessel Press

*To purchase these titles and for more information
please visit newvesselpress.com.*

SERGEI LEBEDEV was born in Moscow in 1981 and worked for seven years on geological expeditions in northern Russia and Central Asia. Lebedev is a poet, essayist and journalist. *Oblivion*, his first novel, was translated into many languages and published to great acclaim by New Vessel Press in 2016.

ANTONINA W. BOUIS has translated over 80 works from authors such as Evgeny Yevtushenko, Mikhail Bulgakov, and Sergei Dovlatov.

RICE PUBLIC LIBRARY
8 WENTWORTH ST.
KITTERY, MAINE 03904
207-439-1553